Wild Acclaim for
Brian M. Wiprud

Stuffed

"*Stuffed* has it all. Albino crows. Russian gnomes. Bear gallbladders. Fertility dolls. A man called Flip! Pygmies! No one in the mystery genre can match what Brian Wiprud has created, which can only be called . . . Wiprudian."
— C. J. Box, author of *Out of Range*

"You cannot write a comedy set in the secret world of animal parts sold for profit unless you are the audacious Brian Wiprud. *Stuffed* is all of that and more—often harrowing, at times macabre, and always original. Wiprud twangs funny bones I never knew I had."
— T. Jefferson Parker, author of *California Girl*

"Brian Wiprud is one of the most imaginative and creative authors working today. His writing is witty and engaging and worth every minute you'll spend reading when you should be doing something else."
— Ben Rehder, author of *Flat Crazy*

Pipsqueak

"First get past the cover. Then the title. Now I dare you to get past the funniest book this year. A dead squirrel, a taxidermist and a crazy mystery that keeps you turning the pages and laughing out loud." —*BookCrazy Radio*

"Fans of author Jeff Strand should stand up and take special notice! A mystery filled with scenes of Murphy's Law: If Things Can Go Wrong, They Will. Fun, hilarious, and warped, this author ROCKS! Recommended to all who want a few laughs with their mystery!" —*Huntress Book Reviews*

"'Zany,' 'madcap,' and 'romp' must have been invented specifically for Wiprud's smart and funny *Pipsqueak*. A lunatic, super-fast mystery."
—Lauren Henderson, author of *Chained*

"Imagine, if you will, Dashiell Hammett's *The Maltese Falcon* as conceived by Robin Williams. . . . Reminiscent of some of Donald Westlake's more inventive and humorous mysteries, but with a comic sensibility all its own. By the time I finally finished reading *Pipsqueak*, my face hurt from the constant grinning." —Reviewing the Evidence.com

"Fast-paced, humorous and highly entertaining . . . Brian M. Wiprud's writing is parallel to that of Carl Hiaasen or Gregory Mcdonald. Quirky and unique, this cleverly plotted story is both engaging and memorable." —Bookbrowser.com

Also by Brian M. Wiprud

PIPSQUEAK

Stuffed

BRIAN M. WIPRUD

A Dell Book

STUFFED

A Dell Book / June 2005

Published by
Bantam Dell
A Division of Random House, Inc.
New York, New York

This is a work of fiction. Names, characters, places, and incidents either are the product of the author's imagination or are used fictitiously. Any resemblance to actual persons, living or dead, events, or locales is entirely coincidental.

ISBN 0-440-24188-X

Printed in the United States of America
Published simultaneously in Canada

www.bantamdell.com

OPM 10 9 8 7 6 5 4 3 2 1

For my sister, Rebecca

Acknowledgments

First and foremost, kudos to Caitlin Alexander, my editor at Bantam Dell, who was instrumental in making this novel all it could be.

I doff my cap to Clay Fourrier of Dovetail Studio, best darn Web guy there ever was. He served above and beyond the call of duty updating my site daily during my summer 2004 tour—I salute you, C-Boy.

Milty Vargas and the boys at the www.wiprud.com control room: incomparable.

And for inspiration, Reggie, my adopted Magellanic penguin, who lives in the third burrow on the left, Isla Magdalena, Straits of Magellan, Chile. Many penguin populations have been decimated in recent years by commercial fishing and deliberate oil pollution. To adopt a penguin of your own, please contact http://www.falklands.net/AdoptAPenguin.shtml.

Stuffed

Chapter 1

I was walking down the creaky steps of a shop called Gunderson's Odds N' Ends. In my arms was a heavy bell jar with a white crow in it. The albino *Corvidae* was dead, had been for a long time, but was still around thanks to the noble art of taxidermy. I was intent on not dropping the bird and was focused on my footing. Ice patches lay in my path, and an impromptu Eskimo cha-cha would likely send the crow to the scrap heap and me into traction.

My '66 Lincoln was close at hand, top down. A nine-foot Pacific sailfish lay on its back in the rear seat. Fish tail sticking out one side of the car, sword out the other. Cut a corner too tight in Manhattan, and I'd have some pedestrian shish kebab on my hands. But I was far from home, in the boondocks of Vermont, and didn't expect much foot traffic.

The backseat was full, so I dodged slippery swaths of snow and heaved the bell jar into the car's front seat. Stretching my back, I groaned and smiled at the bird. It was a birthday gift for Angie, one I thought she'd really like.

"Mister!"

The salutation went right by me. "Mister" is some dude with a pipe, a fedora, and a cardigan. "Mister" is Fred MacMurray, Ward Cleaver, Robert Young, or that dyspeptic Wilson guy next door to Dennis the Menace.

Just the same, my attention was drawn to a husky kid with a PORTLAND COLLEGE sweatshirt. He was running toward me across the village square, past the gazebo and white picket fences and lawns where crocuses were still snoozing.

I am not "mister." I'm just over forty-three, chew bubblegum, and still think of myself as being cardable at the package store, however much of a fantasy that might be. So I looked around for a handy fifties' TV dad and came to the unhappy conclusion that this husky kid was aiming at me. I was already feeling old that day, and this wasn't helping.

I flashed on all the mundane things a stranger could want: the time, directions, possibly to sell me a subscription to *Grit*.

But when he stopped in front of me, panting, I never imagined he would say:

"That raven is mine."

He forced a smile.

I didn't.

And now that the bird was mine, I wasn't going to let it be insulted.

"It's not a raven, it's a crow. A raven is a big bird, with a wedge-shaped tail, coarse feathers, and a taller beak with a slight hook at the end."

"My name's Fletcher," he panted, ignoring my lecture. "My mother gave the bird to Gunderson to sell while I was away. She didn't ask or anything. It's not for sale. I just come back and—"

Frat Boy seemed a little desperate, which naturally made me more possessive. I drifted between him and the bird.

"Sorry. I just bought it from Gunderson." Damn nice-looking bird it was too. Angie loves crows.

"How much you want for it?" Fletcher started fishing in the pocket of his sweats.

"Well—" In keeping with local Yankee custom, I looked to the sky for a divine price check. I would have thumbed my suspenders too, had I been wearing any. "Five hundred dollars." Sorry, Angie—business is business.

Fletcher paled as he picked up his two twenties from the ground.

"You paid Gunderson—"

"Never mind what I paid Gunderson. The crow belongs to me, and the price is—"

"But my mother, she—"

"Well, she shouldn't have—"

"But it's mine, dang it." Now he sounded insistent, if not a little hostile, the fingers of his left hand fidgeting with a bulky silver high-school ring.

Dang? To me, that's a western expression, not something you hear down east.

I turned and drew the seat belt across the bell jar to secure it.

"What do you think you're doing?" He took a step forward. "Don't you understand—"

He was standing a little too close, and I put a hand on his chest, easing him back.

"Look, I had a mother, and she threw out dead things of mine too. Did she ever! That's just a part of life. Like hitting a baseball through a car window or finding out the Easter bunny is an elaborate conspiracy to sell cheap chocolate. You live with it, eat the jelly beans, and move on."

He stood there looking completely devastated, which didn't seem odd to me at the time. I hoped the bit about the jelly beans—particularly clever repartee, I thought—had floored him. As a kid, I would have gone ape shinola over this bird if someone got it away from me, so his mortification seemed an entirely normal reaction. But I should have wondered why a lad like Fletcher would be so attached to an albino crow in a bell jar. Instead, I sympathized and softened my tone.

"Look, Fletcher. I really, *really* like the bird. You had it for a while. Now it's my turn to enjoy it for a while. If you're ever in New York, you can come and visit him."

He didn't much like that. His face reddened, his left fist clenched, and Fletcher went for my jaw.

Completely telegraphed. I dodged to the right and watched that big silver ring streak past my eye.

"Whoa, kid, whoa!" I backed away toward the car. Seemed to me I kept a tire thumper somewhere under the driver's seat. Not exactly handy at that moment.

Fletcher pointed a finger at me. "That bird is mine."

The shop proprietor, Gunderson, and his nor'east shop gal were suddenly on the porch, watching dumbly.

I had no idea what he was on about, but I wasn't letting him near the crow. Fisticuffs are way down at the bottom of my bag of tricks, especially when my opponent is significantly younger and stronger than me. If he'd come at me again, I guess I would have kicked him in the shin. But what with the midlife green meanies eating at me, my first move was to play the commanding adult. Hey, as long as he thought of me as "mister," why not indulge him?

I put a hand on the bell jar, hummed up a good resonant tone like Dad might use, and pointed a stern and reproachful finger at him. "Now, son, just simmer down."

One minute I think I'm eighteen, and the next I think I'm sixty. I sounded like a complete idiot, of course. But as I said, it seemed like the thing to do at the time.

And then, quite suddenly, Fletcher crumpled in a heap on the ground. Straight down, like one of those little plastic push-button puppets, you know, where you depress the button and the horsie goes limp. *Flump*.

I guess you'd have to say he fainted, but it was oddly instantaneous, no staggering or blinking or anything.

Wow. I gave my stern and reproachful finger a look of approval and figured I should use the Dad routine next time I want to move to the head of the line at the DMV.

Just then, the local constabulary happened to roll around the corner in a mud-spattered Jeep. The red strobes on the roll bar and gold seal on the side gave it away. It stopped, and I saw the silhouette of the driver peer our way. He was probably just making his rounds or something. I waved him over.

Gunderson and the shop gal were at Fletcher's side trying to revive the kid by the time the Jeep sputtered to a stop next to me.

A craggy man slowly unfolded from the Jeep. He was the weathered, thick-fingered kind of lout. Looked like he rolled his own cigarettes. His uniform of the day? Brown Carhartt bib overalls and a round badge pinned to one suspender. The law eyed me suspiciously as he bent down and helped slap Fletcher awake. His slaps were more forceful than Gunderson or the maid seemed willing to muster. While they worked on their patient, I helped myself to a stick of sugarless bubblegum.

"What happened, Gunderson?" the cop asked.

"They was arguin' over that thayah raven when Bret, all the sudden like, drops to the ground."

"Fainted dead away!" the nor'east maid marveled.

"It's not a raven," I hissed, mainly to myself.

The kid came around, confused, but quickly picked up where he left off.

"He's got a, uh, thing of mine, that Ma gave to Gunderson," he complained, his finger stabbing in my direction. "Gunderson sold it to this guy, and, like, he won't give me my thing, Constable Bill!"

"Thing? Thing? What thing?" The sheriff pawed his white shock of hair with one hand while helping Fletcher up with the other. "For the love of Sam! What's this about, Gunderson?"

"A crow," I said, snapping a bubble. "A stuffed crow. I've got the receipt." I held the invoice out for inspection. "The kid here wants to buy it with his fists."

"That so, Gunderson?" The cop glanced at the invoice and then locked eyes with me.

"Well," Gunderson shrugged. "Yeah huh."

Constable Bill eyed me a moment longer, my car, my license plate. "That's a big fish, mistuh. You from New York?"

"Yup. Name is Carson. I deal in taxidermy. Just came from Brattleboro, and I'm on my way to Rangely."

"Rangely? Maine?"

I nodded. "I'm on a trip through the northeast buying stock."

He whistled, as if Rangely were a planet just beyond Pluto. He wasn't half wrong, come to think of it. Gets mighty cold there, and it's definitely in an orbit far from New York.

"Didya let Bret here take a shot at buying it back?"

"Yup. He doesn't—"

"He's trying to rip me off!" Bret honked. "He wants five hundred dollars for—"

"Sheriff, what can I say? I bought the bird, I like the bird, I want the bird. It's a birthday gift for my girlfriend. Five hundred dollars could make me get over it."

"For her birthday?" The maid whimpered, and I thought *she* might faint.

"Odd gift, I'd say," Gunderson added bitterly. He was just peeved that I'd conned him out of the bird.

"Five hundred dollahs." Constable Bill whistled again. "S'lot of money. Well, Bret, if you don't have five hundred dollahs, then I guess this fellah don't have to sell it to you." He gave me a cold smile. "Even if he did pay, what, thirty dollahs for it?"

"Fifty." I snapped another bubble, waved the receipt, and got into the Lincoln. As I started the car, I could see Constable Bill trying to reason with Bret in my rearview mirror. Frat Boy wasn't having any of it.

Okay, so maybe I'm a stinker. More than that, I'm a dealer. All in a day's work.

Chapter 2

When the Great White Hunter returned from his safari through the northeast, he'd bagged a plethora of raw caribou racks, the somewhat grim vestige of Alaskan spring floods. The skullcaps smelled a bit funky, but after a good emulsifier bath, a stiff brush, and a thinned application of antler stain, I'd mount the twenty racks on hardwood plaques and unload them for perhaps three hundred apiece. Also in the larder was a bobcat with his butt ripped off. He was only twenty bucks and otherwise a nice mount posed in a sitting position, head tilted, paw raised, fangs bared whimsically, or so I thought. I figured I'd stick the bad end in a nicely finished stump and sell him for two hundred, easy. What can I say? I was feeling cheap and creative. Which is not to say that I didn't nab a few finished pieces.

African stuff is always prime cut, so I sprang for a stout kudu head with massive, curving horns and a matching pair of hoof bookends. In fact, I had to break the bank on that deal because I bought him as a set with a howling coyote, a nasty-looking barracuda, and a wolverine with a small marmot in its jaws for two grand.

And of course it was my pal Rodney—the guy who'd turned me on to Gunderson's—who sold me that whopper of a sailfish. He's not a taxidermy specialist but a sleigh/carriage/sea-chest restorer and dealer. I like Rodney, but sometimes he's a little over the top, the very character flaw that got him booted out of college in our senior year for commandeering a university police car for a trip to Biffy Burger. We were pretty tight in those days, memorable mostly for every extracurricular idiocy possible in a sleepy North Carolina town. You know, like painting ourselves in luminous poster paints and lurking around the cemetery. Or Saran-Wrapping roadkill and slipping it into the meat case over at the Dixie King. And I've still got a snapshot of the giant cardboard squid strangling the college clock tower.

After Rodney's untimely departure, he bought a motorcycle and went off to Alaska to find his destiny. The exchange of postcards dwindled, and in the decade that followed college we lost track of each other. I rediscovered Rodney some years later nestled among his sleighs and sea chests at the Brimfield antiques fair. Two wastrel English majors reunited, not only by our dubious past association, but by our shared passion for swindling people out of their junk. We're buds, and I stop in on him when on safari whether he's got anything for me or not.

My safari came to an end in Rangely, with my billfold ransacked. I loaded up the trailer and got home in time for Angie's birthday.

Birds like me and Angie roost on Manhattan's somewhat cheaper, industrial fringes, which in our case is the west teens. Way, way west. However, we're lucky enough to be on the ground floor of a soot-streaked tenement. Hey, 150 years of grime lends a unique patina to the brick, an architectural style we call brown*stain*. It's near enough to the corner to have a storefront, which is where we live. Used to be a soda fountain, and when we signed on it still looked like one inside.

Nowadays the marble soda bar along the living room is an open kitchen and the back, off the storeroom, is the bedroom. We partitioned half of the main room into Angie's and my studios, and the front where booths still sit in bay shop windows is the living room. We frosted the huge front glass panels halfway to the ceiling for privacy. Metal grating shadows a diamond pattern on the frosted glass from the outside, just to keep folks from throwing a trash can into our living room during the next blackout. What had been a really cool black and white tile floor was destroyed, but a yellow pine floor lay beneath, which after a titanic effort and a bunch of polyurethane now looks like butterscotch.

Yeah, we know it wasn't too bright sinking moola and effort into a place that isn't ours. But how else are we—a couple of freelancers—going to get the apartment of our dreams without a sizable down payment? You can only imagine the look a loan officer gives you when you say that you freelance in used taxidermy. He doesn't know whether to laugh or cry.

I arrived home at four-thirty in the afternoon, just dodging the worst of New York's rush hour because I was going against the flow. I got a space right in front of my building, a feat roughly comparable to a suburbanite finding a space next to the handicapped spots at Sears on a Saturday morning during a white sale.

There are basically two kinds of people who live in New York. There are those who take cabs to work, park their Land Rovers in garages, have their laundry "done," and buy their doorman a cashmere scarf for Christmas. The kind found in Woody Allen movies who really aren't affected by the mundane urban complications encountered by those of us who take the subway and have to brave the opening of our own doors.

The vast majority—myself notable, I like to think, among them—has to put up with a lot of crap. We live in a city governed not by laws but by penalties. Every day New York sticks it to you somehow. There's Saturday at the Wash-O-Mat fighting with Broom Hilda in a housedress who's holding on to a dryer for half an hour just to dry one sock while my pile of wet laundry and I cool our heels. Sunday you can't get the game on TV because an errant backhoe cut the cable. Monday you tangle with an impotent MetroCard at a subway turnstile; Tuesday the newspaper machine robs you; Wednesday you spend an hour looking for a parking space; Thursday you slip on and almost fall into a pile of stray vomit. And Friday you get a ticket from the sanitation department because a passerby tucked a newspaper into your metal-recycling trash can. It's one kick in the teeth after another. I'm sure suburbanites have their sundry mishaps at the strip mall, food court, or waiting for tee times, but nobody can deny New Yorkers have more than their fair share of hassles.

We're a stoic lot. That is to say, New Yorkers don't get mad, they get even. We do what it takes to stick it to the city or someone else to offset these penalties, usually in some sleazy, compensatory way. Cops might eat free at the deli and offer protection by their presence. Firemen might drink free at the bars that pass fire-code inspections despite basements overflowing with oily rags and loose wiring. Petty criminals jump subway turnstiles, and the defiantly indigent randomly harass commuters out of sheer perversity.

Me? When a newspaper box rips me off one day, I prop it open the next day so a local entrepreneur can make off with the rest. When I get a parking ticket, I move my car to a legal spot, take a Polaroid, and plead not guilty by mail. Hey, even if it doesn't get me out of the penalty, at least the city loses whatever it anticipated in the cost of processing my plea. And when I need a parking space at my apartment, I establish my own parking rules.

For the price of a cordless drill, I park with impunity in front of my abode. A signpost directly between my building and the adjoining warehouse has a LOADING ZONE—NO STANDING 7 AM TO 7 PM MON–SAT sign pointing up the block. The sign mounted below it, pointing in front of my building, says NO PARKING HERE TO CORNER. An absurd sign, which if posted in front of some guy's trailer outside Kalamazoo would surely result in someone going postal at the local Parking Violations Bureau. Instead, I simply remove the offending sign when I get home and put it back up when I leave. Hey, it's part of the American dream to have a parking space in front of your home, practically part of the Bill of Rights. While my block isn't heavily trafficked, I suppose some locals may have noticed my handiwork. But New Yorkers—every blessed one of them part mobster at heart—don't rat.

I unlocked the front door to my apartment and sensed Angie wasn't home by the cigarette smoke hanging in the air.

"Otto!" I yelled, hefting the crow onto the soda counter. "You're smoking!"

"Ah, vhat you do!" Otto tossed aside the curtain leading to the back workshop. "My God," he gasped at the crow. "Eetz good, eh?" He stepped up and slapped the bell jar, then took a step back and tweaked his sharp little beard, scrutinizing my acquisition.

"You were smoking in the house, Otto. Bad. No smoking in the house."

"I dunno. Eet not lookink." Otto was still squinting at the crow, his heavily wrinkled face scrunched in deep thought. "Maybe ve must new vood, eh? Bird maybe new vood."

I stepped up to my little Russian wacko and grabbed him by his chinny chin chin.

"No smoking in the house! Backyard." We've got a patch of soot out back just for him.

"Vhat smoke?" He threw out his hands. He gave me his puppy look, like I should be ashamed of swatting him over the nose with a newspaper.

"C'mon, you nincompoop," I snorted, waving him to follow me outside to the car.

"I dunno. Vhat ninipoop?"

Angie's a freelance jeweler, so Otto helps her with her piecework—soldering, polishing, etc. And he fixes up some of my taxidermy—combing, cleaning, mounting, painting, etc. He's what you'd call an old-world, Soviet-refugee artisan, as handy with a brush as with a rotary hobby tool. More important, he's old-world cheap, though often very annoying. Angie discovered him in the subway back when she commuted to a diamond-setting job on 47th Street. On a crowded subway platform, he'd assemble one of those suitcases on folding legs that contained a traveling workshop. He billed himself as *Otto Figs It. Wail You Weight* and actually came to do brisk business soldering brooch pins, adjusting watch bands and eyeglasses, sewing stray dangling coat buttons, and tightening loose ring settings. But after shooing him out a few times, the cops decided to bust him one morning. Angie came forward, bailed him out, and paid his fine. He had no money to repay her, so the post-Soviet gnome was indentured to help Angie with piecework jewelry. As it happened, he also demonstrated a talent for primping used taxidermy. After his debt was paid, well, I guess you'd have to say we'd gotten attached to him, like a barn cat.

Within the hour, Otto and I had everything unloaded and the trailer folded once more into the Lincoln's trunk. When we got back inside and Otto had a chance to inspect the new stuff, he became riveted by the possibilities posed by the bobcat with the missing butt.

"Garv, ve must maybe special. Ket, eetz good, eh? Maybe, ket, eet out come vater, for bird, eh? Maybe, Garv, ket in mouth of great large bear. Great large bear eat ket, eh?"

"Tree stump. Cat from tree stump." I handed him a cup of coffee. "All these antlers, caribou. Clean. You clean antlers. Understand?"

Otto looked aghast. "Yes, of course. But ket, eet maybe in small car, eh?" He flashed his stainless-steel Soviet-era dentistry at me. "Very amusink, eh? Keety ket in keety cat car?" He burst out laughing, slapping his knee. His booming laugh is very literal: *haw, haw, haw—*

The door slammed. Angie was home.

"Yay!" She dropped her bags and threw her arms around me. "My favorite birthday present: my boyfriend! What's with him?" She jerked a thumb in Otto's direction. He was still in the grips of hilarity.

"Hiya, kiddo." I gave her a kiss. "He's out of his tiny, infinitesimal mind, that's what."

She tossed her coat over a caribou rack. "Wow, lotta stuff you got."

"Ket, eet maybe in balloon . . ." *Haw, haw, haw* . . .

"Otto, did you finish that polishing?" Angie sniffed the air. "Otto, no smoking in the house!"

Otto stopped laughing. "Polishing. Of course, yes, I polish. Ket, eet very good, yes?"

I hooked Angie's arm. "One of these days, if we can afford it, one of us is going to kill this evil little man. Bury him in the backyard."

"Yangie, maybe I go to smoke, eh?" Otto tromped back behind the curtain. We heard the back door creak and slam.

I wheeled Angie in front of the bird. "Happy birthday."

"Oh, Garth." She gasped. "It's fabulous!"

I could tell she really liked it.

"How old do you think it is?" Her green eyes brightly admired the specimen, turning the jar on the counter.

"Probably done in the forties by a bird fancier. Too nice to have been done by a hobbyist—Dudley the fastidious exception." I cocked my head and admired the bird's hunched stance, partially spread wings, and open beak. An apt posture for the vocif-erous crow.

She looked closely into the bell jar. "Looks like he's mounted on cedar root, to keep the bugs out, and under glass to keep the dust off. And a good heavy hardwood base to keep it from getting knocked to the floor. Perfect, sugar, perfect. I love it." Angie brushed her short blond hair from her face and carried the bell jar over to her other crow, the black one, wings spread and mounted on a spooky-looking branch I found in Washington Square Park. I'd salvaged him from the remainder of a tourist museum diorama on Alfred Hitchcock's *The Birds*.

"A bit smaller than the last one you gave me?" Angie squinted.

"Albinos run a bit small. They thought it was a raven. Can you imagine?"

Angie answered with a scrunched face, the one that transmitted derision.

"Who?"

"Gunderson, the guy I bought it from, and an-other guy. But it's a crow."

"Garth, it's a real one of a kind." Angie slid the bird onto the table and her arms around my neck. "You did it again."

"Don't mention it, babe. Stick with me and—"

"You'll cover me with dead things, yeah, I know." She rolled her eyes around the apartment and nod-ded in the direction of a small, dusty TV under the wings of an owl. "I don't think we're ever going to graduate from that thirteen-inch color television."

The comment stung, and despite my shrug Angie realized her faux pas. She grabbed me around the waist.

"Garth, you chase that old funk of yours outta here. You know I don't care about the TV. I love you and our life together just the way it is."

"If I could find a slightly used Sony Trinitron, cut back the gums, polish the teeth, put in a new tongue, repair the ears . . ."

"So where you taking me to dinner?" She wasn't one to let me enjoy self-pity. Angie pushed me away suspiciously, hooking her caiman purse from the bear cub umbrella stand. Yup. The purse had been for Valentine's Day.

"Besides . . . I've got some terrific news, something else to celebrate. You ready? Peter Van Putin."

I nodded, clearly not knowing who he was. Or perhaps not remembering.

"Peter Van Putin, the HUGE fashion jewelry designer?"

"Ah."

"They want to see my portfolio!"

"Whoa! And if they like it?"

"Then there'll be an interview."

I smiled, put my hands on her waist, and gave her a kiss. "Sounds like a done deal to me. Once they see the quality of your work, your designs, and, well, you in person . . ."

"Oh, stop snowing me."

"I'm dead serious, sugar."

"Well . . ." She almost blushed, but then turned suspicious again. "So, where is it this year?"

"I thought you liked last year's dinner."

"Kabul Tent was a delightful restaurant." She inspected my hair, an unruly mane of dirty-blond locks that I barely keep caged with the help of Level Ten gel. She jabbed at it with her fingers, trying to tame it. "Really, I didn't mind sitting on a cushion on the floor—"

"Eclectic dining."

"Or eating goat chunks with my fingers from a giant communal pile of rice—"

"French food is so rich."

"But did you have to pay for the meal with a vulture?" Angie gave my hair a cross look and folded her arms.

"They still have that bird." I directed her to the front door. "It's perched right over the hookah pipe. Otto!"

Tossing aside the curtain, Otto swept back into the living room, a cigarette clenched in his teeth. "Ve go?"

"No, we go, you stay." I snatched the cigarette from his teeth and dropped it into his coffee. "No smoking in the house or I won't let you work on the kitty cat."

"But of course. I up the lock, eh?"

"But of course!" Angie and I called back as we exited.

Chapter 3

Angie and I met at a company Christmas party. Some pals of mine were trying to make it in the film business and had taken jobs as paralegals while they wrote screenplays and tried to find opus backers. Back in the early eighties, the big New York law firms were starved for paralegals to catalog warehouses of documents for the many corporate mega-lawsuits. At the time, my college degree landed me a dirt-pay job at a used-record store. But I had a dozen pieces of inherited taxidermy—my grandfather was a big-game hunter—and had struck upon the whizbang idea of renting the stuff out to make some extra cash. I advertised in free classifieds and, sure enough, found gainful employment for my lion, Fred, in a Broadway play that ran for three years. Fred's not a huge lion, about seven feet long nose to tail, but he has a full mane. He's mounted on a wheeled mahogany platform, on all fours and snarling at some imaginary threat. As youths, my little brother Nicholas, Fred, and I used to ambush trick-or-treaters. Bursting forth from the philodendron's shadow, Fred's casters wobbling and squealing frantically, we'd chase clowns, pirates, hobos, and ghosts down the driveway like a panicked flock of ducks. The result? Pinfeathers in their wake. Spilled Mary Janes, Pixie Stix, orange UNICEF boxes, and candied wax lips marked their flight path down the driveway. Hey, for scoring Halloween treats, it beat the hell out of going door to door. Our parents always wondered why no kids ever came by our place for candy.

Of course, my friends thought I was nuts trying to start a taxidermy rental operation, and they tempted me with becoming a paralegal too. Paralegals got cabs home, free food, business trips, and company morale parties with all the beer you could drink. At twenty-four, there's not much more a male of the species could want from life. Except a female.

That's how I ended up at a holiday booze cruise on a boat around Manhattan.

Amid the hubbub, I spied a particular female with a cast on her right hand and forearm. With her left hand, she was trying to assemble cold cuts into a sandwich. It was touch and go.

"Who's that?" I asked a pal.

"Angie. She's a temp. A jeweler with a broken wrist. Give her a try. If you like the smart type."

"Smart type?"

"Does the *Times* crossword over a single cup of coffee. The rest of us can barely do the Jumble."

I watched as this "smart type" cradled a paper plate on her cast and began to turn. Someone bumped her, she stumbled, the plate fell to the floor, and she stepped on her sandwich. I thought that was pretty funny until I saw her eyes begin to tear with frustration.

She began angrily slapping cold cuts onto a new piece of rye. I sauntered over, scooped up the squished sandwich from the floor, and cradled it in my hands.

"Kinda looks like one of those squirrels you find flattened on the highway."

She turned and scowled at me.

"You know, the ones that dry up into a disk and you can pick them up and throw them like a Frisbee?" I dared a cajoling smile and flung the sandwich into the East River. It flew more like a clay pigeon that had been shot, separating into its components on the way down. She still wasn't smiling, and this was my A material, if you can believe it. By all rights I should still be single.

"Yeah, well, here, let's try again." I gamely began making a turkey sandwich. "I'll make the next one."

"I don't like squirrel meat." Her green eyes bored into me disapprovingly. "Possum."

"Possum?" I tried smiling harder.

"Make the next one possum," she deadpanned.

So I made her a faux possum sandwich, gave her

half, stomped on the other, and flung it starboard. It split apart again.

She rolled her eyes in disgust. "You gotta use more salami, with white bread and butter to cement it together. Make the next one jackrabbit."

I was pretty sure she was stringing me along to make a complete fool of me. I'm used to having girls go "eeuuww" with this brand of persiflage, a shrewd pickup tactic akin to dropping a frog down a gal's dress at the church picnic. What was I thinking? Youth is wasted on the wrong people, as they say.

But she was right: With butter, white bread, and a stable luncheon meat, the rabbit sailed like a Frisbee. What can I say? It was true love.

That was back in the days when we used to dance all night at parties and clubs. But you find that by your late twenties, your peers are nest-building. Career and the urgency of reproduction quickly subjugate frivolity. Parties, once fun, turn into wet-bar think tanks about insurance, personal finance, and real estate, with portfolio malaise the inevitable finale. And once the gang has kids, well, the most you can hope for are barbecues, awash in feebly disciplined children and talk of C-sections, day care, and bowel movements. So much for hootenannies.

Angie and I, oddballs that we are, have resisted the urge to spawn and replicate. We're self-employed. *Free spirits.* The Brood Crew likes to imply that we care more about personal freedom than money, kids, and family. Which is true. So what's wrong with that? We eat out whenever we want without having to get a sitter. To each his own, I say.

I'd made reservations for Angie's birthday at Anglers & Co., a chic seafood place on Hudson where she'd always been keen to dine. But no sooner did we sit down than her eye latched on to the dandy Atlantic salmon mounted on the wall opposite her. She scrutinized me as I innocently checked out my menu.

"Don't tell me—" she began.

"Good evening, Mr. Carson." The manager interjected, hand on my shoulder. "Everybody has said how much better the new fish looks. You were right. The old one looked—"

"Let me guess?" Angie fanned herself with a menu. "Like it was baked over an open fire and spackled to a plank?"

The manager spread his arms. "Just so," he chortled. "I've told the waiter no check, just tip, okay? Enjoy."

"Garth, you're impossible." Angie grinned reluctantly, and immersed herself in the menu.

"Order anything you want." I tried to suppress a marplot's smile. "Drinks included."

Then the birthday surprise. I took Angie dancing at Mud Bug Bar & Grille over on Third Avenue. It had a zydeco band that did Little Feat and Professor Longhair. It was a spacious, high-ceilinged club, decorated with discarded Mardi Gras float figures. Big barrels of peanuts sat at either end of the bar, and as the evening progressed, the floor became awash in peanut shells like some bayou roadhouse. Sunday night the place got pretty crowded, so much so that a trip to the bathroom for Angie was a fifteen-minute sojourn. It was during just such a break, while I was sitting alone at our table, cooling off with a Dixie beer after dancing, that an Asian man in yuppie duds and an effervescent mood settled into the chair next to me.

"Hi, Garth!"

I extended my hand slowly, no idea who this guy was. But he had a warm smile, a broad cheery manner, and looked like the kind of guy I'd like to know. Though the pro-shop togs made me wonder. So did his pencil-thin mustache, which wasn't visible until he was up close. He smelled vaguely of cloves.

"You don't know me. Jim Kim is the name."

"Really?"

"I saw that piece on you in the *Times* a while back. About taxidermy rentals."

"Good memory. That was over two years ago."

"Yeah, well, I also know a guy who rented from you once."

"You don't say? Who?"

"A guy . . ." Kim snapped his fingers. "Can't think of the name, imagine that. Anyway, I hear you have quite a collection of taxidermy. Do you sell as well as rent?"

A potential customer, so I figured I ought to be a little less guarded. "Yes, I do. Are you looking for something in particular?"

Kim smirked at me. "Some people I know are looking for a white crow."

There was something odd in the way he said it, and I studied his face for some menace at his core but couldn't cut through the veneer of his clubhouse bonhomie. Finally, I said, "Don't see many of them."

"I hear you just got one in."

I sat forward. "Now, how would you know that?"

"A guy told me." He shrugged. "You know, that guy, can't remember his name."

"Okay, so what's this all about, Kim?" I locked onto his eyes a moment, hoping to fathom his intent in the dark recesses. Bupkes. "You're obviously pulling my leg here."

Jim clapped me on the shoulder. "It's all about the white crow, and how these people want it, and how I think you ought to give it to them."

"Give?"

Kim gave his mustache a sly rub. "It might be better to give it to them rather than have them take it by force."

A vermicular chill wriggled up my neck and bounced around between my temples. "Just what are you trying to say? And what's so funny?"

"I apologize, really, but it's hard not to see the humor in it. That's just my nature, my morbid sense of humor. And no, Garth, I'm not threatening you. I'm just giving you some sound advice. I'm on your side in this, really. Gotta go." He gave me a jolly salute and slid back into the crowd.

I scanned the papier mâché Mardis Gras harlequins grinning down from the ceiling. Their *joyeux* now seemed *sinistre*, like they knew some dark secret I didn't. Had Kim really just been there, or was he a specter, presage's embodiment, like a Greek chorus? Or was he just some loopy apparition brought on by the planter's punch and too many peanuts? You know, like Marley's ghost brought on by a blot of mustard.

"Hey, pumpkin." Angie plunked down next to me in the booth. "What's wrong?"

I had a quick debate with myself and decided not to tell Angie about Jim Kim. I guess I thought it might put a damper on the evening, and it seemed like it would keep until the next day. Or until I could make sense of it. Sink her teeth into puzzle pie like that and we'd be up all night working it over. Remember the *Times* crossword? Can't put it down until it's done. So occasionally I have to try to steer her away from such things, if nothing else so I can get some sleep.

"Just tired, I guess. Shall we split?"

"Yeah, I have stuff to do tomorrow." There are a lot of weddings in June, and Angie had to fill an order of eighty diamond solitaires and some pavé work. She does some of her own design, but her bread is buttered by piecework for art jewelers and the stray factory job.

Normally, we would have done the twenty-minute walk home, but since it was her birthday, we grabbed a cab and were home in five minutes. The front shop door is sealed and we always enter via the adjoining apartment lobby through two locking vestibule doors. There's a side entrance into our apartment tucked back under the stairwell opposite the basement door. When we arrived home that night we displayed our usual wariness of dark corners and potential lurking muggers. New York isn't so openly dangerous anymore, but you still have to have your Spidey Sense about you at night. Make out someone tracking you, either from behind or from across the street, and you have to take evasive maneuvers: Walk in the street between parked cars and moving traffic, where the tracking mugger will be shy of being exposed in the headlights. Or sometimes, if you just stop and stare him down, he'll realize the element of surprise is no longer on his side and go looking for less-suspecting prey. If I'm walking with Angie, the thing to do is for us to drift farther apart so the hunter can't corner us together, thus frustrating his decision about which of us to target. His window of opportunity is usually pretty small, less than thirty seconds before the quarry is back in the safety of the pedestrian herd at a well-lit intersection.

We instinctively drifted apart, checking the perimeter as we approached the door. They sometimes like to pounce while you're preoccupied unlocking the door and collecting the mail. But the coast was clear. We entered the vestibule and stepped into the hall.

Safe at home.

"Hold it, hold it!" A husky, masked figure emerged from the basement door, which is usually locked. He was pointing a pistol at me, and my first thought was that it had to be fake. Then it occurred to me that a toy gun in New York is almost harder to come by than a real one.

Angie slid behind me, and I just stammered, my heart sinking like a gazelle surrounded by lions.

"I'll kill you, I'll friggin' kill you." Husky started waving the gun, I guess in response to the stupid grin on my face. I snorted, still grasping at the notion that this wasn't really happening. I wonder if a cornered gazelle ever experiences denial. Then I turned and saw two more masked men. All of them wore jeans, black pea coats, and ski masks—must've been a sale at the army surplus store.

All I could think to say was "What are you, nuts?"

A hand grabbed me by my shirt collar from behind, and I hissed from the sting of fingernails scratching my neck.

"What's that, pardner?" The voice behind me was raspy, vicious and yet mischievous, like a desperado robbing a stagecoach.

"You're crazy, we don't . . ."

I turned, straining against the grip on my shirt. The whites of his eyes turned red, and he smacked me in the head with a gun. Take it from me, don't try this at home, kids—getting gun-whipped hurts like sin.

Angie yelped louder than I did. I was bent over

with blood running off my scalp and down my arm, the vision of warm red fluid dripping from my elbow making me a little woozy. Nice mouth, Garth.

Next I got a kick in the ribs, my hair was pulled, and I fell over on the floor. There was arguing among the attackers. Even with the imp of agony dancing on my skull, I was reminded of the stagecoach robbery scene from *The Man Who Shot Liberty Valance*. I was James Stewart, naive lawyer from the East, confronted with the business end of Lee Marvin's bullwhip. I seemed to recall that "Duke" Wayne didn't come to the rescue then either.

"Back off, man, back off!" This third intruder had an accent, a brogue of some kind. I didn't remember Father Duffy being part of Liberty Valance's gang.

"I'll wup this shit seven ways from Sunday!" Lee Marvin couldn't have delivered the line better.

"Christ, let's not have another stiff!" Brogue implored. "He's down, can't y' see?"

C'mon, Duke! Where are you? If only somehow, by some miracle . . .

I heard Angie shriek, "Stop!"

"Shut her up!" There was the sound of Angie struggling.

I wheeled around, fresh hormones flooding my noggin with the imperative to protect her. That's when I felt another blow to my side, and then to my head again. Next thing I knew I was looking up, and the world was fading purple. Now the three ski-masked men, one holding Angie by the neck, stood over me.

"What is it you want?" Angie yelped. "Garth, stay down, darn it! Anything . . ."

"Open the door, dang it," one of the bandits barked. "Hear?"

Raspy put his foot on my head, pushed me back down. "Next time, fellah, you watch your mouth. Who's crazy now, huh?"

He had me there, all right. Only an idiot or a lunatic sasses a man with a gun, and I preferred being bonkers—at least there's some hope for a cure. I'd pretty much resigned myself to the ugly reality that we were completely at their mercy and there wasn't a damn thing I could do about it. Duke wasn't going to show. A policeman wasn't going to peer in the front door. I'm not what you'd call a religious person, but at a moment like that, you find yourself praying, the last resort of the helpless. Or in my case, the hapless. If God wanted me to go to church, sacrifice goats, proselytize on subway cars, or hand out pamphlets in Penn Station, I'd do it if he'd just get us out of this.

I was trying to keep my eyes trained on Angie, watching to see if one of them laid a hand on her, when I saw a fourth figure—a tall, broad one—appear from around the corner. No army surplus here. He wore an oversize hooded sweatshirt, his face obscured by shadow. But I could see the glint from his eyes, two bright stars, and I could feel the intensity of his stare. My heart skipped a beat: He looked like the Grim Reaper. I didn't suppose he'd let me have a go at playing him in chess.

The others looked to him, as though waiting for instructions, but the Reaper said nothing.

I heard Angie fumbling with her keys and our front door scrape open.

"Into the basement, lady," Raspy commanded. "Throw him in the basement too. Now."

Husky started pulling my hair.

"I'll take him!" Angie protested. "We'll go, just don't hurt—"

"Shut up—"

I heard a slap, and then felt myself sliding on my back down the stairs, my jacket cushioning the trip only slightly. A door slammed and we were left in the dark. I heard Angie crying. Maybe I passed out for a minute or two, it was hard to tell. I could smell the emulsifier that the caribou antlers were soaking in, the cedar oil we spray on the mounts to mothproof them. Well, at least Otto had been busy while we were out. The next I knew, Angie had me cradled in her arms, and she was holding something to my head to staunch the bleeding. I could hear her sniffling, felt a tear hit my face, heard her heart pounding in her chest. My legs were still partially on the basement steps. One of my feet felt cooler than the other, and I could feel the sock down around my toes. I waved my foot in the air in a vain attempt to see what was going on with my foot.

"Where's my shoe?" Hapless, hopeless, and now slaphappy. "I had two."

"Shhh," she said back to me. "When they're gone . . ." Angie left it at that.

I may have passed out again, but suddenly light flooded the basement, and in a blur I could see the stairs leading up to the doorway. Angie shifted and started to pull me away from the stairs. I think she thought it was the attackers again. But I saw my naked foot and a very distinctive silhouette creep into the open doorway.

"Oo, my Got! Garv! Yangie! Not lookink!"

Chapter 4

Even though there's a lot of nice domestic wildlife taxidermy around and a healthy market in commercial interior decoration, I can't deal in top-of-the-line exotics. The dinguses in demand by folks with bushels of money I'm not allowed to sell. Like lions, tigers, polar bears, and over a thousand other species listed in parts 17 and 23 of CFR 50, a rule book written by thirty-six countries through an authority known as the Convention on International Trade in Endangered Species and Wild Flora and Fauna (CITES). However, this doesn't necessarily keep me from owning them, provided I submit U.S. Fish and Wildlife form 3-200 and receive approval in the form of a permit. And it doesn't keep me from renting or "lending" them for commercials or photo shoots. And it doesn't necessarily keep me from buying and selling them, provided said merchandise is packing a New York State Department of Environmental Conservation form 82-19-21 certifying it was harvested legally before 1974, though taxidermy with "papers" isn't as common as it should be. And if I want to sell an endangered or protected piece I bought in New York in Maine, I need a comparable permit from the other state. Welcome to the taxidermy paper mill.

In order to sell endangered animals killed after 1974, even if they were road kill, you basically have to prove it's being used for educational purposes. I have an easier time acquiring such pieces because I supply schools, museums, and tourist traps that pass for museums. But usually such institutions aren't real moneymakers and can't pay what the things are worth—i.e., what the black market would pay or what pieces with "paper" would get on the open market.

The pelts of some endangered species have considerable value on the black market. Some folks ignore CITES authority and sell ivory, crocodile leather, and exotic pelts permit-free to private collectors. I've crossed paths with shadowy types who deal both on the fringes and in the fold of this black market, and they have a compelling incentive for continuing their crimes: money. And not just from pelts and rugs but from animal eviscerae. Asian apothecaries turn all manner of animal vestiges into costly folk medicine, and while some of it's taken legally from bears by hunters, a lot of it is taken whenever and however. Machine-gunning hibernating bears in their dens is one popular method. Then there's rhino horn and tiger penis, which are never in season but can be purchased just the same, though usually you're just being sold very expensive ground arrowroot. Aside from the devastating effect this sleazy activity has on biodiversity, it's an inexcusably rapacious crime that might just put me and PETA in the same lynch mob.

The reason Big Bro makes it such a pain to collect endangered and protected species, even those taken before the ban on captive animals, is fairly obvious. A legal market for the stuff would encourage even more poaching, which is already alarmingly common. Now, I'm not sympathetic with those who think nothing of making animals extinct to alleviate lumbago or to sport a nifty wrap at the club social. By the same token, I take a dim view of zoos or "conservation parks"—habitat penitentiaries that amount to animal jail. But I can't help but commiserate with those who want to collect animals freed by natural death or harvested legally, a dignified end for some of Mother Nature's most exquisite creations. Taxidermy is the ultimate form of flattery.

Be that as it may, I was less than disposed to the assault team that ransacked my collection and smacked us around. After a chat with a couple uniformed cops, I paid a visit to the hospital for stitches to my scalp, an X-ray, and a sleepless night. The next morning found me at home, playing host to Agent Renard, a plainclothes ECO (Environmental Control Officer) from the New York State Department of Environmental Conservation. He was a balding and tawny black guy with reading glasses and the disposition of an indifferent schoolmaster. Only by virtue of the fact that I'm a longtime New Yorker, exposed to every conceivable ethnic variety, could I venture to say his clipped, lilting accent was West Indian—Haitian, perhaps.

Also enjoying my hospitality was a New York City Police Department detective named Walker, who looked on with distaste. I knew him from our local precinct. That is to say, he had been gently harassing me for years, convinced that my entrepreneurial bent with taxidermy was somehow a crooked enterprise. Police have always just seemed to have an innate feeling that I'm up to no good, ever since I was a kid. With my younger brother, Nick, it was even worse, though in his case it was justified. And I did have a great-uncle who was a bank robber. Maybe it's genetics—I got the felon's pheromones but not the inclination. Walker had gotten a rotten whiff off me right from our first encounter.

Angie sat on the couch, hunched glumly over a cup of tea, holding an ice pack to her bruised cheek. I had an ice pack of my own clamped over the back of my head where I'd been gun-whipped. But I was too agitated to sit and paced back and forth in front of Fred. Even though he's a fairly valuable African piece, I guess the attackers figured he was too cum-

bersome to grab quickly. I should really have him
spring-loaded, so whenever an intruder enters, Fred
lurches forward and scares the bejesus out of them.
I can still picture those trick-or-treaters running
down the dark driveway.

Renard cast a sleepy eye over my list of missing
property, cleared his throat, and read it aloud:

"Skins: two leopard, five zebra, one tiger, one
panther, two lioness, three lion, one grizzly. Rugs:
two polar bear, two Kodiak, one lion. Skulls: three
ocelot, one tiger, four lion, one cheetah. A pair of
carved ivory elephant tusks . . ." He paused to inhale. ". . . And one white crow in a bell jar.

"Tell me." Renard closed his eyes, and for a second I thought he'd dozed off. "You have papers for
this, and the rest of your collection?" His eyes
tweaked open, peering closely at a snipe on the
shelf by his elbow.

Papers? Put him in a black leather trench coat
and he'd be a shoe-in for the Gestapo. Most ECOs
use the word *documentation*.

I knew Renard's predecessor, Pete Durban, a
bold character who had once been a lion tamer. No
lie. Circuses still need lions tamed, after all. Durban
had come to trust that I was on the up-and-up.
He'd gone through all my *documentation*. Now I had
to break in the new kid, and at a time like this.

"He's got paper up the wazoo," Walker laughed,
"if you think that means anything."

"Detective Walker is a big fan of ours," I said,
trying to get Agent Renard to look at me. "He's

been over for tea and scones lots of times, you know, just to check up on us, make sure we're all right."

Walker flushed. "Patrolmen seen all kinds of things going in and outta here. Five'll get you ten this operation isn't completely kosher, Renard. And what's it with this character? This Russian? Hey." Walker snapped his fingers at Otto. "You saw these bandits?"

Otto was posed in the booth by the window like a Rodin bronze in the clutches of some existential conundrum.

"But of course. Workink many job. My vife, Luba, not happy, so I vurk. Vhen voman like Cossack, not good go to home, eh? Not lookink."

"What's this guy talking about?" Walker sneered.

"He was working late, Walker," I growled. "He was out back smoking a cigarette when it all went down. He heard the commotion, looked in the window."

"Yes. Vindow I look. KGB come, take. Not lookink. I fraid, because for me, is at very difficult. I vait, then come to find basement Yangie and Garv."

"What the f—"

"Muggers, thieves—bad people—he calls them KGB. *Not looking* means wrong or bad."

"You'd think these people come to America, they'd speak American, for chrissake. Okay, so what did they look like?"

Otto donned an expression of dismay. "KGB always like KGB. Verink black. But!" Otto jumped to his feet. "Boss man, off he take black mask face, eh?" Otto stepped up close to Walker and winked. "I see boss. Teeth big, vood in leeps."

"What's this creep talking about?" Walker pleaded.

"Big teeth and a toothpick," Angie translated.

"Is that it?" Walker poked Otto in the sternum.

"But of course, eh?" Otto poked Walker in the sternum. "Otto big eyes."

Walker looked like he was going to head-butt Otto, but he turned crimson instead. "Renard, I tell you, between this creep and these animals there's something very illegal here." Walker rocked on his heels, grinning wolfishly. "And I'm gonna find out what it is too."

I cleared my throat. "And when he catches us red-handed with a crate brimming with bald eagles, the police chief himself is going to make him detective sergeant and invite him over for a pool party."

Walker took a step forward, and I was ready to do the same—I'd had about all I was willing to take from him. But Renard swung out an arm toward a small brown bird, blocking Walker's advance.

"And this." Renard twinkled an eye in my direction. "A long-billed dowitcher. Part of your collection?" Still with the black-leather trench-coat stuff.

"That's a snipe you're looking at, and this is not a collection. I told you, I'm a dealer, I rent. This is my stock. The numbers at the bottom of that page are my personal tracking numbers."

I tossed him a small key and gestured to a file

cabinet in the corner. "The files on them are all in there, along with complete records of everything I've bought and sold over the last two years, where it was bought, where it was from, where it went, organized *Aardvark* to *Zebra*. Records from before then are in the basement in bankers' boxes."

Angie brought me a breakfast beer, and I rolled the icy bottle along the bruise gracing the side of my head. She ditched her tea for a cold one herself, still holding the ice pack to her swollen cheek. You'd think we were a couple of Canadians the day after a rousing midnight curling match.

Detective Walker chuckled. "Miss, do you mean to tell me that nobody touched your supply of gold wire and diamonds? That they didn't even go through your studio, open any drawers?"

"Left my studio alone, sorry to say. At least my stuff is insured." Angie sighed, and perched on the arm of a chair.

"Gimme a break." Walker snorted. "They came in here just to steal these dusty old dead animals? Maybe these characters were some of Carson's business partners who double-crossed him, a deal gone bad."

"KGB not lookink." Otto grunted, and he left for the backyard and a smoke. He'd been brooding fitfully all night and all morning about failing to save us from Liberty Valance's hooligans. Now I think he'd had about as much as *he* could take of Walker.

Renard was playing with a calculator, his brown eyes shining.

"Detective, these 'dead animals' add up to at least sixty thousand dollars' worth of merchandise. They have a very high resale value, better than most stolen property. And they were highly visible going in, going out, and on display. Thefts from large private taxidermy collections are not all that unusual. By comparison, the jewelry is small, and the diamonds are probably kept in a plain-looking little envelope in what to the untrained eye doesn't necessarily look like a jeweler's bench."

Walker was fed up. "So, Carson, sell any bear gallbladders lately?"

"He doesn't deal in that stuff anymore." Angie looked at Renard. "In fact, he went undercover for you guys to break up a chop shop. Two years ago."

I'd have preferred this not come up. The gallbladder incident had netted me $52,700 and got Walker on my case in the first place. I didn't want the black leather trench coat to get any inkling that my dealings weren't completely on the up-and-up. I could get along very nicely without any more of Renard's sly innuendos.

"See?" Walker began, waving a finger in my direction. "They sent him in to rat out his pals."

I gritted my teeth. "Check it out in your files, Renard. The agent I dealt with is named Pete Durban, guy who used to have your job before he went to U.S. Fish and Wildlife. When I reported this character named Park to the New York DEC, they had me go back and buy fifty thousand dollars' worth of endangered skins for Candid Camera. And believe me, this guy was not a pal. He ran an animal chop shop."

"Park?" Agent Renard raised his eyebrows at me, like his alarm clock had just now pulled him from a deep sleep. "Gallbladders. A lucrative business," he added dryly. His sleepy indifference returned and he flipped randomly through a folder of my permits.

"Damn right. I dealt only once in bladders, when I brokered them for a taxidermist friend out west." I'd made a nice chunk of change during that short stint too.

"And so: Why did you give it up?" Renard shoved the file closed and tossed me the key.

I pointed to the bandage on the back of my head and winced.

" 'Cause of this kind of rough play. Sleazy characters. It was like doing a drug deal. Not to mention that it's now illegal to sell gallbladders in most states."

"I see." Renard buttoned his jacket. "Did you mark your stolen acquisitions in any way that—"

"My pelts and rugs are branded on the underside, dead center, with my name and the ID number. Head mounts I brand behind the plaque, on the neck stopper. Skulls have a yellow sticker inside the skull cavity that's a bitch to remove. The tusks have my brand on the stump, but that won't help much once they chop them up." It hurt just saying it.

Those babies were part of my personal collection. "Dammit."

"Carson, it's not like they cleaned you out." Walker was calling me a crybaby.

"Oh, yeah? Imagine, Detective Walker, somebody breaking into your house and stealing everything but the veggies, fruit, and condiments from your refrigerator." I raised my arms toward the aviary of predatory birds hanging from the high ceiling, then at Fred, then waved my ice pack at the stand-up bear, the full-body albino deer, the badgers, beavers, otters, porcupines, bobcats, muskrats, weasels, martins, and polecats. "All potatoes and no meat. What's left doesn't add up to what was taken. This is mostly domestic, a few nice pieces, but nothing like the African skins. I still have a few cat mounts, but . . ." I smacked an armchair with a fist.

"What about the man Garth told the officers about?" Angie sidled up next to me and gave me a squeeze, trying to calm me. She'd already reproached me for having held back my encounter with Kim until we were at the hospital. "That guy in the bar who asked Garth about the crow."

Walker flipped a page in his notepad. "Do you have any idea how many Kims are listed in the phone book, and how many of them might have changed their Korean first names to Jim? Forget about it. Probably a phony name anyways."

"A Korean?" Renard knitted his brow, a bad dream disrupting his sleep. "There was a Korean asking about the crow?"

"Said I should give the crow to some people he knows who wanted it, before they took it from me." I sighed. "But I dunno. These guys took a lot more than the crow."

"Indeed? Well, Mr. Carson, I should think you're most fortunate that you two weren't more severely injured." Renard fitted a blue plaid porkpie hat on his shiny head. It had what looked like a red salmon fly in the hatband and was the kind of thing Perry Como would have worn. "You do realize they could have killed one or both of you, on purpose or by accident? Doesn't seem worth it."

I rearranged the ice pack on my head and squeezed Angie's hand.

"You're right about that," she sniffed.

"I'll put the list on the wire." Renard opened the door. "By the way . . ."

I knew the sound of that opener. It's the "one last, small question" ploy detectives use just as they're going out the door, when the suspect's guard is down. His spin on it was to yawn first, like he was just turning in for the night and was about to remind me to set my alarm. I found myself wondering what kind of pajamas he wore. Stripes, plaid, or polka dots?

"Any idea why they took the white crow? Why the Korean warned you?"

"Nope." I was too disgusted to even think about it.

"I see. Where did you ever find a white crow?"

"Bermuda, Vermont. That important?"

"I'll be in touch." Renard ducked out the door.

"By the way, Carson," Walker grinned, "I don't suppose you noticed how the parking regulations keep changing in front of your building?"

I gave him a smarmy squint. "Teenagers: such a handful."

Walker slammed the door behind him.

Angie and I sniffled back tears and sat for a while without speaking, as we finished our beers.

The apartment suddenly seemed unbearably quiet. No solace in this sound of silence, just the victim's mute and relentless echo of frustration. I'd never been the victim of violence before, not like this, and it made me angrier than I think I've ever been, mostly with myself for failing. Failing to protect Angie, failing to capitulate, failing to anticipate. I didn't ask Angie whether she felt the same. But I know we both had that nasty lump of humiliation in our throats, which in combination with my anger had me ruminating on all sorts of fantasies where I locate the bastards and hack them to pieces with the sawfish bill on the wall over the sink. And naturally, I felt somewhat emasculated. It was the first time either of us had been "mugged" in all our years in New York, something that only happened to other, less savvy people. I guess we should have felt lucky. That's what our friends told us. Then again, none of them had been gun-whipped, kicked in the head, had their partner smacked around, and then been thrown down a flight of stairs and locked in a dark basement. But mostly I think we couldn't get over coming so close to losing each other, all for a mere sixty thousand dollars of dead animals.

Had my prayers in that dire moment been answered?

Please, God. Don't ask me to hand out pamphlets in Penn Station. Goat sacrifices, you say? We'll talk.

Chapter 5

As if the attack by burglars wasn't bad enough, the morning-after cat-and-mouse with the fuzz left Angie and me feeling at loose ends. We sat around staring at the vacant spots on the wall, a bad taste in our mouths. We slept fitfully for a few hours, then went out to a coffee shop and found we had nothing to say, except to rehash our unfortunate episode, upon which we were clearly tired of dwelling. We gave up. Angie hopped the subway to catch up with fellow goldsmithies uptown.

I had work to do. There was an Elks' convention in town, and I was supposed to get back to them about supplying an elk head for above the podium. At a film studio in Astoria, they were shooting a Freezy Cone commercial and wanted some stuffed penguins to fill in the background behind some live ones. I had to get my six Magellanic penguins over to them by eleven-thirty that morning, if for no other reason than I wanted to talk to the live-penguin wrangler to make sure he'd keep his birds away from mine. Live ones will viciously attack the taxidermy variety—I've been told they think the stuffed ones are sitting so still that they're nesting on their turf. Never mind that they're in a television studio and not on an ice floe. I lost one of my squad members (poor Sneezy, RIP) in just such a tragic incident two years before. The penguin squad is almost always rented as a set—nobody ever wants just one penguin, for some reason.

This particular variety of penguin is not protected by CITES and is quite prolific along the Pacific coast of South America, though commercial fishing has put a serious dent in the Falkland Island populations. Estimates of breeding pairs is around 1,600,000. However, you do have to know your penguins to stay out of trouble, because the Magellanics can easily be confused with jackass penguins, from Africa, which are classified as "vulnerable" and thus protected. The jackasses (named so for their braylike utterances) have been decimated by habitat degradation at the hands of guano prospectors. The way you tell them apart is by the markings. The Magellanic has white brow markings that do not connect to the rest of the tux.

I also had to pick up my zebra skins at the Expedition Club uptown, which I figured I could do on my way out to Astoria. (At least some of my zebra

skins were out of the shop and thus spared.) You'd
~~think they would~~ have had enough of them lying
around over there at the Expedition Club, but they
needed a few extras as part of buffet table settings. I
suspect that they preferred to have Richard Leakey
and Robert Ballard spill wine and gravy on my pelts
instead of theirs. So a light coating of Scotchgard
goes on mine before I rent them out, and the tough
stains come out with a dynamite little product
called Furz-B-Clean. You'd be surprised how many
people on the Upper East Side want to serve their
cocktail weenies from a table cloaked in zebra skins.
Better that than as a rug. Soak 'em in pinot noir, if
you must, but nobody scuffs the hair off my skins
with their boots. I don't rent them as rugs, ever.

I called the Elks and got a machine. So I rolled
my penguins in bubble plastic and boxed them in
foam peanuts. Appropriately, they looked like they
were frozen in ice and up to their necks in snow. I
had just grabbed my car keys when the phone
rang—I hoped it was the Elks so I could save myself
an extra trip.

But it wasn't the Elks. It was Pete Durban.

"I heard" was all he said.

"Word travels fast."

"Wanna talk about it?"

"Not really. My penguins are waiting for me."

"You going out drinking with your penguins
rather than me?"

"Who said I was going out drinking?"

"That's what guys do when they feel sorry for

themselves," Pete said. "And believe me, I'm a much better listener than your seven dwarfs."

"Six. Remember the refrigerator commercial?"

"Right." Pete sighed. "Poor Sneezy. So, what say we get drunk and toast his memory?"

"Can't. Got business."

"A wet lunch, perhaps? One o'clock, the Mexican place?"

"I'll be there."

Pete's a high-school dropout who literally ran away with the circus. Hard to believe that sort of thing has even happened in the last fifty years, but he apparently had a full beard at seventeen and they weren't particular. He started on the lowest rung: cage cleaner. But like most people who really adore animals, cleaning up after them comes with the territory. That's how he got close to the lions and mentored with the lion tamer, a man who had lost his own son in a car crash three years earlier. Pete stayed until his late twenties, when the circus went into receivership and threw everybody out of work. His mentor retired, but the bank hired Pete to care for the lions and find buyers. Well, to make a long story short, some of the buyers who came sniffing around weren't exactly legitimate, and Pete helped the New York State Department of Environmental Conservation and the feds nab a chop shop, which in this case was a black-market operation that sold exotics for parts. The DEC had an opening for someone who could make big cats purr instead of devour and was relatively fearless around dangerous animals. So once the lions had new homes, they signed him up.

We were meeting at a Mexican place over on Washington Street, which is walking distance from my place. I'd picked up my zebra pelts and found them to be relatively clean—Jim Fowler and Sir Edmund Hillary must have used their plates. Made my penguin delivery and duly admonished the penguin wrangler to keep his beasts' beaks away from my squad. He showed me that his birds were suitably contained, penned up in a chicken-wire enclosure at one end of the set. They jostled and squawked like a bunch of wobbly bowling pins. I would have thought they were cute if they weren't crowded at the end of the cage closest to my birds, casting their beady eyes at the nearest box. They must have picked up the scent. You could see the little bastards already gleeful about the prospect of shredding Doc, Dopey, and Grumpy.

Arrived home, no messages from the Elks. Hoped they hadn't found another source.

As I walked down Washington Street, I wondered how this latest development in my life bode for my burgeoning midlife crisis. I felt like I was against the ropes. At least before the sacking of Garth's Castle, things were fine. Not great, but fine. Now things were crappy, which isn't great and isn't even fine. A setback or a sign of things to come?

Pete is not your strapping lion tamer of lore, the one with the black handlebar mustache, but a small, hairy sinewy guy with a red handlebar mustache, small wire specs, and thin, frizzy hair. You can see he's one of those guys who has to try to figure out where his chest hair and beard begin and end. Pete chose to shave to the edge of his T-shirt collar. In keeping with his character, it was always a little dangerous visiting with Pete. Ever since he roped me into that chop-shop sting operation, he'd somehow gotten the impression I was a fellow thrill-seeker. He specializes in going undercover for the feds, often as a redneck but on occasion as a Dutch trader, a befezzed Turk, or an Australian magnate. And no matter how preposterous the ruse, he always manages to keep a straight face and avoid getting drilled by the humorless folk on the other side of the law. Well, so far.

We sat in a booth in the back that had pictures of Ernest Borgnine covering the walls. Why, you ask? Because it was the Ernest Borgnine Memorial Booth at my local Mexican restaurant. That's New York for you.

"Y'gotta try this, Garth." Pete held out the animal perched on his arm. I tried to make my recoil look like I was hailing the waitress.

"Better box that critter before someone freaks out." I glanced at Borgnine as the lead in *Marty*, and he looked disapproving. The waitress approached, and Pete put the arm with the critter under the table.

"W-we're ready to order," I stammered.

"Black beans and rice for me." Pete beamed.

"And a shot of tequila, a can of Blue Ribbon, and a slice of peach pie with whipped cream."

"Beef burrito and a Corona. No fruit."

"He'll have a tequila too, won't you?"

"Well . . ." I looked at Borgnine as McHale, and he seemed to be urging me to have one.

"Give him a tequila." Pete gave her a wink. "He needs one."

As the waitress retreated, Pete brought his arm back up onto the table and said, "Uh-oh." His arm was empty, his pet gone. Did I mention Pete collects venomous animals?

My reaction to the escaped pet was immediate and much to Pete's amusement. Several other diners came to help me off the floor and right the chair I'd tripped over in my haste to exit the booth.

"Don't worry, Maddy's back in the box." Pete giggled like someone who'd just fooled me with a joy-buzzer handshake. Once I was seated again, he insisted on giving me a last look at his humongous emperor scorpion. "Don't like the bugs much, do yuh, Garth?"

Too large to hold in one hand, the damn thing looked like an ill-shaven patent-leather lobster. Can a big, black, hairy, shiny, and bumpy animal that waves pincers and a stinger be anything but evil? You could hear the creak of its segmented tail as it flexed like a gunfighter's nervous trigger finger.

"Lordy, Pete, that's not your everyday mantis or cicada or anything. I collected beetles as a kid, my dad was a butterfly collector, and I can take cockroaches, giant walking sticks, and the occasional tarantula even. But that thing looks like a freakin' alien being. Too big to stomp on is just too much bug." If I hadn't known better, those rats covering Borgnine in the still from *Willard* could have been emperor scorpions.

"Awright, I'll put Maddy away. But she's a pussycat, really. Scorpions like this with big pincers look mean, but it's the ones with itty-bitty pincers that'll zap you but good." Pete shoveled the evil bug back into its box and slid the lid shut. "Thought Maddy might distract you from your recent woes."

"I appreciate the thought, but . . ."

"You got smacked around a bit, that's for sure. Sonsabitches." Pete waved a pinky finger at the stitches on my head. "You find them, you let me know. We'll kick their ass. I've got a Malay cone snail that is absolutely vicious. This tetrodotoxic bandito boy is like a gun and can shoot its radula—*pffft, pffft, pffft!* Those bastards'll be in such incredible pain . . . they'll wish they were never born. Ha!"

Patrons seated in our vicinity did their best to ignore Pete's bravado.

"Cone snails? Let's not break out the big guns right away," I jibed.

"Why not?"

"Pete? I was kidding." The idea of us kicking anybody's ass with or without snails was ludicrous, yet the notion of Pete on my team in a revenge plot was oddly reassuring.

Our drinks arrived and I wrapped my bubblegum in a paper napkin. "Anyway, I've got other prob-

lems, like Agent Renard, your replacement." There
was a lime in the top of my beer and I removed the
offending fruit. As though under the power of sug-
gestion, the words *no fruit* never fail to sail right
over a bartender's sphere of consciousness. "He's
starting to bust my chops already."

"Thought Detective Walker was your number-
one porcupine?"

"He was there too, adding color commentary."

"Never met this hombre Renard. But I took a
glance at his resumé before leaving the DEC.
Worked out of the Albany office tracking export of
domestic fauna. More the office type, a bean counter
who issued figures on the black market. West Indian,
from Guyana, originally. Used to work for Guyanese
Customs, and then for some Asian shipping outfit
that moved tropical fish, I think. Don't understand
the transfer south from Albany, tell you the truth.
Some guys just itch to get out in the field, get some
action. Garth, y'gotta figure on him giving you the
business at first. He's gotta let you know who's the
bear, that kinda hoo-ha."

"As a victim, I could do without police harass-
ment just now. I mean, it might actually be nice if
the DEC was circulating a flier on my stolen property."

"Leave it up to Pete." He downed his shot of
tequila and gave me a wink. "I'll get the list from
Renard and pigeon it out to every police bulletin
board in the country. U.S. Fish and Wildlife is

better connected than the state outfits. Hey, mucha-cho? You okay?"

"Gee, I dunno." I rolled my eyes, and gestured at my cut scalp. "Do I look okay?"

"You know what I mean."

I squinted, and he continued.

"I can see it in your eyes. The green meanies have got you, am I right?"

"Green meanies? Green meanies?"

"Don't kid a kidder. I know that look 'cause you had it two years ago. You were in a funk about your life. About your career. And now this."

"Yeah, well . . ."

He pulled a folded paper from his pocket. "I know we talked before about looking into a job at U.S. Fish and Wildlife."

"I don't want a job. I have a job."

"You don't sound so sure, amigo. Here." He handed over the paper and I unfolded a copy of an e-mail.

I scanned the paper. "What is this?"

"That, muchacho, is a job interview with USFW."

My bruises suddenly felt warm. "An interview? For a job?"

Pete looked exasperated. "That's what I'm talk-ing about. You keep thinking that you need to get out of taxidermy brokering. Well . . ." He pointed at the paper and folded his arms.

I concentrated and managed to read the e-mail. He'd set up an interview for me the day after next, at 8:00 A.M., at their offices downtown.

"What made you think I'd be available at this time?" I waved the paper.

"Are you?"

"Well . . ."

"Look, Garth, these openings don't come up often. You're exactly the kind of guy they need to help their department crack down on the trade of endangered species. You'd do very much what you do now: travel around to all these little stores, and to some big ones, and report the violators."

I groaned.

"This is a job with the U.S. government, Garth. Can you say *pension? Health plan? 401K?* Angie could be on your insurance plan. Just go, and if you decide it's not for you, then turn it down. But once you make your choice, you're going to have to stick with it and be happy."

"I'll go," I moaned. "I'm sorry, Pete, and I'm grateful to you for your efforts. But mostly I'm conflicted, you know that."

Pete punched me in the shoulder. "Okay, *Señor* Carson. But if you ask me, you take all this way too seriously. Do whatever you feel is right and no regrets. Life is too short. Hey—" He fished through a pocket and handed me a slip of paper. "Maybe this will cheer you up. When you said over the phone you had a white crow in the lot that was stolen, it rang a bell."

The document he'd given me was from some sort of Internet search vehicle and read: *MOOSE*

HEAD 4 SALE: MUST GO. U HAUL. NORTH-EAST U.S. (888) 901–4123.

I smiled. "Hey, a cheap moose head!"

"Not that. *Below that.*"

I read on: *WANT MY WHITE CROW BACK. No questions asked, finder's fee. P.O. Box 34, Wells ME 04090.*

"Egads. Another white crow. That is quite a co-incidence. But this moose head . . . if they say *U HAUL* it sounds big. And *MUST GO* means cheap."

"Still hooked on cheap moose heads, eh?"

"I'm not without my vices." A cheap—but good—moose head is like a dream. A fantasy, perhaps—my criteria are pretty demanding.

Antlers: Perhaps the most important part of a moose. They should be large, more than sixty inches, with expansive palms and well-curved tines, no bullet holes. The antlers should be masterful, imposing, threatening.

Pelt: Egads, do I see a lot of baked moose heads that have been mounted over the fireplace. Stick your finger between the hair on the neck and press. It should give without cracking. Pet the moose. No crunching, no falling hair. As if taxidermy isn't tran-sient enough as it is, a dried-out mount of any kind is ruined and effectively worthless.

Ears & Dewlap: Whole, free of cracks, glue, or bug shucks. Ears are one of the first things to get damaged on any mount, and next to noses and maybe cat lips they're the most prone to drying and crumbling.

Eyes, Nose, Lips: I can live with small cracks. Patch them up with plastic wood, paint them black. But shriveled facial derma is a distortion nobody can repair well.

Pose: Chin up, snout slightly turned, ears forward, and by all appearances alert to the hunter's approach. Or, if I could find it, a grunting moose, mouth open, tongue partially extended. That would approach moose-head quintessence.

Of course, if I really wanted the damn thing, I could find it. I could go to a world-class taxidermist and buy a museum-quality mount. I could do that, and pay full price. But I'm a dealer. It's more than an occupation. It's a creed. I live for deals. And to me, moose heads have come to represent the ultimate deal, though perhaps an unattainable one. You see, over the last fifteen years, people claim to have seen—at a garage sale, a thrift store, an estate sale, the Salvation Army—a moose head selling for fifty dollars. The result is that I can't bring myself to buy a moose for more than that because I'm deluded, foolishly convinced that any day I might just stumble upon the mythical cheap head. Or better still: Where is the estranged wife of the great white hunter who thinks her dear departed's giant moose is a worthless monstrosity and will *pay me* fifty bucks to haul it away?

Silly? Well, I prefer to think of it as a natural part of the human condition. Everybody seems to be

searching for something—a lottery jackpot, con-
sensual sex, a great lawn, true love—that is so improbable it crosses over from seething aspiration
into apotheosis.

"Garth? Hello?"

"Sorry, Pete, I was just—"

"Yup, I know, dreaming about the perfect
moose head. I thought the white-crow ad would
interest you."

"It does, it does. Where'd you find it?"

"We have a special Web program that searches
eBay and online classifieds nationwide. It looks for
animals on sale that might be protected. The only
reason I saw the crow was because it was next to an
African pelt ad. And white crows are rare enough
that I didn't forget it."

"That is weird. This crow ad was dated three
weeks ago. Think someone is out to corner the
white-crow market?" Of course, I was talking crow
but still thinking about the moose.

"Hard to say, hombre." Pete twirled his mustache
thoughtfully. "Seems like the thieves who took the
crow, this clipping, the college kid in Vermont—
albino crows are suddenly downright popular.
Funny they'd take all your other critters if they
went to the trouble to send that Korean fellah to tip
you off. Brainteaser. Let me know what you dig up
in your investigation."

"Investigation? No, sir." I showed him my palms,
pushing the notion away. "That gallbladder stuff I

did for you guys was the end of it. I've got no love of danger."

He smiled. "C'mon, don't kid. Admit it. You were pumped after we busted those bladder guys."

"If you recall, I ended up gun-whipping you."

"By accident." He crinkled his nose and waved it off like I'd merely nailed him with a spitball. "That was nothing. I mean, if you shot me, I'd have been a little peeved, especially if I died. A gun-whipping? Could happen to anybody. Anybody who's pumped, that is."

"You got me all wrong, Pete. I leave the cops-and-robbers stuff to you, Renard, and Walker. Let me guess. Even now you're probably into something that's liable to seriously jeopardize your health. Other than scorpions, that is?"

"All very hush-hush." Pete leaned in. "Something's going down in Chinatown. Something big."

"Yeah? What's it this time?"

He winced. "All I can tell you is that there's some guys from Korea coming to town with alligator briefcases so full of money it looks like a Brinks truck crashed into the Everglades."

"Could be almost anything. Ivory? Rhino horn?"

"Yeah, could be." Pete shifted gears and raised his can. "Anyway, here's to recovering your varmints."

I raised my bottle and glanced up at Ernie bullying Spencer Tracy.

"Here's to staying out of trouble."

Chapter 6

Two days later, I returned to my apartment after my interview with U.S. Fish and Wildlife and found my phone ringing.

No, it wasn't the Elks. I'd finally reached them and toted my giant bugler over to the Sheraton where their convention was being held.

No, it wasn't the penguin wrangler telling me my birds were pecked to ruination. As far as I knew, his beasts were being kept at bay and my two-tone dwarfs were still A-OK.

No, it wasn't the cheap-moose people. I'd left a message as soon as I got home from my lunch with Pete—not a peep. Probably snatched up already, dag nabbit.

It was the Massachusetts State Police. They'd found my stolen taxidermy in the safety net at a bridge rehabilitation project over the Connecticut River. I thought that pretty odd, and so did the Massachusetts State Police. But as you can imagine, my puzzlement was secondary to joyous relief at recovering my prime pelts. I didn't waste any time pondering the whys or wherefores. After dancing around the apartment, whooping and kissing Fred on his cracked nose, I was out the door and headed north.

The weather was convertible-friendly, so Angie came along for the breather. She got a kiss too. I was in a kissing mood and gave her a few extras.

We had to swing by a TV studio farther up the West Side to drop off Aunt Jilly. She's a standing bear Angie affectionately named after an aunt of hers. I never met the woman, but Angie claims she had thick black fur on her arms and beady yellow eyes. So up to the Network Theater we went. While Angie waited in the double-parked Lincoln, I wheeled Aunt Jilly into the stage entrance. I found the guy who writes the checks; he signed the rental agreement and handed over the deposit. By the time I got downstairs, Angie had circled the block twice to avoid a ticket.

Then we hit Peter Van Putin's town house on the Upper East Side, where Angie ran inside and delivered her portfolio. I drummed my fingers on the steering wheel for half an hour before she came trotting down the steps.

"Sorry it took so long. But Peter was right there, and we got to talking. . . . Garth, it went really well, it was almost like the interview. We flipped through the portfolio together. . . ." She crossed fingers on both hands.

Angie had been trying to break into the high-end art jewelry scene for a long time, first on her own and then on the coattails of someone like this Van Putin character.

"Tremendous. You'll probably get it, but don't get your hopes up too high, okay? You've had disappointments before, so just take it easy."

"You're right." She pinched her eyes tight like she was making a wish, an affectation that looks like something she picked up from *Bewitched*. She can be Samantha anytime she wants, but don't expect me to be Darrin. "Whatever happens, happens."

We charged across the 97th Street Transverse through Central Park, back to the West Side Highway, up the Henry Hudson Parkway, and got our butts outta town before noon. We were approaching the Henry Hudson Bridge before we said much of anything.

"Where did you go so early this morning?"

"Hmm? Oh, I had to go down to the DEC about permits. Get there early, avoid lines."

"You wore a tie."

"Hmm?"

"I said, you wore a tie."

"Yeah, well . . . they treat you better if you wear a tie."

Angie didn't say anything to that. She just made a

humming sound that I knew meant she wasn't completely satisfied with my answer.

Why was I lying? Well, I wasn't lying, was I? I *was* down at the DEC. And the job did concern permits. And at an interview, they do treat you better if you wear a tie. So it wasn't a lie. But I didn't much like telling her a half-truth either.

See, if I told her about it, she would give an opinion. Or even if she didn't, I'd read something into whatever she said, thinking she wanted me to take the job or not take it. Then, if I did what I thought she wanted me to do and I regretted it, I might hold it against her, or stick with a job I hated to please her, which might lead to more resentment. Then again, if I did what I thought she didn't want me to do and I liked my choice and she didn't, then she might resent me. Of course, she might encourage me to do what she thought I wanted rather than what she really wanted, and if I countered by doing the opposite of what she said she wanted and it turned out badly, we might resent each other. Or not. Whatever—it made my head hurt working all the permutations. I felt the decision was mine alone to make in the vacuum of my own panic.

They had offered me the job on the spot. It paid roughly what I was making now *plus* the benefits. How could I turn it down? I had a week to let them know.

"Tell me again how they said your stuff ended up in a safety net?" Angie smiled into the sun, the wind whipping her hair. She looks great in sunglasses of all kinds, sort of the way women can look great in all kinds of hats. Sunglasses were her accessory vice, and she owned dozens. Catty black shades with rhinestones had been chosen for this trip.

"Dunno." I gulped, suppressing thoughts of *the job.* "Someone must have thrown it off the bridge. I figure it wasn't for safekeeping. Man, I can't believe the luck of it. Getting all my stuff back. Never thought I'd see it again. Wanna find the E-ZPass?"

"How do you mean?" She opened the glove compartment, found the transponder, and held it up to the windshield.

"How do I mean what?" The tollgate flipped up.

"Throwing it off the bridge."

"What I meant was, someone was trying to throw my stuff into the Connecticut River and didn't see the netting. Animal lifers?"

Angie adjusted her sunglasses and made a sour face, the one she makes at a crossword puzzle that doesn't fully cooperate. "Drove a long way just to dump the goods. Most of those animal lifers want their stunts publicized. No publicity in just dumping it off a bridge. And they usually break into places when nobody is there. These guys were too confrontational. Didn't seem like PETA types to me."

I bobbed my head in agreement and gunned the Lincoln onto 9A. "Well, whoever they were, they took a greater risk getting caught by going out on that bridge with all my animals. Why not just bury them in the woods somewhere? Or burn them somewhere publicly so it would make the news?"

"Hmmm." Angie nodded. "It's like they just wanted to make the loot disappear, y'know? Say they panicked. Or maybe the bridge was on their way somewhere else, or they were just driving and had this impulse."

"Why go to all that trouble?" I adjusted the rearview mirror. "And why take the booty so far away?"

"Unless this was near where they live, or, like I said, on the way somewhere."

"So you're suggesting they came all the way to New York from Massachusetts to case our apartment and steal my livelihood? Some shiftless Gloucester fishermen happen to be thumbing through the Manhattan yellow pages and say, 'Hey, let's rip this guy off.' Quite a stretch, sweetie."

"I'm just thinking out loud." She stuck her tongue out at me. "Did the police say whether anything was damaged?"

"All he said was that it was in plastic garbage bags, except the tusks, of course. Should at least have been kept reasonably dry."

Our quizzing subsided into mutual perplexity, so Angie set upon the latest *New York Times* crossword book as I took us from the Cross County to the Hutchinson Parkway to 684 to Brewster, then headed east on I-84. It was a gorgeous day, uncommonly dry and warm for late May. Angie besieged me with crossword clues for a couple hours. She answered most of them herself, of course, but I miraculously got three in a row. Across, three-letter word for percentage: *VIG*. Down, beginning with V, a nine-letter word for reprisal: *VENGEANCE*. Across, beginning with G, a six-letter word for a penguin's nest: *GABLIT*. You could see where my mind was. We passed through Hartford, and once on I-91 we off-ramped for a pit stop. I filled the Lincoln's tank and Angie emptied hers. Back on the road in a jiffy.

"Y'know," Angie began, pointing a Slim Jim at me, "it could be that the thieves were on their way to sell the booty, like in Rangely or something."

I taxied the Lincoln onto an entrance ramp. "Still doesn't explain why they dumped the stuff."

"I wonder if the crow got all futzed up," Angie pouted. All I could envision was someone with a hacksaw cutting up my tusks, or my beautiful tiger rug sitting in the mud on the bottom of the Connecticut River. I had dismissed the loss of the fifty-dollar crow, not to mention the issue of whether anybody would go to such extremes to possess it. Until, that is, we reached the Massachusetts State Police barracks. My possessions were all there and in good condition, even the tusks. Everything except for the crow. I looked up at the officer holding the pen and clipboard out to me.

"Is this all of it?"

"Yessir. Damn lucky they were inspecting the bridge this month and that net was there, I'll say."

"But there was no crow."

"A what?"

"A crow, a white crow in a bell jar?" Angie chimed.

The trooper looked suspicious and jabbed the clipboard at me. I took it.

"Just what you see here. Sign the top, bottom, and middle. Press hard."

Angie and I stowed all ten leaf bags of beasts in the Lincoln and drove off to find an early dinner. Along the way, we crossed a bridge over the Connecticut River.

I pointed to a sign. "Hey, this is the bridge."

"French King Bridge?"

"Yup, that's the one he said."

"Pull over." Angie waved at a rest area on the far side of the bridge. It was connected to a pedestrian walkway that followed the length of the bridge. There was a terrific view up the river, and the bridge seemed monstrously high. I had trouble looking down without vertigo kicking in. But I looked long enough to see the net where my taxidermy had been found, about forty feet down. Five'll get you ten Liberty Valance and his thugs dropped their ill-gotten gains at night and didn't even see the net.

Back on the road, we quickly found one of those humdrum middle-America places called Bob's Family Restaurant. The kind of die-stamped joint that's in every mall from Miscoganie to Missoula. Once outside New York, the eateries are so repetitive from Palookaville to Palookaville, you'd swear you were driving in circles.

A young waitress came by and took our orders, and when I asked if I could have my fries well done, she said, "Sure, mister."

As she sauntered away, I turned to Angie. "I ask

you, why am I suddenly *mister*? Not *bub*, not *fellah*, not *sir*. But *mister*. Do I look like a *mister* to you?"

"This is weird, Garth."

"I know. I don't feel like a *mister*."

"Could you stop obsessing for a moment? I was talking about the crow. The crow is weird, id-jit." She straw-slurped her cherry cola.

"I'll get you another present." I gave her my squinty, vexed look. "The point is that—"

"I know: You got your treasures back. What I mean is—"

"Right, right—that the crow was missing. Nothing to do about that. I feel damn lucky to have gotten any of it back. I'll assume the loss as a sacrifice to the gods." I knew where Angie was trying to go with this train of thought and vainly attempted to steer her away.

"Lucky, sure, but you should feel spooked too. Those guys obviously came all the way from somewhere up here to swipe that crow. Like Jim Kim said."

"There are at least a dozen other explanations—"

"Name 'em."

"Okay." I held up a hand and began pointing to my fingers. "They threw the crow in the river separately and it missed the net. It was heavy and tore through the safety net. They dropped the crow somewhere else. One of the construction workers who found my stuff kept the crow. The burglars decided to keep the crow. . . ."

She grabbed my pinky. "That net is meant to

catch hefty construction workers who slip and fall, ya big dummy. Can't see how the bell jar would tear through. Don't you think it might be that they took the other mounts just to make it look like they weren't stealing the crow?"

"Like the crow was packed with cocaine or something? Microfilm? What?"

"Garth, don't get like that with me."

"Like what?" If Pete Durban is a terrier, Angie can be a pit bull when it comes to puzzles, brainteasers, and the like. I sometimes kid her she'd be better off hitched to Alex Trebek. He drives a convertible, I'm sure.

"Sarcastic. And blind. It's just like that gallbladder thing. You didn't want to see what was going on because you were afraid to find out."

"Damn right, Angie. And I've got a lot to be afraid of if that Fletcher guy came all the way to our house to steal that crow." I glanced at some gawkers at the next table and stuck my tongue out at them. I lowered my voice. "If there are Colombians, Nazis, cultists, or terrorists who want the crow that bad, they can have it, because after what almost happened to us—"

"Fletcher?" She arched an eyebrow. I hadn't bothered to tell her about Frat Boy.

"What?" It had occurred to me in the days since the robbery that maybe, just maybe, one of the attackers had been that Bret Fletcher who tried to fight me for the crow back up there in Bermuda. But that was pretty damn far-fetched.

Our food suddenly arrived and I got busy putting ketchup on some cold, undercooked fries. Angie messed with her sticky-looking nachos.

She was dead on, of course. There was the distinct possibility that they were after the crow and stole the other stuff to cover their motives. So if, for the sake of argument, one of the thieves had been Fletcher, who were the other two guys? As much as I was completely earnest about not tangling with these characters, that grub of vengeance was squirming in my brain. I don't think of myself as that kind of guy. Life is too short to be spent defending every little slight. But when I pictured that guy's hand on Angie's neck . . . well, it made me want to have some Malay cone snails at the ready. Or at the very least, see these bastards in jail.

"Garth?"

She woke me from my dark reverie. "Hmm?"

"Don't think I've forgotten about Fletcher."

And so it was that the Lincoln found its way back up to Bermuda.

Chapter 7

There's something decidedly sinister about a New England village after dark. The byways are empty but awash in the light of eerie green streetlamps. Wizened old maples and sycamores shroud sidewalks in the sporadic shadows of branches swaying in the wind. Spatters of lamplight skitter like ghost crabs across picket fences and white clapboard houses, the surge of rustling leaves like waves breaking on rocks. Fix your gaze on each grizzled trunk as you pass: Is someone hiding there, sliding to the far side of the tree? Stop. Listen. Were those footsteps behind you, matching your steps? That guy in the window, reading, rocking back and forth: a zombie, normalcy's pretense, the town in the grips of Satan's most ominous coven?

Angie and I looked up at the bear holding a

scripted CLOSED sign. I imagined his eyes might just glow red with Cerberus's incarnate evil, followed by the sound of a distant calliope and chanting clowns. In case you hadn't already guessed, my psyche is burdened with formative years devoted to *Creature Features*.

"Things seem pretty damn quiet in Bermuda." I shivered, the little hairs on my neck standing at full attention. "What say we drop in on Gunderson in the morning and ask about Fletcher then? Tonight we'd better backtrack to that roadhouse and nab a room."

"About five miles back," Angie sighed in agreement.

Wind whistling over the convertible top, I cranked the heat and we barreled down the country road.

"Angie, what would you think if I, you know, took a job?"

"A job?"

"Yeah, you know . . ."

She gave me a hard look. "I think you'd have to buy a real tie and mothball that pony-skin tie you have, that's what."

"I'm serious."

I saw her roll her eyes in the dashboard's lime glow.

"Garth, you say that every year. What kind of job? Let me guess. At U.S. Fish and Wildlife?"

"Pete Durban said if I ever get tired of hauling

dead animals hither and yon I should give him a call."

"Well?"

"Well, what?"

"Well, are you tired of your stupid taxidermy racket?"

"A stupid racket? What the hell's that supposed to mean?"

Angie gave me a sneaky smile. "It means that if you still react so defensively to that wisecrack, you don't hate your craft as much as you think. Not enough to toss it for some job you want just because it's steady."

The problem with being in love with a smart person is that you have to put up with them being right a lot of the time. Not that I admitted it at the time, mind you.

The motel came into view and the discussion came to a timely close. The Maple Motor Court was essentially a tavern with a crescent of tiny white cabins behind it. You checked in at the bar by the light of a Narragansett beer sign. But while the barmaid fussed over the key rack and I signed in, I sensed something amiss. Scanning the sundry plaid patrons, nothing remarkable caught my eye. Two were looking toward but not at me, the way townsfolk check out strangers. Nothing odd in that. There was a full mug at the bar stool next to them, and I heard a toilet flush. I chalked up my spookiness to *Creature Features* and one too many Hammer films, signed the register, took the key from the barmaid, and headed for Angie and the Lincoln waiting out front.

I passed into the foyer and through the second door. I glanced back into the bar. There was someone at the empty bar stool, and he was looking in my direction.

It was Bret Fletcher, who looked like the dean had just caught him in the girls' dorm.

"Son of a—" I may not have wanted to practice my pugilism the last time I saw him, but now I wanted to take a poke at him. The more I thought about it, the more I figured he must have been one of those bastards who roughed us up.

I doubted he saw me looking back, what with the light being on his side of two separate panes of glass. I got into the Lincoln, drove us to our cabin, and told Angie I was going to step out for a beer and catch the Late Nite Show, maybe see if Aunt Jilly made the program. There was no TV in the cabin, and Angie always reads before bed.

Creeping along the shadow of the tavern, I peeped through the darkened kitchen window and into the barroom. All I could glimpse was the back of Bret's red plaid coat and occasionally his arm as he gestured to his cronies in some sort of animated conversation.

A battered green pickup came rattling down the road and roared to a stop in front of the tavern, tooting its horn. Bret's two cronies stood up abruptly and headed for the door. But before they left, they gave Bret a glare that put fresh mojo on my little neck hairs.

These two were older than Bret, and considerably more weathered. The taller, slimmer one had pretty big teeth. And a toothpick. He wore a felt cowboy hat, atypical antlers for folks around these parts. And the hat wasn't some sort of white job with a big red feather that ho-dad ranch-hand wannabes wear. This was sweat-stained, rain-freckled, and well worn, complete with brim nicks from barbed wire and cigarette burns from smoking in the saddle. Or in the back of a pickup. Beat up as it was, it didn't come off shabby because he obviously worked to keep the creases sharp in the crown, and the brim had a uniform curl. He wore it at a slight angle that might lead you to believe he'd swung a few pool cues in his time. When Slim gave Bret a parting smile, those giant teeth looked ready to bite.

Slim's pal was short and stocky with a bush of red hair. Fiery eyebrows framed dark, button eyes. Hands in his pockets, he shouldered the door in Slim's wake.

I took a few steps forward to peek around the edge of the tavern as they opened the door and climbed into the cab of the truck. I couldn't get an eyeful of the driver.

Yep, these two could be the guys. The one who'd popped out of our basement with the gun might have been Bret. It clicked with his frenetic performance at Gunderson's, complete with breaking voice.

The guy with the raspy voice easily could have been Slim, a smoker. He certainly fit Otto's bull's-eye description: "Teeth big, vood in leeps."

I watched as the old truck lurched and rattled its way down the road, a blue haze of exhaust floating in its wake.

Options presented themselves. They'd spotted me, no doubt about that, but probably felt I had no way of connecting them to the ski-masked assault in Manhattan. My return to Bermuda would be setting off alarms, though. They would figure that I may have recognized one of them somehow, and since I'd only seen Bret before, they'd deduce that I'd come up here to track him down. Or track down the white crow. The Three Amigos would have to stop me cold or blow town. And they didn't look like they were headed for the hills in that old green pickup.

So: Did they plan to do something about me? That very night?

I waited in the shadows until Bret finished his beer, left the tavern, got into a dented Honda Civic, and whirred off down the street. Lucky nobody happened by or I might have been chased down the street as a peeping Tom. I guess angry Vermont mobs don't lynch perverts—probably drown them in maple syrup.

Am I plum loco? My assumptions were galling. Was my secret greed for vengeance playing tricks on me, putting square pegs in round holes, making three hapless strangers into the ones who had assaulted me and Angie? I went through it again, point by point, looking for a lapse in judgment. Basically, other than Bret having been angry about the crow, what possible reason would he have for stealing it? Let me guess—it was a family heirloom? A deceased pet? A substitute security blanket, his very own pink blankey, Bret all curled up in bed with a cold bell jar, sucking his thumb?

And the bridge over the Connecticut—why drop my dead stuff there? It was over a hundred miles away from Bermuda. But at night, it was probably pretty desolate and they had little chance of being spotted.

And how did they find me in Manhattan, after all? Perhaps the business card I gave that shopkeeper Gunderson? The yellow pages? Both possible, but anybody could put my pin in the map that way.

And if they were the ones?

Well, I could roust Angie and we could pile back into the Lincoln and make for the interstate. But maybe they were waiting for us down the road, the pavement littered with carpet tacks. I'd end up stooped behind the car, gripping a car jack in the glow of the red taillights, my back to the dark forest. Then where would we be? Alone on a desolate country road, at the mercy of insane killer clowns from another planet? I'd seen that kind of thing in way too many horror pics.

I decided to stay where there were lights and phones and an innkeeper who probably had her twelve-gauge side-by-side loaded and at the ready in case the local cocktail set had one too many cosmos and decided to trash the place.

I went into the bar and asked for a second cabin, farthest from Cabin #1, which Bret's pals had seen me sign for.

The barmaid eyed me, and I shrugged.

"We have these awful fights."

Her eyebrows went up, and I went out with the key to Cabin #9. Jostling Angie from her slumber, I said the barmaid had mistakenly given us Cabin #1, the hut with the rat, and that we should move to the cabin on the far end if we didn't cotton to bedding with scaly-tailed vermin. Angie wiped the Sandman from her eyes and swiftly gathered her belongings and relocated to the new cabin without too much protest. I left the Lincoln at Cabin #1, told Angie the Late Nite Show was about to come on, and excused myself to the bar.

Was I convinced they were really coming back for a little midnight slice n' dice? All I could be sure of was my bristling neck hair—that and my determination to protect Angie. Of course, the logical move would have been to tell Angie what I saw and suggest we vamoose. Not that she would have gone, mind you. Knowing Angie, she would have wanted to help me set the trap.

If I sound a little like a man with suspenders and a belt, I think I have a right to add duct tape to the mix. During my stint with Pete Durban, my feel for impending danger was sharpened, as was my fear of getting caught with my pants down.

Gallbladders. I almost got killed because of bear gallbladders, if you can believe it. Therein lies a tale.

Chapter 8

I didn't used to get into trouble. But I can tell you how and when mortal danger entered my life, and it can be summed up in the word *Smiler*.

It was a couple of years ago. A taxidermist I know in Wyoming, named Sinclair Jones, specializes in bear mounts, and over the years he'd accumulated a bunch of bear gallbladders in his freezer. Seems he wasn't getting a very good price for them and had heard they sold for considerably more in New York's Chinatown. Did I have any connections? Said he was looking for at least ten but hopefully as much as fifteen dollars a gram for them. A ten percent commission would be my reward. At the time I didn't know much about the trade of bear parts. So I asked Pete Durban, my seemingly mild-mannered ecological control agent at the time, if it was legit for me to broker them.

He frowned. "On a federal level, it is for now. In New York, yes. Where are the bladders coming from?"

"Wyoming."

"That's legal too. Both states allow the sale of both resident and nonresident bear parts. But there are thirty-two states where it's completely illegal. So be careful."

"Be careful? Gallbladders?" Pete hadn't yet lured me into any of his Wild West antics at that juncture in our relationship.

He tried to smile. "You ever seen a bear gallbladder? A North American black-bear bladder looks like a prune, weights about twenty to thirty grams. Asian bear bladders are bigger, up to sixty grams. Little ones, like from cubs, at ten grams are cheapies. But they all look like prunes of different sizes, and there's no telling where they come from."

"Ah. So the legal ones from black bears are mixed in with the illegal ones. . . ."

"*Right*. And nobody can keep track of it, so nobody does and so a lot of the wrong people are involved. So just remember what I said."

What he didn't tell me was that what makes bears' bladders so valuable is that they are the only natural source for tauroursodeoxycholic acid (UDCA), a substance more commonly known as bile. Bear bile has been used for centuries by practitioners of traditional Chinese medicine to treat everything from menstrual cramps to lymphoma. Does it work? Western medicine is much more tentative about its benefits and synthesizes an artificial form of cow bile to treat cirrhosis and dissolve gallstones. The Chinese have realized the limits of the harvesting from the wild and have actually developed farms of over seven thousand captive Asian bears raised specifically for their wonderful, lovely, scrumptious bile. *I scream, you scream, we all scream for bile!* If you don't believe me, look it up.

In Chinatown, I had an importer named Chuck Woo who sometimes got me gazelle pelts. His shop was your classic Mott Street denizen, replete with all manner of Chinese and other imported exotica like coconut carvings, miniature fountains, freeze-dried display piranhas, fertility dolls, Indonesian skull beads, Javan shadow puppets, Turkish water pipes, Mali masks, and Mexican *Día de los Muertos* paraphernalia. He was also the largest New York importer of Ecuadorian *Jívaro* shrunken heads, hand-crafted by Jivaro Indians from goat skin with the same attention to detail as if they were the noggins of rival tribesmen.

I dropped in on Chuck shortly after my talk with Pete, and Chuck was his usual bubbly if somewhat profane self.

"Garf! You old fuckar! Come in! I haf many pelts for you, you fuckar!"

"Hiya, Chuck." I pumped his hand, never having bothered to tell him that it wasn't exactly kosher to go around calling people *fuckar*. I didn't know him that well and so always figured someone close to him would get around to breaking the news. And I can see how he came to use the word so casually—from the example set by everyday American vernacular.

"You want Dutch water, you big fuckar? Yes, let us make Dutch water!" A bottle of Johnnie Walker Red appeared in one hand, two tumblers in the other. I don't like scotch, but found a glass in my hand just the same. Never could figure out whether he was an alcoholic just looking for an excuse to dip his bill or whether this was some kind of custom. But whenever I visited him, I always had to gird myself for some "Dutch water," his peculiar name for scotch. I kept swirling it, hoping to make the vile amber liquid evaporate faster.

So after he showed me some pelts and I dumped the scotch in a potted plant, I finally got around to my question.

"Chuck, my friend, you have the very best pelts. I only buy from you, the best." He beamed and I continued. "But I don't have any buyers for pelts today. I come to you, my friend, because I have something to sell."

His eyes went shifty on me. I don't think he knew quite how to make the transition from friendly seller to shrewd buyer. They were two distinctly different people, one accommodating and the other a son of a bitch.

"Chuck, a friend has some bear gallbladders, and he wants to sell them."

He was motionless.

"I understand there are people in Chinatown who will buy them. Do you know someone who buys bear gallbladders?"

A word or two of Chinese fell absently from his lips before he said, "Garf, I am fuzzled by your inquiry. I will see if anybody wants these worthless items and can make them go away for you." He took my glass. "Come back, my friend, in an hour."

When I came back, the CLOSED sign was in the door. As I turned away, the door suddenly opened.

"Garf, come in, bastard!"

I edged past the smiling Chuck and found myself in front of two frowning Chinese men in shiny Hong Kong suits. I tensed reflexively when I heard Chuck throw the bolt on the front door. My neck hairs didn't stand up—they didn't know any better yet.

One of the suits tried to smile, but clearly he was out of practice. "We can help you dispose of the bladders." He had a pinky ring, gold cuff links, sideburns, and a pompadour. His glasses were tinted and had oversize black frames that put Philip Johnson to shame. I don't know shoes, but his loafers looked expensive and had a gold clasp. Yeah, this guy was the one in charge, all right. His pal was the heavy.

"Are you a buyer or broker?"

"Buyer." Smiler took a step forward. "We must see the product. Do you have it?"

"I have this one." I pulled a Styrofoam box from my shoulder bag and opened it. Wisps of fog cleared to reveal what looked for all the world like a small dog doo nestled in dry ice. Not exactly the unveiling of the *Mona Lisa*. "I can get more in a few days."

Smiler held out a hand, and I intuitively began to sweat. I had a sense he wouldn't give it back, so instead of handing it over, I stepped closer so he could see it more closely. He produced a mini flashlight and a jeweler's loupe and set upon a close examination.

I heard a metallic snap and saw his compadre holding a switchblade. I froze.

Smiler took the knife and poked the turd until he got a small sample from one end. He deposited the sample into a plastic vial.

"If it is as it seems," Smiler began, trading glances with Chuck and his compadre, "and of consistent quality and size, we will pay you ten dollars a gram. That is our top price."

"Twenty-five for those over thirty grams. Fifteen for those over twenty grams." Who the hell said that? Yikes! It was me. A dealer's reflex, even though the ten a gram met my supplier's asking price.

"These are only American bladders." Smiler tried smiling again but failed miserably. "I said, top price."

I snapped the foam box shut and tucked the turd back into my bag. Dealing is dealing, the world over, whether it's for a moose head, Chiclets, or gallbladders: You never accept the first offer. These

guys were crafty, and they were lowballing me—
just as I would if I were they.

"Nice meeting you." I smiled, but sweat was
drenching my back. I turned to go and Chuck
stepped into my path.

"Garf, how many do you haf?"

I glanced back at the two suits. "Sixty-eight. Including this one. All plump and greasy. No dinks in
the lot. *And they're all over thirty grams.*"

The three Chinese exchanged glances.

"Look," I said amiably, "I know you men may be
strapped for cash. It's okay, really. I'll find someone
who will pay the twenty-five, who won't be incon-
venienced by this transaction."

Smiler almost rolled his eyes. Instead, he slowly
unwrapped a stick of Fruit Stripe gum, slid it into
his mouth, and chewed for a moment. "Bring all
sixty-eight back here on Saturday. We will pay you
your twenty-five. But only for those over thirty
grams."

"Works for me," I said, as Chuck opened the
door. I left, trying not to walk faster than normal.
There it was, fifty thousand smackaroos doing the
hula in my brain, all for a couple hours' work. Who
could resist?

Two afternoons later, I was at a corner table at the
Red Dragon dim sum palace. If you've never been to
one of these places, they're refreshingly different
from Bob's Family Restaurant. I imagine it's like attending a Chinese wedding banquet. This one was
decked out in gold wallpaper and adorned with scroll

paintings of red dragons and paper lanterns strung from one end of the ceiling to the other. Dim sum is usually enjoyed in the afternoon, and this place was bustling. Just the same, nobody seemed to pay any attention as Smiler weighed his bladders and I counted my cash. After about forty minutes, I was closing a picnic basket chockablock with wads of twenties thick as egg rolls. Smiler and his heavy hefted their coolers of frozen dog poo and slipped out a nearby fire exit. Done deal. Hula hula!

Now, in my line of work, I often withdraw and deposit fairly large sums of cash, and the bank officers know me and the peculiarities of my business. In fact, I give a five percent discount to anybody paying cash. Sound stupid dealing with so much cash? Well, what's stupider are bounced checks. What's stupider is paying a vig to MasterCard. What's stupider is "invoicing" where they pay you a year or two after the sale, or hiring collection agencies to try to strangle your money out of someone, or never getting paid at all. But I know that deposits over $10K are scrutinized by the FBI. So I guess I was overly insouciant when I waltzed into my friendly neighborhood bank with $52,700 in a wicker picnic basket. Maybe if I'd brought it in a Halliburton attaché I wouldn't have been scrutinized.

They were polite, too polite. I should have guessed they were stalling until the cops arrived. This, of course, is where I met my pal Walker, and where we grew so fond of each other. Even though

I didn't know Pete Durban that well at the time, I felt he knew I was basically on the up-and-up, so I gave him a call and was gratified when he came right down to the bank to vouch for me.

But then he asked to speak to me in private. He showed me a fuzzy telephoto picture of two Asian men walking on a Chinatown street.

"Know these two guys?"

It was Smiler and Compadre. "You must know I do."

He smiled. "When you called me about the bladders, I figured you might be dealing with them. We've had them under surveillance for some time—slippery characters. This one is named Park." He pointed to Smiler. "He's the head honcho. We want him. Garth, the department will vouch for you on this business with the cash, but we want a favor."

I shrugged. "Sure, Pete."

"Great." He slapped me on the knee and stood up.

"Uh, Pete? What's the favor?"

"How about I come over to your place tonight and explain it over some of Angie's goulash soup?"

"How do you know about—"

He grinned. "We have our sources."

A week later I found myself in the back of a dark police van at 1:00 A.M. on a lonely industrial stretch of Peck Slip, a wharfside street in lower Manhattan. Microphones had been threaded into my jacket lapels and a camera was lodged in my belt buckle. Angie was there with Pete, several technicians, and a bunch of flickering, humming, and blinking surveillance gear. I was sweating up a storm. All I needed was a soil sampler and parachute and NASA could have shot me into space for a Mars landing. One day I'm just minding my own business, paying bills, making a living, doing the day-to-day, and the next I'm being made into an underworld probe.

"A favor," I muttered, wiping my brow with a bandanna.

Pete patted me on the shoulder, but I was looking at Angie. "It's nothing to worry about, Garth."

"Oh, really?" I squinted. "Then how come you have a bulletproof vest on?"

"Purely routine. Like flossing."

"Like flossing?" I snorted. "With bullets?"

Angie put a hand on my arm. "They've got police all around, Garth, and we'll be listening the whole time, isn't that right?"

"Right," Pete chimed in.

"Wait a second," I said, shaking Angie by the shoulders. "Aren't you supposed to be the one who says *Garth, this is too dangerous. Please, I'm too young to be a widow.* And then I say, *Angie, someone has to stop these villains.*"

"If it uncovers a chop shop, someone does have to stop them. And you already dealt with them once, so they'll trust you. Pete wouldn't have asked you if it were really dangerous."

I sighed heavily, my chest tight with anxiety and microphones. "Angie, I really wish you hadn't come along." Pete got a stern glance from me. "I have a bad feeling about all this."

"Don't look at me." Pete held his palms up. "She said she'd only let you do it if she could come along to make sure we kept you safe."

I'd been hearing nothing but the words *chop shop* all week. Most of these places are overseas, in certain Asian countries where they have tacit protection from the local government just as they would if they were processing drugs. Periodically, they attempt to establish one in the U.S., if for no other reason than they have less bribes to pay, fewer middlemen, better quality assurance, and more inventory control. The valuable parts range from pelts and organs to horns and claws. Big cats usually constitute a large proportion of these animals, everything from servals to Siberian tigers. Penises and testes of these cats are highly sought after, but so are assorted other organs such as brains, paws, claws, and various glands. All of them are used in traditional Asian medicine to treat everything from impotence to bad luck. You'd think Viagra and Match.com would have made this stuff like a lozenge for the flu. Go figure. The United States has a huge Asian customer base that will pay top dollar for what amount to cherry Sucrets.

But bears were more plentiful and in demand at the time, not only for their gallbladders but for their paws. There were rumors that a single serving of bear-paw soup in South Korea could go for $1,400. I wondered if that came with oyster crackers. And it was Pete and Fish and Wildlife's belief that Smiler & Co. were primarily in the business of moving a lot of bear parts, far more than they could account for legally. The feds aimed to shut them down, and I was the chump who had to stick his neck out and take a look around.

Would taking down a single chop shop stymie the entire trade? Well, one less sure wouldn't hurt. So did I want to help out? Yes. But I'd watched too many movies to think wearing a wire wasn't without considerable risk. I was having flash-forwards of Smiler ripping the mike from my jacket, strapping me to a saw table, and flicking the switch. The buzzing blade heading for my midsection, I'd say: "So, Park, I guess you expect me to talk?" Him replying: "No, Mr. Carson, I expect you to die." Next thing I'm soup with oyster crackers, probably at two bucks a bowl. Causes lapses in judgment.

Cowardice is more ally than enemy, and bravery is prodded at the sharp end of dilemma's horns. The only reason I didn't run screaming from the van was the snorting bull of pride standing behind me. To back out would wave a red flag in his face.

The plan was for me to meet Smiler & Co. at the corner of Peck Slip and Front Street, a pretty lonely spot at that hour of the morning. I had a duffel bag packed with $50,000 in small bills. I'd contacted Chuck. "Garf, you dog sucker!" Between his mutterings, I told him I could move some exotic pelts if Smiler could arrange such a thing. It didn't take long for him to set up a meeting with Smiler, who said I should come prepared to buy as his inventory had a high turnover and he couldn't hold anything for me. I wondered if they didn't just intend to get me in a desolate spot and then deploy thugs to rip me off. Actually, I sort of hoped that they would, in which case I'd calmly hand over the money and walk.

Well, I did all the way up until Pete's parting words. He smiled, patting me on the shoulder. "Relax. Here. It looks like a cell phone, but it's a GPS tracker. Don't lose it or we'll lose you. But it'll go smooth as silk, and we'll be right with you all the way." As he climbed into the van, he added as an afterthought: "And be careful with your money."

"My money?" There was something in the way he said it, the spark in his eye.

He tried not to smile as the van started to pull away. "We didn't think you'd mind if we borrowed some."

Son of a bitch.

It was a night in April, which is anything but springlike. The sky was overcast, it was chilly and it was misting, but I hadn't bothered with a raincoat. I was nervous, and hot, and didn't want to sweat excessively for fear of looking nervous. Besides, I remember a movie in which somebody wearing a wire starts to sweat, the electronics short-circuit, he starts to freak from being singed, is discovered, and . . . and I seem to remember it ended badly for this fellow. Or what about that movie where the guy with the wire goes to a Japanese restaurant with his underworld cronies and is asked to take his boots off? The boots with the tape recorders in them? Or the one in which there's a guy with a wire posing as a driver at a mob funeral, where the squeal of feedback on his mike gives him away?

My reverie was such that I didn't hear the town car roll silently up behind me.

Compadre was in back, and from the open door he motioned for me to join him. I tossed in the bag first, and paused. He could easily have zoomed off with the money—I still hoped he would—but instead looked impatient. Not the brightest penny in the gumball machine.

I clambered in, carefully, like I was crawling into a cave that might have a bear in it. No angry bruins—just Compadre. We drove around in circles for a while, and when we finally disembarked, I recognized our locale: the 125th Street meat district, all the way on the West Side in Harlem. It was an industrial area of meat-packing establishments, dicey-looking parking lots, and warehouses, tucked under an elevated section of Riverside Drive. At that hour, on a Sunday, the place was pretty much deserted. You could go there for a late-night stroll—if you were naive.

But it made sense for a chop shop to be tucked into the meat district. The Dumpsters full of the operation's residue—bones and carcassess—would blend in among the Dumpsters of fragmented livestock. And at a meat wholesaler, they'd have plentiful and spacious refrigeration at their disposal for all those dead animals.

I was in my usual sport coat, running shoes, chinos,

and white shirt. The sport coat I kept unbuttoned, hoping the 007 camera in my belt buckle would make sure Pete Durban knew where I was. In case the batteries on my "cell phone" failed or my particular satellite had a fender bender with a meteor. But it was dark. I thought about saying something about where we were, for the mike in my lapel, but thought that might tip my mitt.

No, Mr. Carson, I expect you to die.

I kept mum as Compadre led the way past drums of foul suet and bones for rendering. In my top-ten least favorite aromas, before vomit and after burning hair, is that of meat districts with their lard-infused sidewalks that make dandy rat licks. Bean curd and carrot juice at the Chipper Sprout briefly seemed a palpable alternative to the Neanderthal Platter at the Steak N' Swill.

I was led upstairs into a den. I say a den because it wasn't an apartment, and it wasn't exactly an office, though there was a sprawling desk where some work—possibly accounting—was performed. But there was also a large sectional sofa, a wall of mirrors, one of those patent-leather bars from the seventies, and copious track lighting. It was supposed to be classy but looked worn and tacky like a strip club. Part den, part den of iniquity.

A sizable poker table was centered in one half of the room by a large array of grimy factory windows, the kind that open bottom out. Two shady-looking guys stood at the table, one in a yellow sweater, one in a vest. Ten rolled skins were stacked on the table before them. I looked around for Smiler. He wasn't there.

Compadre swept his hand over the rolled skins like a caterer displaying his finest canapés. I snapped a bubble and wondered if I'd deafened the technician at the other end of my microphone. Hoped I had, him all snug in that police van, me here rocking on my heels, facing down the buzz saw.

I pulled the string on one skin after the other, unrolling them and draping them one by one over a spare chair. When I was done, there were six leopard skins of varying quality, a cheetah, two smallish, mediocre tigers, and a huge, drop-dead-gorgeous Siberian tiger. Just skins, no heads or paws. They'd been cut quite carefully, with good tools, cleaned and brushed, but were untanned and without any felt backing. As is, they were suitable for wall mounting, but could still be tanned for clothing. Although I don't know where you could wear a Siberian tiger jacket without raising more than just eyebrows—such as hackles. And they were one hundred percent genuine. You can tell fakes quite easily, because cat fur has a distinctive stacked or layered pattern when you bend a pelt and flex it. But a good pelt is lush and plush, and these two tigers looked like ill-fed captives. Some of the leopards had scars from rough treatment in transport.

Were I unscrupulous, I could get between five to seven thou each for the better leopard skins, less for the cheetah and small so-so tigers, and God knows what for the Siberian tiger. Take that figure, chop off fifty percent for my profit margin, and you had about forty thousand, ten less than what I had in the attaché case.

What I should have done at that point was just follow my instructions, buy the skins, and be on my way—let the troops come crashing in after I left. But the smattering of rare skins, probably a mere crumb from the whole pie, made my gum go soft—there was more, and I wanted to see it. I was working at my profession now, authenticating and appraising. So the dealer inside me elbowed his way past the panicky guy wearing a wire. Okay, so my kneecaps were trembling and I was chomping my bubblegum like my jaw was stamping out license plates—other than that I fancied myself a paradigm of CCC: cool, calm, and collected. I wanted to get an eyeful of the good stuff, like the Siberian. This was just the way shrewd dealers like Smiler worked. Try to unload some crap at top dollar, hope to wow me with the Siberian, and in a package deal get a prime markup on the so-so stuff. It couldn't hurt to ask, just to look, could it?

"This is interesting merchandise." I gestured to the unrolled skins. "What else have you got? I mean, I can move some of it, but some of it is just plain shit. My clients pay top dollar and demand the good stuff. I bring cash and am hoping to give you all of it. *For quality merchandise.*"

The sweater, the vest, and Compadre exchanged glances like there was an unexplained bad smell, then a few staccato words of Chinese followed.

Compadre turned and stepped out of the room. To call his boss, no doubt. If nothing else, maybe Smiler would show up and insure that he didn't slip through the net.

Sure enough, Compadre reappeared, his eyes tight with annoyance. He shook his head.

I looked at the skins, and when I turned back, the three of them were standing in a row, arms folded, the Pep Boys via Seoul. But I don't think they wanted to rotate my tires. Rather, make up my mind. But I have a stubborn, single-minded, and determined streak that serves me well in the day-to-day of doing business. And this approximated the day-to-day, so it came naturally, if unfortunately.

"I wanna speak with your boss." My voice broke slightly, and when I cleared my throat I almost spit out my gum. "If there's more, I don't see why I should only have this to choose from."

Compadre dialed his cell phone, exchanging glances with Sweater and Vest again, like he'd been the one who cut the cheese.

That reminded me of my own "cell phone," and I gave a pat to my jacket pocket to make sure it was still there.

Mistake.

Sweater and Vest had guns in their hands fast as cobras nab a rat. My hands went up very slowly, not so much as a surrender as a gesture of non-intent. My kneecaps froze. It had happened so suddenly that I had trouble getting my breath.

"Whoa, hey . . ." I croaked, stroking the air like I was petting a freaked-out kitty. Nice kitty.

Compadre was talking Chinese into the phone as he came over and reached into my pocket, snatching the phone and showing it to Sweater and Vest, who deflated. The guns went below the table. He tossed the "cell phone" on the table.

Moments later, footfalls scuffed on the stairs and Smiler entered the room, a frown on his beak like that of a baby magpie. A bodyguard was with him, a rotund man with a jowly, irritable face and tiny feet in delicate-looking loafers. Why is it a lot of fat men have tiny feet? They need big ones, yet they get the small ones. His looked like a ballerina's.

"We have showed you merchandise. Do you want it or not?"

I couldn't back down now but tried to soft-pedal as much as possible, so I babbled.

"Look, I just asked if these ten were the whole bunch. Y'know? If there's more you're not showing me, I just want to know why I can't choose from the whole lot. Y'know? I mean, if you don't want to, that's . . ."

Smiler squinted at me, and I didn't like it.

"I don't know you." He shook his head. "I don't like you. That is why. You buy from this, later you see more. That's how it works."

I held my hands up, giving in. "Okay, okay. So . . ." I gestured to the table. "How about I take the Siberian, these two leopards, and, um, this tiger . . ."

"Seventy."

"Whoa, these aren't for me, this is resale. Y'know? I mean, I've gotta have my profit margin." The knee-caps were pumping like pistons.

He stepped up to my duffel bag, put it on the table, and snapped his fingers at Ballet Boy.

The bodyguard wrenched open my duffel bag. After rifling through the stacks of bills, he turned from the untidy jumble and grumbled something to Smiler.

"You have fifty. I give you all ten. Final offer. Get more money, come back for more. That's it."

That was an outright affront to my alter ego, and I had to forcibly shove the dealer inside me into the backseat. My kneecaps were revving. I took the steering wheel and said, "Okay, but promise me you'll let me at some of the really good stuff next time." I'd already pushed my luck. High time to pop the clutch, smoke my slicks, and make tracks.

His answer was a smirk, which displeased dealer Garth a great deal. He was making a chump out of me and he was enjoying it.

But he took to studying me a moment, and I wondered what he could possibly want now. In a more conciliatory tone, he ventured: "You see much merchandise, yes?"

I shrugged an acknowledgment.

With a grunt of satisfaction, he reached into his inside jacket pocket and handed me a well-worn sheet of paper. It was folded, and when I opened it I found a one-sided photocopy of what appeared to be a page from an old manuscript. The characters had little circles that I recognized from the signs throughout the Korean district in the East 30s.

In the midst of the text was an illustration. Of what I wasn't sure. A rather long and anemic gallbladder? But it was shown twisted, slightly corkscrewed, one end somewhat pointy.

"You see this?" he commanded. "Find and bring to me. I pay top dollar."

"Sure." I handed it back and gave him a cavalier pat on the shoulder. Though he might just bite my fingers, so my hand ran and hid in my pocket. "I'll keep my eyes open."

He tilted his head at Ballet Boy, who zipped my duffel bag closed, turned, and thundered down the stairs with it. Smiler followed without looking back. I was left with the Pep Boys, who grinned with satisfaction, just like on the matchbooks.

I sighed, turned toward the table, and started rolling and tying my skins. I glanced up at my Manny, Moe, and Jack and hoped they didn't plan any fast ones. Maybe they were hoping the same thing about me.

That's when I heard a shout down on the street. Then a bang, followed by a long string of pops that sounded like gunfire. Automatic gunfire.

Before I knew what happened, Vest had me by the back of the collar, those knees of mine buckling as I tumbled to the floor. I looked up and saw a pistol in my face. The other two were on the floor too, shouting in Chinese to each other.

Then one of them said in English, "It's the Fu-King tong!" Fu-King? Or . . .

As gunfire continued down on the street, Sweater crawled behind the bar and came back out with a small crate. Oranges, at a time like this? He flung the top off and started tossing smooth, black, apple-sized spheres from the box to Compadre.

Not oranges. Pineapples. Pete never said anything about friggin' grenades!

Sweater crawled over to the light switch and the room went dark. Vest's grip tightened on my collar. Compadre's silhouette appeared in front of the grimy industrial windows, and he cranked one open, peering down at the street.

I couldn't understand how Pete could have let this happen. What went wrong? I'll tell you what went wrong—when Pete asked me a favor, I said yes.

Suddenly the window exploded, shards of glass gushing into the room as machine-gun fire strafed the entire front of the second floor.

I saw Compadre's silhouette stagger backward from the volley of bullets. I felt something moist mist onto my face, and it wasn't sweat. I smelled my hand, and my feet went cold. It was the tinny smell of blood. But I knew it couldn't have been mine—or could it? I shuddered violently and thought I was going to black out.

Vest scuttled away from me in the darkness. There was a thud as Compadre's body flumped onto the floor.

Then I heard a sharper thud.

I smelled an acrid smoke, heard something clunk against the chair leg next to me.

My eyes zoomed in on a faint red glow by the chair. My hearing, amplified, detected a faint sizzle.

A live grenade? All I did was sell some gallbladders! They're legal!

My instinct was to jump and fly away from there like a grouse, but lacking feathers and wings, I kicked like a mule instead. I shot my feet out frantically and heard the grenade skedaddle to the far side of the room. I was on my knees when it went off, a bang like a truck backfiring, followed by the sound of splintered wood and shrapnel ricocheting off the walls and skittering around the floor.

Bursting out of the room in full flight, I was confronted by hands and wide eyes in the stairwell: It was Smiler's fat bodyguard, sweat running down his face. I grabbed him by the lapels to throw him out of my way, but that was like trying to fling aside a hippo. He threw his arms out to the side, waving them in a desperate attempt to keep his balance on that top step. Our eyes were locked in panic as we teetered, a couple of ballerinas in a wind tunnel.

"Oop!" he grunted, wet jowls trembling.

One of his tiny feet waved in the air desperately, a dancer's *balançoire*.

"Oop!" Ballet Boy's arms waved, a veritable *grand port de bras*.

"Oop!" *Adiós, Swan Lake*—we both knew we were going down those stairs.

He toppled hard, and through his prodigious

belly I felt the reverberation of his spine cracking. My grip on his lapels almost gave way, but the shelf of his stomach helped hold me in place. My feet thunked along as I sledded down the stairs on all that erstwhile Balanchine blubber.

I closed my eyes reflexively, but when I opened them again, we'd stopped at the bottom of the stairs.

Panting with desperation, I looked up from where my face was buried in Ballet Boy's navel. Before me was the flickering green fluorescent light of a short hallway and an open door filled with the orange glow of streetlight at its end. It was the way I'd come in.

Ballet Boy's weapon was suddenly wobbling in my shaking hands. It was a slick-looking automatic. Was it empty? Was the safety on? Was it cocked and ready to fire? I can tell a lynx from a bobcat at a glance, but I know almost nothing of guns.

I rolled off my chubby toboggan, got to my feet, and hid around the corner from the hallway, my chest heaving.

To my left was the dark recess of the rest of the meat-processing plant; Lord knew what gun-slinging monsters were lurking in the cave. To my right was the open door; at least I knew the terrain outside. I can run damn fast when I have to and could envision myself making some serious tracks down the street.

But I waited, frantically hoping to see flashing lights, some cops, some sign of safety beyond. Hadn't this racket, this O.K. Corral under Riverside Drive, alarmed somebody enough to dial 911? Of course, from the time the shooting started, to the exploding couch, to my little ride on the Tubby Express, this brouhaha had probably lasted all of sixty seconds. To me it seemed like sixty minutes.

I squeezed back into my niche, a bat in the shadows. My breath seemed like the roar of a jet, and I tried desperately to slow it down as my heart pounded, my head throbbed, my ears sizzled.

Someone had said it was the Fu-King tong. A rival Chinese gang? Where was the cavalry? What was keeping them? Of course, it seemed like I'd been hiding in my cubby for another hour instead of a drum roll.

My heart stopped, I swear it did; one step, then another, scuffed in the hallway. I needed all the oxygen I could get but had stopped breathing. If a gnat had burped, I would have heard it. The footsteps drew closer.

I blinked and my eyes stung with sweat, either mine or Ballet Boy's. How could this have happened? How? I sell taxidermy. I'm not a gangster. I had definite plans to die in my sleep, preferably while taking an afternoon nap after a nice lunch, maybe some wine. Getting shot in a meat-processing plant was way, way off target.

My eyes refocused—a foot slid around the corner. Rats! My reverie and outrage had wasted a few precious moments of mental preparation. Something felt funny about my neck, and I realized it was the short hairs standing straight up. My entire body was tingling in dread and anticipation.

My hand tightened around the barrel of the gun. I lifted it, like a tomahawk at the ready.

Now. Now, Garth. NOW!

I missed my intended target—his head—but the gun slammed the side of his neck like a solid karate chop.

Pete Durban went down next to Ballet Boy without so much as a pirouette.

A flood of agents and their radio squawks suddenly filled the hallway. One of the agents shot me a disgusted look and took my gun as paramedics crowded in.

Back toward the door. Into the night. Fresh air. Noggin filling with tiny bubbles. Vision swimming. I staggered, sat on a car hood. Flashing lights swirled and swirled. Tiny bubbles fizzing. Don Ho. Hula girls. Singing "Tiny Bubbles." I closed my eyes.

After you go through something like that, through an incredibly intense, adrenaline-charged experience, what follows is the exact opposite. Your brain shifts to neutral and you coast, you float. Or in my case, you get Don Ho, who began singing "Pearly Shells."

"Oh my gosh! Garth!"

I opened my eyes, looked at Angie, and said, "Aloha and mahalo."

Next thing I knew I was flat on my back in an

ambulance, muttering, "Take me Coconut Grove—it's opening night," all the way to the hospital.

Turns out a rival gang—actually named Fu-King—had followed Smiler to the meat plant and tried to ambush him when he left. Pete and U.S. Fish and Wildlife had no choice but to jump into the fray as all hell broke loose. And wouldn't you know? The armored surveillance van was riddled with bullet dents. So nice to know Angie was out of harm's way.

The authorities rounded up Smiler's crew, found a stash of pelts and some bear bladders. But the operation was well compartmentalized, and it was widely believed that they only got a fraction of Smiler's hoard. I got my money back and a USFW travel mug for my trouble.

One other thing they didn't get: Smiler. He made it to the Hudson and dove in. Police boats searched for hours, but they never found him. Or his body. Just his oversize glasses and one of his Brioni shoes.

Danger? Been there.

Aloha.

e, paranoid?
How about preemptively cautious?

With Angie snug in Cabin #9, I crept to the Lincoln's trunk, grabbed a tire iron, the jack, some twine, and one of the grizzly rugs that had been re-covered from the bridge safety nets. Crafty as the Grinch, I had a diabolical plan to make Bret go boo-hoo.

Inside Cabin #1, I pulled the flimsy mattress off the bed and used the sheets to tie it around the bed-post, over which I draped the grizzly rug. The looming beast I'd built was tall, hunched, ferocious, and ready to pounce on any intruder. I looped the twine around the ceiling-lamp fixture, suspended the jack about chest and face level, then tied the twine to the curtain rod opposite the door with a slipknot. The loose end of the twine I ran under the bed, around a dresser leg, and across the doorway at shin height. If an intruder pushed the door all the way open, or stepped into the room, he'd pull the slipknot loose. While he stared at the towering grizzly, the jack would swing out of the corner and smack him in the chest or head. Wile E. Coyote, eat your heart out. I only hoped it turned out better than most of Mr. Coyote's snares.

The trap set, I slipped into the cold May night, planted myself in the shadow of the tavern, and held vigil over Cabin #1 with the tire iron in my grip. In the hour that followed, I heard the barmaid eject the last patrons and throw the lock on the front door. The kitchen phone rang, and she had a long chat while doing the dishes. Then she went into the back room and asked her cat—or perhaps a dog—if "my weedle fat boy wanna have a yummy." (If it was a husband, God bless.) She and her pet then settled down to watch the Late Nite Show, recognizable by the brassy, hyperbolic theme music and protracted adulation of the audience. Aunt Jilly never left the green room, taking a backseat to Stupid Bird Tricks and the latest teen idol. Thin walls. Hey, I don't care if A.J. makes the boob tube, just as long as the check clears.

Here we go again, I thought as I huddled next to the heating-oil tank. I'd let my curiosity—and no little amount of Angie's, thank you very much—get us involved in something sinister. Unlike the gallbladders, I did recognize the white crow for what it was when it wasn't recovered from the bridge nets. I knew that it was probably missing for a reason. *Knew* may be too strong a word. *Felt* may be more like it. But how often do you *feel* something and it turns out to be wrong? Besides, like most people, I don't just feel one way about things. In my case, there was a cootie of vengeance needling me, a seam squirrel of malevolence in my shorts, vendetta's weevil burrowing under my skin. People throwing yours truly down the basement stairs and smacking Angie rub me the wrong way. To tell you the truth, I was expecting to come up to Bermuda, not find out much, and put all this behind me. But reprisal's lice and I were hoping we would find the culprits.

In the shadow of the motel, I started getting itchy just thinking about the vengeance prickling my brain. Go figure.

Groans chorused from a row of spruce behind the cabins as the wind gusted and bent the huge trees. Shards of light from the streetlight danced through the trees across the green cabin roofs and white siding. I saw Angie's reading light switch off, and before long everybody was asleep. Except me.

The wind swirled some leaves around the parking lot for a while, then got bored. Around 2:00 A.M., I was less itchy than cold and coming to the conclusion that I was a complete lunatic. Nothing was going to happen, no Road Runner was going to slam into my trap. A trap? What the heck is wrong with me, anyway? My imagination took flight and my senses with it.

What a chucklehead. Now I'd have to get up

early in the morning to dismantle the whole thing. I'd rather have sung "I'm a Little Teapot" in a biker bar than have Angie get a load of this idiocy.

I dusted the leaves off my pants and trod the shadows back to where Angie was fast asleep.

There must be something wrong with me. First, an excellent job offer has me in a panic, and now this. I seriously wondered if some professional help wasn't in order. Most people don't do these things. They get a great job offer, they smile, and they take it. So why was I different? Why was I building booby traps and shivering in the shadows of an oil tank? Was it a chemical imbalance? Had I clicked over 100,000 miles and needed Miracle Lube in my crankcase, a healthy dose of Prozac and Viagra to unstick the valves in my brain?

I went straight to the bathroom, gloomily brushing my teeth in the dark. The cabin was chilly and so was I. The clothes would stay on until I made my dive for the covers.

I had just spit and was tapping the water from my toothbrush when I heard a car whir slowly down the road. I listened. The car started to pass by.

Then it slowed.

Then it killed its engine.

I dropped my toothbrush. Sure as shinola sounded like the whir of Bret's old Honda.

Tiptoeing past the bed, I stuck a finger in the blinds. All I could hear was Angie sawing balsa. Outside I saw nothing. At first.

Then a shadow crossed the streetlamp's glare.

I felt around on the chair where Angie's clothes were for the tire iron, which fell with a clunk to the floor. I froze, and Angie rolled over with a slight groan, her golden hair fanned out across her pillow, a sleepy smile on her lips. She gave a protracted sigh, and I knew she was still out.

This could be anything, Garth. Somebody with car trouble. A bread delivery. A garbage pickup. A traveler stopping to look at a map, check the oil, take a whiz. This could be anything.

I was itchy again as I eased the front door open. Moving lightly off the porch, I slipped around to the back of our hut.

It didn't seem cold out anymore even though it was. I stared toward the streetlight and the long shadows it cast across the lawn and driveway. My ears were sonar, as though the pinging in my brain might help me hear danger's approach.

A shadow flicked the edge of the light and my heart skipped a beat. My hands began to sweat, and I caught my breath as I saw someone skirting the shadows in the direction of Cabin #1.

I was actually trembling with excitement. By golly, I had to admit to myself that it was fun lurking in the shadows and trying to catch this guy in my trap, and I felt very clever indeed. Like I'd invented that Milton Bradley brainchild Mouse Trap. Player opens door (A), which pulls string (B), causing slipknot (C) to release jack (D). Jack swings into unsuspecting intruder (E), intruder flies back through door (F) onto porch (G) into an unconscious state (H).

Although my mouse was in dark clothing and wore his ski mask, I could tell by the assassin's lumbering gate that it was Bret Fletcher. It was the same way he'd come at me across the square in Bermuda the first time I saw him, splay-footed, chest out, arms back. I guess Slim and Scotty held Bret accountable for my involvement, seeing as how he'd lost the crow, and now had sent him to do the dirty deed. I didn't doubt they were somewhere nearby.

Bret didn't appear to have a gun. But you never know. *How come I don't have a gun? I have a lousy tire iron. Other people always have the guns when this crap goes down. First thing tomorrow, I'm getting me a friggin big-ass Dirty Harry gun.*

Then I remembered the smell of the hand grenade, Compadre's blood spraying my face, hiding in the meat-packing plant hallway, listening to Pete Durban's footsteps.

I realized I'd zoned out for a second, just like in the meat-packing plant, and my jaw seized with panic. I'd lost track of Bret. I rubbed my face, blinked away the cobwebs.

Checking my perimeter, I felt I'd better move to a spot where I could see beyond Cabin #8. I darted along the rear of the cabins until I was flat against the back of Cabin #2.

I jockeyed an eye around the corner of Cabin #2, and Cabin #1's porch came into view.

Like a strobe light, muzzle flash projected the grizzly's silhouette on Cabin #1's window shade.

Echoing gun blast masked the sound of glass raining from the window. But it didn't block out the
clank of the bumper jack against Bret's head.

Like a cowpoke ejected from a saloon, Bret
crashed backward through the cabin's screen door,
pistol held loosely in one hand while the other
groped for stability. He flipped over the porch rail,
another shot cracking flame off into the sky as he
crashed into a yew bush. Bret pawed at his face,
cursed, and staggered to his feet.

Lights popped on in the tavern's back room, and
Bret stumbled a few indecisive steps toward the
road. Flood lamps flared in the yard and there was
Bret plain as noon, ski mask dangling in one hand,
the gun in the other. Blood smeared his face like the
winner of a pie-eating contest. Cherry pie.

He wheeled and galloped gridiron-style across
the lawn toward the road.

And for whatever reason, I bolted out after him,
itchy as all hell.

I'm no cornerback, but I almost did catch him,
just before the goal line. Perhaps the tom-toms
from his heart, the indoor gun blast, or the clank to
his head deafened him to my approach. And to the
approach of the pickup truck.

Perspicuous to a fault, I yelled some concise
warning like "Hey!" or maybe "Whoa!"

If Bret heard me, it may have only made him run
harder, which in itself might have helped. If he'd
been faster. Or if he hadn't stopped right in front of
the truck.

The truck pegged him right to the macadam. You'd have thought Frat Boy would have flown into the air, or off to the side. But one second he was upright, the next he was flat. And I mean flat.

Flecks of streetlight and shadow from the trees sliced through the truck's windows. From the fractured imagery in the driver's side I was sure I saw the profile of Slim's hat. But from the passenger side, as it passed not three feet in front of me . . . I don't even dare say what it looked like. But I saw something, a shape that didn't make any sense.

I didn't hear the truck hit Bret, maybe because I was making some unintelligible exclamation like "Guh!" at the time. But a millisecond after it, there was just the sound of the truck trailing off down the road, steam hissing from its radiator, bent metal and valves rattling as if nothing had happened. I looked at Bret and noticed first that his shoes were missing, socks hanging from his toes.

Gloved hands were twisted into the air, fingers tightly twitching like he was working an invisible piccolo.

More likely a harp. Needless to say, Bret was extremely dead.

Chapter 10

Would it surprise you to learn that I spent that night, or shall I say morning and the next day, in jail? Well, I have to admit that if I were the cops, I would have been pretty leery of letting me slip away. I looked Constable Bill straight in the eye and told the whole story of the white crow, but as I got to the part of how I came to build that bear n' bedpost booby trap, the way he scratched his big head of white hair seemed to signal that he'd heard better fish stories.

Of course, I now see how my actions that night could be construed as reckless endangerment, or even manslaughter, what with me effectively hitting Bret in the face with a jack and chasing him into traffic. In my favor was the gun, which with any luck would have Bret's fingerprints on it, as opposed to mine. Then again, nobody actually saw Bret shoot the bear rug, not even me, which might not necessarily be viewed as intent to shoot me. For all the cops knew, I tried to apprehend him, shot, missed, and chased him into a fatal collision.

And I could now see how it sounded improbable that I might have chased an armed man with a tire iron, and that he suddenly stopped in front of an oncoming car. My case was further weakened by the bar owner, who sided with the roadkill rather than the stranger. She told Constable Bill that she knew I was trouble when I rented the second cabin. Great.

On top of all that, Angie, bless her heart, was furious with me for not clueing her in to my cunning trap. She also kindly pointed out that if I hadn't insisted on being so clever and brought her in on what was going down, I might have had a corroborating witness to the fracas with Bret.

Yeah, and I seem to remember thinking I was very clever when setting the trap. Sitting at the cigarette-scarred institutional-blue table in the Brattleboro courthouse basement, I felt like a dunce. But mostly I was still stunned by what I had witnessed. Bret smashed into the pavement, his fingers still wiggling . . . It was the first time I'd seen anybody killed. Or seen anybody dead, outside of a funeral home. I don't count Compadre—it was dark and I didn't really see him die. And Ballet Boy survived being a toboggan, though life in a wheelchair meant no more *Nutcracker*.

"If you thought you were in danger, why didn't

you call the police?" the State DA said, twirling his glasses by one ear rest. I looked up at my public defender, Phil, who shrugged at me. He took the pencil from his mouth.

"My client was merely suspicious. He couldn't be positive of the assailant's potential. C'mon, Danny, Mr. Carson set up a grizzly bear in his room to lure this guy in there so he could murder him? That doesn't make sense."

Danny DA stood up and began waving his glasses.

"I'm just trying to establish what led him to believe Bret Fletcher meant to harm him. That's all, Phil. I mean, somehow he says he knew Fletcher was going to come and try to kill him. From what he said to Constable Bill . . ." Danny DA fished around some papers and came up with one that made him smile. "He said, 'I saw him see me in the tavern. He was there with this cowboy and a Scotsman. After I left the bar I watched the cowboy and Scotsman leave, and they gave Bret a knowing look kinda thing.'"

Phil the defender looked at me and shrugged— like he had fathered the village idiot—and put his splintered pencil behind an ear.

"My client had a hunch, Danny. What was Carson supposed to tell the police if he did call them? He was just being cautious—Constable Bill even said Bret took a swing at Carson outside Gunderson's a couple weeks back, so Carson had good reason to think Bret might want to harm him.

Don't forget, Bret's car was there, on the side of the road. And he had a ski mask in his possession."

"Doesn't mean he was sneaking in with a gun. It was cold, so he wore a hat. You know how many kids wear hats just like that down at the mall? Carson and Fletcher could have had a meeting, been discussing a deal, and it went sour."

Defender Phil gestured at me hopelessly.

"A deal? A meeting? The barmaid said they didn't talk in the bar. My client didn't flee the scene or ditch the gun. Carson's got no record and was not in the possession of any illegal goods. Your case is a load of crap, Danny, and you're gonna have to substantiate some of this to make the judge buy into it."

Danny smiled sardonically, pointing to the police report in his hand. "Flipper?"

I felt my face warm, and I resisted looking at Phil, who stammered.

"It says here," Danny chimed, eyebrows wiggling with delight, "that: *Carson reported that he could not see the occupants of the truck except that the driver had a hat similar to the one worn by the man in the bar with Bret. In the passenger side, Carson reports he saw . . . a flipper.* Really? What kind of flipper? Like a dolphin?"

"Okay, Danny." Phil stood. He was blushing too. "You've had your little joke."

"A joke, Phil? Not at all. Please, Mr. Carson, tell us, what kind of flipper was it?"

I expected Phil to jump in, but when I raised my

eyes from the floor, I found them both looking at me expectantly.

"I can't explain it," I muttered. "But that's what it looked like. It was brown, and it was up against the driver's side window. Maybe it wasn't a flipper. It happened very fast. I dunno."

Phil gestured at me like a trick dog. "See? He's doing his best to tell you what he saw, Danny. What more do you want?"

"What more do I want?" Danny slapped the police report down on the table and started twirling his glasses by the earpiece again. He fumbled them and they fell to the floor. He ducked out of view, below the table. "What I want is to see what comes up on the gun, that's what I want. And I want to see the autopsy."

"Autopsy?" Phil snorted. "Bret's cause of death seems pretty obvious. When are they gonna get around to this autopsy? My client's supposed to sit in jail all that time? The arraignment's this afternoon."

"We'll see" came from under the table.

And we did. Basically, the crusty old guy in judge robes was confused. He kept asking about the bear and if it was in season. By the time he had it all straightened out, the judge blew his nose thoughtfully and said, "The fool should have looked where he was going before he crossed the street." His gavel banged, and he turned toward the bailiff, saying, "Never should have canceled that show *Flipper*. I like fish."

See? The justice system does work. I walked, pending further hearings and more hard evidence—like the truck-as-murder-weapon.

Angie drove us to some German brathouse just off Interstate 91 where the waitresses wore lederhosen. Our zaftig server accessorized with a two-pound wooden tag that read *Hallo! HELGA. Willkommen!*

"For the last time, Angie, I was trying to protect you. Sure, if I'd been thinking only of me, I'd have dragged you out of bed and put you in harm's way so that you could go to jail too." I looked up at the woman in leather shorts. "I'll have a Bud, Wiener schnitzel, no kraut." Helga frowned.

"Gimcrack!" Angie sniffed.

"Gimcrack?" I winced back at her.

Angie ignored me and handed her menu to the waitress, sighing away our running argument. "Helga, I'll have the bratwurst, a Dinkel Acker, and I'll take his kraut, please." Helga smiled and left.

Gimcrack was a new one to me. Angie is physically incapable of cursing and so substitutes some of the most absurd exclamations for the old Anglo-Saxon standards. She once told an irate bus driver to *go splint a leg*. Worse yet, I can only exercise my profanity muscles when she's not around, lest I be subjected to bench-pressing the full weight of her indignation and disappointment. Her current displeasure was trifling by comparison, a mere dumbbell of disappointment.

"You know, Garth, I really resent that, like I'm a

silly female who needs the protection of a big, strong man. I can take care of myself, you know. And we're supposed to be a team, you and me."

"Angie, I'm not saying you're silly or stupid. What I am saying is that I love you and feel responsible for you almost getting killed twice now. Last night would have been the third time, the unlucky time."

She gave me a scowl, like the one I got for offering her a squirrel Frisbee back when we met. This one was for keeping her in the dark.

"Look," I continued, "what would you have said last night if I wanted to set up that booby trap?"

Her mouth squirmed. "It was stupid, if you really want to know. I was cold and sleepy and probably wouldn't have helped you anyway."

"You might even have talked me out of it."

"Maybe not. But you're on notice, Garth. You owe me one for leaving me out."

"One what?"

"One, that's all." She threw up her hands and closed her eyes, Angie's body language for *The Matter Is Now Closed*. "So what now?"

I trained a bloodshot eye on darling Angie. "Now? Now we sit in a motel room, keep our noses clean, and wait for the DA to say we can leave the state."

"What about—"

"No, I'm not going to go looking for Slim and Scotty."

"They were really like that? A cowboy and a Scotsman?"

"Yes."

"If I'd only seen them, I could have—"

"Angie, these guys are killers. Right before my eyes they ran Fletcher into the asphalt."

"But you said—thank you, Helga." Our beer arrived with a thud, and Helga left. "You said you didn't see who was in the truck."

"I think Helga might just be Otto's type."

"The truck?"

"I just know it was them, that's all. Were they holding flashlights to their faces? No. But I caught a glimpse of Slim's hat." My Bud was tepid, and I suspected Helga wasn't too broken up about it.

"And what about that other thing, the—"

"Don't say it! Don't say the F word." Again we got stares, and I lowered my voice. "I bitterly regret even mentioning it to Constable Bill. I feel like enough of an idiot as it is. I have no idea what it was I saw."

"Again, if another pair of eyes were there . . . Anyway."

I could see Angie's mind was elsewhere. "What are you thinking? If you're thinking this is one of those situations where I've gotta clear my name with the cops, forget it. Once they do the autopsy, once they find the truck, once they—"

"I just thought you might give your old friend Pete Durban a call, see what he makes of all this.

He might know why someone would steal a white crow."

"Nah."

"He might. You might even call around, do a little networking with all your cronies, like Rodney. You know, you're always telling me how you saw some piece or other in Brimfield, then saw it later at the Boukville show or in an antiques store."

I paused, musing. "There's this really nasty—and I mean downright ornery—raccoon that's been turning up for years. Thing looks like it's choking on a tapeworm." I looked Angie in the eye, and I suppose she knew she had me.

Chapter 11

Needless to say, we had moved out of the Maple Motor Court and into some utterly unremarkable motel just outside Brattleboro and near I-91. I wanted a clear shot at the interstate when I heard we could leave Vermont.

Strangers in a strange town, we sought out my pal Rodney—the troika, carriage, and sea-chest collector—and his bride for dinner. I had some pleasant restaurant in mind, with decent wines, a good carbonara sauce, hot crusty rolls, a passable tiramisu, potent cappuccino, and competent, unobtrusive service. The kind of restaurant common in New York, but also the kind I keep forgetting doesn't really exist outside major metropolises. Not that there aren't a lot of pretenders, places that have the look. But overcooked spaghetti, garlic salt on a hot-dog bun, and a "bottomless cup" of Sprite don't measure up.

"Won't 'ear of it, Garth!" Rodney bellowed into the phone, and then yelled off into the house, "Lorrie! Company for dinner!"

So Angie and I wended our way out to Dogville. As usual, I got a little lost on the dirt roads but found his house all the same. It was Angie's first visit, and she got out of the Lincoln hesitantly.

"Three, two, one . . ." I pointed to where hounds stampeded around the dilapidated house in our direction.

"Gads, you weren't kidding, Garth. You sure this is the place? If the lawn weren't cut, I'd say this house was vacant. Or a dog pound."

The front door wiggled, and I could hear Rodney cursing.

"Lorrie, the blasted doorknob is off again!"

"Window!" Lorrie hollered from somewhere.

Fortunately, Angie loves dogs, because a moment later she was surrounded by ten or so, alternately announcing our arrival in their hoarse howl, the one that means they're purebred bloodhounds.

I saw Rodney struggle with one window but then manage to open the next. He got one foot over the sill trying to climb out but couldn't squeeze the rest of his beery bulk through. As we stood watching, he gave up.

"Come 'round back the house," he hollered, trying in vain to shut the window he'd just struggled to open. "Lorrie!"

There's a porch in back of the house, along with the kennels and the smell of too much dog. Lorrie met us there, strands of gray-black hair hanging in her face. "Away, beasts!" She shooed the dogs, then pointed at us. "Not you two—come on in!"

Their house was cozy, neater than the outside, and it smelled mainly of wood smoke and cedar. The decor was heavy on Americana, like patchwork-quilted toaster covers, Shaker-style chairs with cushions, and cedar chests at every turn.

"Why, this place is lovely," Angie said, with more than a little surprise in her voice.

Rodney immediately wrapped Angie in a bear hug.

"How'd you get mixed up with this scrounger?" He tilted his shaggy head at me and held her at arm's length. "Couldn't you see he was gonna be such a bit o' trouble?"

"I understand you can be quite a handful too, if you're half the lout you were in college. I've heard that story about you stealing the squad car, oh, maybe a hundred times?"

"Aye!" Rodney winced. "Garth, 'ow come you don't broadcast my finer qualities? I'm not without some refined tastes, Angie."

"Well, I'm a sucker for a man with taste," Angie sighed, batting her eyes.

"Me too," Lorrie groaned, "a man with a distilled taste for Old Milwaukee. Ouch, Garth, that's a nasty bruise—"

"Speakin' of which . . ." Rodney interjected, two Old Milwaukees in his outstretched paw. "Did you hear the one about the woman who went to the doctor? She says: 'Doctor, every time I sneeze I have an orgasm.' The doctor shakes his head, worried-like, and says, 'Well, what have you been taking for it?' The patient replies: 'Black pepper.' "

Never fails to open with a ribald joke, no matter the audience. He'd caught Angie off guard. She blushed, then she burst into a peal of laughter. Lorrie and I rolled our eyes.

Rodney roared with laughter at his own jocularity and led me from the kitchen to the living room. I could still hear the cascade of Angie's laugh in the kitchen.

While the women got acquainted as Lorrie minded the meal, Rodney and I went through "how's business" preliminaries and our beer before dinner was served. And I can't say I've had better meat loaf and mac n' cheese. Dogs, antiques, fairs, and jewelry were all topics of conversation, it being tacitly understood that my legal problems were dessert and coffee talk.

Angie and I had some instant coffee and crumb cake, while Rodney had another beer. Lorrie made no apologies about spreading out some newspaper and scraping shutters next to the couch as we talked. She'd removed all the shutters from the house and stacked them in the living room. Some women knit. Lorrie peeled paint.

They listened attentively to our story. When I was finished, Rodney brought me an after-coffee beer.

"A white crow, y'say?" He scratched his stubble, winked, and stomped off into the other room. We chatted with Lorrie about puppies and weaning for fifteen minutes while Rodney rummaged through drawers full of crumpled paper. He found one he liked, came over, and spread it out on the table in front of me.

"Mind you, I 'aven't seen this bird. But I reckon it does sound like the bit you described, don't it? Look, here at the bottom."

Rodney poked a stubby finger at the flier for an auction that had been held last March in the town of Remington, New Hampshire.

Angie leaned over and read aloud: ". . . *rocking chair, mission bed, tractor seat, bamboo fly rod, white raven*—Rodney, it was a crow, not a raven."

Rodney suppressed a belch. "There a difference?"

"Damn right there is." I smiled. "But Gunderson didn't know the difference either. I wonder if Poe did?"

"We gonna check it out, Garth?" Angie brightened.

I gritted my teeth and turned away in thought. Lousy white crow. Still, there was the distinct possibility that understanding the crow's past might provide information to help capture Slim and Angus. Not exactly Black Bart and Macbeth, but let's face it, they were murderers who knew who I was and knew where I lived. Angie and I wouldn't be safe until they were apprehended, and I didn't have a lot of faith in the State of Vermont effecting their capture. I don't think the DA even thought they existed.

"Okay, we'll check it out." I stood. "Thanks, Rodney."

"Don't mention it." He clapped me on the shoulder, guiding me doorward. "Tho' I suppose the Chinese food'll be on you come my next visit to New York, what?"

"This pans out and I'll even buy the Tsingtao. Assuming I don't find myself back in the hoosegow."

"Better not." He clapped me on the back. "I'll be in New York next week to deliver some sea chests. And to drink your Tsingtao."

Chapter 12

The next morning Angie visited a local specialty jewelry tool manufacturer, and I took time out to make some calls.

Yes, about my predicament . . . but since I'm self-employed and don't get any paid time off, I have to keep the training wheels of capitalism turning back at my industrial hub. So I called my office manager.

"Otto?"

"Yes, of course, Garv! Vere you are, Garv?"

"We're in Vermont. We've had some trouble and have to stay, maybe a week at most. Can you stay at our place for a few days, keep an eye on things? Take the mail, deliveries, you know . . ."

"Oh my Got! Trouble? Yangie, how Yangie is?"

"We're okay, Otto. Angie is fine, and I'll tell you

all about it when we get home. But we need you to help us."

"Garv, I very happy." I heard him inflate his chest. "Otto is friend and make all looking. All very nice. I tell my vife, Luba, that Garv and Yangie need Otto."

While I was sure his hulking and by all accounts disapproving wife, Luba, could use a break from winging plates and shouting at him, the thought of leaving him in charge of our apartment was daunting. But I had little choice on such short notice. Some other friends who were a tad more reliable, like Dudley the bird taxidermist, I couldn't reach.

"I'll call every day to make sure . . . Otto? Otto?"

He'd hung up. Russian phone etiquette. You never knew when he might think the conversation was over.

I checked my messages and found I had a call from the Freezy Cone people and from the Network Theater about Jilly. Nothing from the Elks.

I was relieved to find that my squad was unharmed and that the Freezy Cone shoot was a wrap. The same could not be said for the wrangler's live squad. One of the little guys, Reggie by name, had swallowed an errant felt-tip pen and met an untimely end. The wrangler wanted to know if I'd like to have Reggie, more or less compensation for the last time when I lost Sneezy. After expressing my sorrow for Reggie's passing, I said *yes indeedy*. Put him on ice. (Sorry, but I don't think there's any way of asking someone to freeze a dead penguin that doesn't sound somewhat flip. At least I didn't follow that up with *He would have wanted it that way.*) I told them I'd have Otto come get him and my squad in the next day or so. I have a chest freezer in my basement for just such mortuary moments. I'm sure my birdman Dudley would love to take a crack at mounting a penguin.

I called about Jilly but the party wasn't in. But I knew what the call was about. Since she wasn't on the program the last two nights, they wanted to extend the rental. Fine. The Elks and the elk head could wait.

Now down to the important stuff: no, not accepting the job. And not *not* accepting the job. I couldn't even add that problem to the mix. My brain was like a pinball machine that releases ten balls at once.

I called my public defender, Phil. Found out from his coworker that they still had no word from the DA's office on my status. I said I was going to be out all morning but that I'd call again that afternoon. In the following half hour, I worked my connections looking for leads on the white crow. Spoke with three message machines, two dealers, and an auctioneer to put out feelers.

Then Angie returned. She was shaking her hands in the air like they were wet, but I knew it was because she was excited.

"Garth, guess what?"

I thought about it a second. I like to try to guess. "Van Putin?"

She clapped her hands.

"I checked my messages from a pay phone. He called, wants me to bring in some of my work to show him."

She got a thumbs-up from me. "Way to go. Foot solidly in the door. Wanna go for a drive?"

"Now, let me guess. To Remington, to check on that white crow?"

So we drove through Brattleboro, which, if it weren't for my predicament, would have seemed a much more pleasant burg. It's perched on the side of a hill overlooking the Connecticut River, the main drag cutting diagonally through a quaint red-brick shopping district dotted with restaurants, too many of which were still fixated on pitas and sprouts. At the bottom of the hill is a trestled bridge, which took Angie and me to New Hampshire and about forty minutes later due southeast to the town of Remington. Yeah, I know we weren't supposed to leave the state, but I don't think anybody really differentiates between Vermont and New Hampshire. Let's just say we were prepared to play dumb.

Not much to Remington, just four corners really, one of which had a brief strip mall. All but the tattoo parlor dealt in junk. One shop was an auction house, and the sign on the door said SORRY! WE'RE CLOSED! I always wondered why those signs had exclamation marks. Were they shouting at me? Or were they just cheerful that they weren't open?

But a man in a sweater and bifocals was mucking

about inside, and I motioned him over. He started speaking even before the door was open.

"(blah blah blah) . . . until Wednesday night, like it says on the door. You show up an hour early to preview. Now—"

"We were looking for some information on a white raven in a bell jar you auctioned in March," Angie said cheerfully.

The man checked his pocket watch like an unhappy train conductor.

"Why? Why are you looking for some white raven in a bell jar we auctioned in March? If you wanted the white raven, you should have come—"

"We only just got the flier, from a friend. Do you remember it?" Angie prodded, holding forth the crumpled paper.

"No. Yes, well, I can't remember everything that we—"

"Was it under glass?" I said.

"Glass? No. Well, I don't know. Look . . ." He started playing with his pocket watch again.

"Did you know that ravens are a protected species under the Migratory Bird Treaty Act, which, although it allows the hunting of ravens, prohibits the sale of ravens? Any idea how much U.S. Fish and Wildlife would fine you for selling that raven?" I smiled, just on the inside.

His unshaven jaw dropped and his bifocals slipped to the end of his nose, the pocket watch dangling from his hand, unmolested for a change.

I tried again. "We are very interested in finding

that raven and whoever you sold it to. Otherwise I'll fax this flier to U.S. Fish and Wildlife, they'll come down and look at your ledgers, and maybe find that you've sold a few ducks, maybe a blue jay, which are also illegal to sell. So how about you save us all some fuss and go look in your roster and find who bought the white raven?"

Could I bust the chops of guys like this 9 to 5 for U.S. Fish and Wildlife?

He pushed up his bifocals and favored me with a dyspeptic sneer, then drifted back into his cluttered office, where I heard him rummaging about and muttering to himself before he emerged a few minutes later. He handed us a slip of torn notebook paper. Forcing a coffee-stained smile and without so much as a fare-thee-well, he closed the door in our faces.

"What's it say?" Angie pulled at my arm.

I shrugged and handed it to her. *Item: White crow in bell jar on rock. Buyer: Guy Partridge, dealer, Mallard Island, Maine.*

"On a rock?" Angie frowned. "Not on a stick?"

"What it says." I shrugged again. Rock, stick— whatever. How many white crows are out there, anyway? Darn few. This was probably the same crow. So how did it make it from Guy Partridge to Slim and his gang? We needed to know more. Or a lot less. I was getting sucked into this thing and knew it. But like a cat at a fishbowl, I wouldn't be satisfied until the carpet was littered with broken glass, stinky water, and flopping guppies.

We climbed back in the Lincoln and roared along the rocky Ashuelot River back to Brattleboro. I don't know how to pronounce *Ashuelot*, but I've been told it's best to try while sneezing.

"Ever hear of a dealer named Guy Partridge?" Angie queried.

I wagged my head. "Sounds vaguely familiar, but no."

Angie sulked a moment, stray blond locks lashing her face.

"Where the hell is Mallard Island?" She started fussing with the maps in the glove compartment, unfolded one, and let the wind rip it a bit. After a few moments, she bit her lip the way she does when she gets a crossword clue. "Mallard Island, just south of Kennebunk," she said in mild wonder. "That's a ways from here."

"We'll call first. Going a few miles down the road to Remington is one thing. Heading for the coast is another. I don't want to blow my release deal with the judge. He likes fish."

"I could go. I'll rent a car."

"You don't even know if it's the same bird."

"What are the chances? I mean, how many other white crows have you seen in your travels?"

"Exactly? One, I guess. In a taxidermy museum, in northern Vermont. A white crow, wings out, not folded like this one. Doesn't mean there aren't others."

Before long we were back in Brattleboro, and I slid the Lincoln in at a hydrant. While Angie waited in the car, I ran up to see if Defender Phil was at the courthouse. I found him outside a courtroom next to a sneering, scruffy-looking teen.

"Garth!" He spat little yellow flecks of pencil paint. "I only have a minute. Bobby, stay there, don't move, okay?" The kid eyed the bailiff. "C'mon, Garth." Phil led me into a vending-machine alcove.

"Here's the scoop," he said around a pencil in his teeth. "They found the truck. Someone tried to drive it into a lake, but it bogged down in the mud. Then they tried to torch it, but only burned the cab. There's a dent in the front grille, just like you said, and a couple of Fletcher's teeth and a button from his shirt inside the bumper. They look like his, anyway. A full autopsy, dental check, and all may take a while. This isn't New York, if you know what I mean."

"So, can I leave town or what?"

"Don't. There's more. Fletcher was officially unemployed, though his mother told the police he'd been out west working a carnival, probably off the books."

"Think he was with one of these carnivals when Mrs. Fletcher gave his feathery prize to Gunderson?" Must be where he picked up the word *dang*.

"Looking into that, but it would have been winter, not carnival season. He also used to work with some outfits here on the East Coast during the summers." Phil glanced back to see if his wayward youth had run out on him. "Graduated college out in Portland two years ago, worked odd jobs since.

Had a record, petty stuff, drug possession, DWI. Hanging out with carnies, so what do you expect? Police are trying to track down where he was out west and who he's been seen with recently. Still nothing on the two men you saw him with. You sure you can't tell us more about them?"

I laughed. "I think I gave the cops a hell of a description. The hat, the toothpick, the red hair, heights, approximate weights, builds—what more do they want? A cowboy and a Scotsman. I don't think it could be more descriptive."

Phil winced. "That description doesn't sound good. Let's say the guy with the hat and the guy with red hair."

"Fine. Doesn't the barmaid remember them? Don't the other patrons who were there that night?"

"She's local and on Bret's side, sorta a hostile witness. Can you draw? Can your wife draw?"

"Draw," I said dryly.

"Yes." Phil edged out the door. "Drawings of these two suspects would help."

"My drawing of Binky from a matchbook couldn't get me into correspondence art school when I was eight, so I seriously doubt my spazoid stick figures would help much. Don't the police usually have some kind of artist that—"

"Sure, when they believe it's relevant. This isn't one of those times. They don't believe you."

"Hey, I know I'm from out of town and all, but I've got a clean record and—"

He cleared his throat. "Technically you have a clean record."

"What's that supposed to mean?" My eyes narrowed.

"Seems they spoke to a detective in New York. Wilkens? Watson? He wasn't helpful to us."

I gritted my teeth. "Walker!"

"Yup, that's the guy." He started drifting back down the hall toward the courtroom. "See if you can draw that picture. I gotta get back into court now."

Hands on hips, I frowned as I watched him disappear into the throngs of court reporters, witnesses, police, and court functionaries.

Walker. My pestiferous nemesis wouldn't rest until he caught me red-handed, and even if he didn't, he was going to enjoy being a hard-ass and making my life difficult. Stupid flatfoot was hanging his hopes for detective sergeant on me, of all people. Okay, so I change a sign now and then. But Machine Gun Kelly I'm not. And he was certainly no Melvin Purvis.

I was fuming as I went down the stairs. Now he had these cops against me too. I'd be damned if I'd let that numskull ruin my life.

Betcha anything there's a matchbook correspondence school for becoming a detective overnight, but I was still bitter about my failure to accurately depict Binky. Perhaps Walker and the Brattleboro cops didn't realize it, but letting me know they were more or less working against me meant I had little choice but to at least put myself to work trying to clear me. If nothing else to show Walker he couldn't bully me.

Would that I had any confidence in my public defender Phil, but I pegged him as a cocktail fork against the Mongol horde: useless. Unless the Mongol horde in question was serving cocktail weenies. Which they weren't.

What I needed to do was locate those guys, find out why Bret was pals with them. Bret's mom and maybe the barmaid needed visiting, and I was just the guy who didn't want to do it.

I tromped down the steps to the parking lot, more exasperated than angry by the time I got back to the car. Angie was gone. In her place was a note:

Sweetums: Rented a car, gone to the coast—I'll call from there—Stay out of trouble—XXXOOO. P.S.: Don't be mad. Remember: I owed you one.

"Son of a . . ." I snarled. "Gimcrack!"

Chapter 13

I pulled up to the Fletchers' modest Cape Cod, which was more a bungalow than a house, two bedrooms tops. The place was so cozy that I surmised Bret was an only child. The phone book listed only Mrs. Fletcher, so I further surmised that Mr. Fletcher was dead. Which figured. Bret had the frantic behavior of a mama's boy gone haywire. I had a mind's eyeful of his room already, pennants on the wall, plaid comforter on the bed, gun in the sock drawer.

Yes, there I was, subjected to doing my own legwork to make sure there wasn't some sort of gross miscarriage of justice on my behalf.

Toggling the rearview mirror in my direction, I tried to corral my hair. What was I going to say? "Hello, Mrs. Fletcher, I'm the guy who chased your kid into traffic?" *Watch out for the old lady's fry pan,*

Garth! Bong! Maybe I could claim I was an insurance adjuster, or—

"Can I help you?"

She'd snuck up on me from behind, grocery bag on her arm. I knew her immediately. She had Bret's rosy cheeks, downy complexion, and thin brown hair.

And she suddenly knew who I was too. An excruciating silence followed before I stammered, "Mrs. Fletcher, I want . . . you to know that I, uh, well . . . Bret—I'm very sorry about it." Her eye glistened, and she reddened a bit more. I clambered out of the car. "I never wanted, intended for this to happen. You see . . ."

Mrs. Fletcher brushed past me like I'd just won a bake-off with *her* cobbler recipe. I winced, wiped sweat from my brow, and pursued.

"I'm trying to find out who it was in the truck, Mrs. Fletcher, that's why I came. I thought maybe you knew—"

"I knew," she tremoloed without stopping.

"What?"

"I knew Bret was with some bad crowd, I knew it," she sniffled. "Carnies."

"Carnies? Do you know who?"

"Don't you think the police have asked me? I don't know. I should have known, but I didn't. A mother gets scared of the truth sometimes. For all I know you was one of them. I talked with the police, I talked with the reporter. Go away." She climbed the three steps to the screen door and yanked the mail from her mail basket.

I was about to lose her and figured I could endure another lashing to get in a good question. But I got ambitious.

"Where did he get the white crow?"

The mail crunched in her fist. Turning slowly from the door, she held up a trembling, bony hand. I took a step back. The look on her face was . . . The eyes looked right through me, like those of some kind of evil centaur.

"The devil himself," she hissed, "is in that crow." One of her bony fingers swept past the hedges and flower beds and toward the backyard. Looked like a heck of a storm had done a number on some large trees there, which had been uprooted, their gnarled roots like bony black hands clawing the earth. Sawdust and piles of logs were evidence that a cleanup was in progress. Funny, but none of the neighbors' trees looked any worse for wear.

"Look at what it did. Burning. I should have burned it," she spat.

I was too stunned to say anything more as I watched her recede into the dark house and shut the door.

Burning? The devil? Felled trees? Jeez, welcome to New England, home of H. P. Lovecraft. The bloated corpulence of Cthulhu and the boundless demon-sultan Azathoth probably lived in the split-level next door like Ozzie and Harriet. Must be a fearsome sight when they turn out to trim the azaleas.

I smoothed the goose bumps down on my arms and made tracks for the Lincoln. I felt like a heel for bothering the old gal, but she seemed a little far gone anyway. But the apple doesn't fall far from the tree—Bret was a wacko in his own right.

It wasn't until I got back to the car that I smacked myself in the forehead. She'd spoken to a reporter. Of course. There would be an obituary.

The Lincoln and I wheeled over to the library, which I'd noticed on my way back and forth from the courthouse. I went to the research desk and asked the tie-dyed kid at the counter for yesterday's local paper. I took the papers to a nearby table but didn't find Bret's obituary.

I went back to the counter. "Do you have today's paper?"

"Dude over there." He pointed. "When he's through."

I sank into a chair opposite the man behind the paper and waited politely. He merrily bounced one crossed leg and hummed softly, the white of his sock blinking at me from under his slacks.

"Shame," he said from behind the paper. "Boy that young, hit by a truck. Shame."

I smelled cloves, and a familiar shiver wriggled up my spine. The man lowered his paper. It was Jim Kim and his happy grin. "Here to read about your handiwork?"

I had so many things I wanted to say, or ask, or do that my circuits locked. I was only able to stab my finger impotently in the direction of my mystery pal, my unknown best friend, my anonymous confidant, my Korean shadow.

"Yes, Garth, his obituary is in today's paper." He moved into the chair next to mine, handing over the paper, which was folded to display Bret's obituary. "I'm finished. And if you don't mind me saying so"—he patted my forearm like a dear old chum, his voice subdued but no less jocular—"I think you should finish up here. Got your stuff back, didn't you? Believe me, things are well in hand. Go back to New York, get some decent Chinese food, for Pete's sake."

"Who are you? What do you want?" I finally blurted, which got me cross looks from the bookstack shushers.

"It's me, Jimmy. And I want the same thing you want. Only more."

"So you're not going to tell me who you are, is that it?"

"I'll tell you who I am, Garth. I'm your friend."

"Look, if you don't mind me saying so, Jimmy, you're a very creepy guy. To tell the truth, you—of all the people mixed up in this business—have convinced me I'd have a healthier future if I back away from this thing. But the State of Vermont has different ideas."

"Creepy?" Kim looked genuinely hurt, stroking his thin mustache. "I never thought of myself as creepy. If it was anybody else, Garth, I'd be offended. And here I am trying to help you extricate yourself from the jam you're in."

"Help me? You know what's going on, right? You can help get me out of this mess?"

"What are the magic words?"

"Okay," I sighed. "I'm sorry. I'm sorry for calling you creepy."

"That's okay, Garth. You're under some stress here." He slapped my knee. "Look, how about I see what I can do—as a friend—to sort of pave your way south, get the district attorney to see what a good egg you are? You'll go home then, won't you? Leave this dirty business to me?"

"You betcha I will. I'll try."

"Try?" He tittered.

"This crow is like gum on my shoe. I wipe it off and step right back into it."

"That's not entirely true. You didn't have to go back to Bermuda, now, did you? For a fifty-dollar crow?" He stood and gave his knuckles a self-satisfied crack.

"Scout's honor, I'll forget about the crow. You and your friends can have him."

He smiled, turned to go, but came back and leaned over me. "By the way, Garth, this is just between you and me, okay? You wouldn't want to spoil everything."

I shook my head. "Believe me, if it means getting out of this and back home, scot-free, I'm your best friend."

Now, what should I have done?

A. Call the police. (Yeah, right . . .)

B. Call my public defender. (Remember the weenie fork?)

C. Follow him. (Hell, I didn't even want him following me.)

D. Threaten him. (With what? My disapproval?)

E. Punch him. (I liked this idea a whole lot at the time.)

I still don't know. As a New Yorker, though, my instincts are not to go to the cops about somebody who may well have influence. In the Big Apple, you don't rat out someone who can put the fix in to make the traffic cops go easy on your block's parking tickets or get the postman not to crumple your mail. Cops have their own wiles, their own secret ways and motivations. The way I always figure it, the police are in a really difficult spot, floating in a Bermuda Triangle between the criminals, the public, and the courts, and the whims of either on a given day may set their moral compasses spinning. DAs are all about convictions, so definitely not on my side. Go to pencil-muncher Phil, who's already doubting me, with a story about a threatening, friendly Korean? Don't think so. Anyway, I finger Jimmy, or follow, or do anything to irk him . . . Who knows? He could make it worse for me—I could get twenty-five years.

It briefly made sense that he might be in cahoots with Bret's cohorts, sent here—as before—to steer me away from the crow. But he'd talked about smoothing things over with the DA for me. I just couldn't fathom how someone with connections like that, someone with political pull, would be involved with those lunkheads who'd stolen my stuffed crow. From the way my preppy Korean friend talked and dressed, he didn't seem like a confederate of Slim's. Jimmy wasn't at the Maple Motor Court bar, and he was definitely too tall and far too composed to be one of the guys who pillaged my apartment. He was slick and would have had pros do his dirty work. Clearly, he had interests of his own. No doubt he wanted the crow for himself, or at least for Bret's crew to have it.

But why? Whose interests did he represent?

Motives? Love or money, and my money was on money. Whatever was going on, there was a lot of moola involved, that was for sure.

Throw it in a pot and boil it down, I had no one I could trust to act in my best interest other than me. Clearly, the best path for me wasn't to find some stuffed crow of no intrinsic value or to track down the people who accosted Angie and me. There was no reason to put my neck on the line. None at all.

On the other hand, forsake not the fig leaf of prudence for naked practicality. I mean, it wouldn't hurt to try and get a little more background on the players, just in case Kim didn't command as much influence in this affair as he claimed. For now I was still in dutch, so it couldn't hurt to make a few phone calls, could it? I dropped a dime and photocopied the obituary.

Chapter 14

Where was Angie? There were no messages back at the hotel, and I was worried. She'd been gone about four hours and should be at Mallard Island already. But I managed to calm myself somewhat. At least she was far away from Slim, Angus, and my "friend" Jimmy. Among all the other wacko stuff coming down the pike, I found that reassuring, I can tell you.

So I turned my attention back to Bret's obituary, which read:

Bret Fletcher, 25, of Brendille Lane, was the victim of a hit-and-run accident outside the Maple Motor Court. He was pronounced dead at the scene. Circumstances of his death are still unclear at press time. It appears he was chased into the road by one of the motel guests, who mistook him for a prowler.

Fletcher graduated from Daniel Webster High

School, and subsequently took several credits in veterinary sciences at Portland College, Oregon. He worked two summers with Faldo Amusements, a traveling carnival. Last summer, Fletcher took an internship with the Primate Department at the Portland Wildlife Conservancy.

Bret Fletcher is survived by his mother, Bernadette Fletcher, of Guilford. Services will be held at the North Guilford Funeral Home this coming Saturday.

Well, *Phil*, looks like you didn't quite have the whole story. Or chose not to tell me. Or didn't care enough to tell me.

Primate Department. That didn't set off any bells, but it was a whole heck of a lot more to go on than carnival workers.

I got on the horn to the conservancy in Oregon. "Yes, could I please speak with someone in the Primate Department?" They switched me around.

"Yello?" somebody sighed in Portland. She sounded like a refugee from a truck-stop lunch counter.

"Hi, my name is Carson, and I've been retained to investigate the circumstances of Bret Fletcher's death. If I may, I'd like to ask—"

"The police already called. If it'll make you happy, I'll tell you what I tol' them." Truck Stop didn't give me a chance to answer. "Bret was a bright kid, good with the animals. He was almost always on time and a good summer intern. Most of the folks in the department are older than him, an' since we didn't socialize, I don't know who his friends are. He had a basement apartment a few miles from here." Truck Stop sighed again. "Look, I gotta go, awright?"

"Did you ever see him with a white crow?"

Another sigh. "A what?"

"A white crow?"

"Like a bird? No. Just primates. Simian anthropoids. Apes."

"What duties did he have?"

"Whadda you mean? You mean like cleaning cages, feeding? What's this, the third degree?"

I felt she was about to hang up, and I figured my sex appeal wasn't going to keep her on the line. After sex and money, guilt usually proves a pretty good motivator. "Sorry to cut into your coffee break, but Fletcher's mother, a little rosy-cheeked old lady in a little white house surrounded by posies, is crying her eyes out right now, brokenhearted. Her only son is dead and she needs to know why." I surprised myself; a sob caught in my throat. "Are you going to help Mrs. Fletcher or hang up on her?"

"Dang . . ." Truck Stop said slowly. "I didn't know it was 'xactly like that, y'know."

"So, what animal did he spend the most time with?"

"But I don't see what use . . ."

Neither did I. Just trying to open this clam. "I assure you, these questions have a direct bearing on his murder."

Truck Stop harrumphed. "Glenda and Gobo. He

spent lots of time with them. Not common with in-
terns."

"Excuse me?"

"Bret liked taking care of Glenda and Gobo.
Mountain gorillas. Wasn't like we let him get in the
cage with 'em. You know, a rapport. He fed 'em.
Same you get with a cat. It rubs against your leg
when it knows you got tuna. Except they'd probably rip his brains out by his nose. Yello?"

"I'm here. Very interesting. Did anybody else
take care of the gorillas?"

"Of course. You don't think we're gonna let a bio
intern be in charge of a half million bucks worth
of ape?"

"Half million?"

"Look, he had nothing to do with the Glenda
and Gobo thing, if that's what you're gettin' at."

"Pardon?"

"Look, I'd like to talk, but—"

"What Glenda and Gobo thing?"

"Dang, don't you read the papers?"

"I'm out east." Boy, Truck Stop was as annoying
as Mrs. Fletcher was damning. "What Glenda and
Gobo thing?"

"Gobo died on accident, got hold of some cleaning fluid."

"*On* accident?"

"On accident."

A little flicker, a little tingle, a little notion
popped into my head. As morbid as it sounds, I have
a contact, a disinterested techie at the World

Wildlife Conservancy Fund, who lets me know when something interesting dies at a zoo. They track captive-animal mortality. Tiger cubs, chimps, and other endearing critters I don't make a bid for, knowing full well that the zoo would have political if not staff problems if they sold the carcass. Besides, many of those are dissected for pathology studies. Deceased birds of prey and parrots I almost always inquire after and often get them in exchange for a donation. It works out for me, because having exotic birds stuffed isn't usually as expensive as exotic mammals.

"What did they do with the body?"

"Who is they?"

"What happened to the body?"

"Buried. Buncha folks in town here put together a collection for the funeral." There was a soft chuckle. "People get pretty soft when it comes to gorillas. Bought a plot for her an' everything."

"In a pet cemetery?"

"Uhn-uhn. In a human cemetery. I thought it was kinda sick, embalming, a coffin, an' all that." The tone darkened suddenly. "If they wanted to do something nice, they shoulda planted Gobo in a rain forest, in a nice nest of leaves. Public relations, don'tcha know. Yello?"

"Who was at the funeral?"

"Everybody."

"Could you narrow it down a bit?"

"Everybody from the department, a lot of donors, the mayor—stuff like that."

"And Bret, right? Was he with any friends then? A happy Korean guy maybe?"

"I tol' you, I never met or saw any friendsa his, happy or otherwise. Bret was there with the department and the funeral director."

"Who?"

"With us. But he was the one who found a funeral parlor that would do the embalming. So he was with the funeral director a lot, y'know, for the arrangements."

"What funeral parlor?"

"MacTeague's . . . Yello? Yello?"

"Guy with black hair?"

"Hair as red as a clown's, actually. Scotch, I think."

"Thank you very much for your time. Sorry to trouble you."

"Yeah, okay."

I depressed the receiver and let it up to make the next call.

"Yello?" Truck Stop was still on the line.

"Good-bye, thanks a million!"

This time I held it down for a full minute.

I called information, then MacTeague's Funeral Home.

"Yes, is Mr. MacTeague there?"

"Regrettably, no." A soothing voice replied, the antithesis to Truck Stop. "He's away for the week. My name is Norman. May I serve you?"

"Well, yes, um, I had spoken with Mr. MacTeague about some arrangements."

"Ah yes, arrangements. Our continuing condolences." Norman's timbre could smooth over a bed of nails. "Name?"

"You see, well, we never got as far as that, we only spoke briefly. I'm out east, in Vermont, and we were thinking of a burial out west. He said he was planning a trip here and that we might consult in person."

"Hmm, yes. Too bad. He's currently in Maine, on other business. He's due back tomorrow. Let me take your name, and I'll have him call."

"Thanks just the same." I hung up.

I was beginning to feel a bit more like a detective. But I decided to fight the odds and see if I couldn't make a few honest bucks.

I called all the chums I'd tried to reach that morning and predictably found that nobody knew of any white crows except the one at the Terry Brisbane Taxidermy Museum. At the same time, I managed to conduct a little more business, which was good, because I was living on Visa and running my business into the ground by staying away from the shop.

I had a call on my machine from Gillie, a fifties' retro dealer in Charleston, who said he had a customer who wanted a moose, which are slim pickins down thataway. I left a message on his machine that I could ship one out to him next week for eight fifty plus crating and shipping, which probably would let him cut a couple hundred out for himself. I asked, by the by, whether he had any dolphin (the fish, not the mammal), which are a hot item in the northeast but overflow the back rooms of some taxidermists in Florida. A lot of tourists catch fish but balk when it comes time to foot the bill.

Then I called Oscar in Rangely (who almost always has a couple midsize, fair-priced Bullwinkles) and rounded out the deal, copping a hundred for yours truly. But that wasn't going to excite my checking account any, so I asked Oscar if he could move any dolphin. I heard him scratch his stubble, then say, "Just might," which in his lexicon meant yes.

May seem easy, but it's not every day that I can clear three hundred for the price of a few phone calls. Might even break even for the week if I could work a little more magic. Which reminded me that I had to call the Network Theater again and check on my bear. Turns out they'd used her the night before, in a taped segment. The bit went well, and the celeb host Buddy wanted to rent Aunt Jilly for a month. Hot damn. They could have bought her for two weeks' rent, though I had little doubt the thing would be returned in bad condition after all that time in a studio. The dry heat of stage lights combined with sloppy stagehands really takes it out of a mount. So I leveled with them, said they might as well buy the bear. No way. Had something to do with how their budget works. Fine.

I pulled a piece of paper from my wallet, the one Pete Durban had given me in the Ernest Borgnine booth, and unfolded it. I ran my finger above the bit about the white crow to where it read *MOOSE HEAD 4 SALE* and then dialed the number.

A sleepy female voice answered tentatively: " 'lo?"

"Hi, I'm calling about the moose head, the one that must go, you haul?"

"Yes. What?"

"You have a moose head for sale?"

"Why, yes . . ."

"I'm interested in buying it. Do you still have it?"

"Hello?"

"Moose head. You have one for sale."

"Why, yes . . ."

"How much is it?"

"The moose head?"

Is it just me, or are there some days everybody else seems to be running on AAA batteries?

"Yes." I winced. "The moose head. How much is it?"

"When can you come by?"

"I don't know where you live," I sighed.

"It's fifty dollars."

My fist tightened around the receiver.

"Where do you live?"

"On Dewberry Road. When can you come by?"

I jotted the road down.

"I'll come right over as soon as you tell me what state you're in."

Nothing.

"Hello?"

Still nothing. I heard a click. The line was dead.

I redialed and found the line busy. Waited five minutes. Still busy. Was someone doing this to me on purpose? I could picture an old woman in a TV lounger in front of *Golden Girls*, still cradling the receiver, mouth open, eyes closed and snoring. For crying out loud.

Next call: home. Now, in person, it's difficult communicating with Otto. Over the phone, well, it's like talking to your dog. But like any bad dog, he knows a few key words.

"No smoking in house!"

"Ah, Garv, very nice!"

"Everything okay?"

"Vhat? Eetz looking, yes, of course. Garv, how Yangie? Eh?"

"Good."

"Vere you, Garv? Vac-ate-ton? Eh? Wodka, maybe svimming pool, naked veemin? Naked veemin beach?"

"Vermont, Otto. No nude beaches."

"Ah, good, eetz looking: Vere Mont. Many trees, bird, air good. Maybe I go Vere Mont, yes? Otto verk all time. Maybe Otto vac-ate-ton, eh?"

"Look, Otto, get a pencil. . . ."

"Pencil, yes . . ."

"I want to let you know where we are. Ready?"

"Yes, I ready."

"Angie and Garth are at the I-N-T-E-R-S-T-A-T-E M-O-T-O-R L-O-D-G-E." My enunciation was as elongated as possible. "That's in B-R-A-T-T-L-E-

B-O-R-O, V-E-R-M-O-N-T." I capped it all off with the phone number. "Got that?"

"But of course, Interstate Motor Lodge, Brattleboro, Vere Mont."

"Okay. We'll see you soon."

"Soon? *Ahoyatilne!*" That last exclamation is yet another Russian tidbit, one based upon a certain aspect of the male anatomy. It could mean almost anything but was always an exclamation. "Eetz looking, Garv! I see you soon, yes, of course. I very heppy." There was a click and he was gone.

I called him back.

"Garv! Very nice speaking again, my friend."

"Don't hang up until I tell you, okay?"

"Yes, of course."

"I need you to pick up the penguins. They're in Astoria. The address is on the rental-slip pile on my desk. Do you understand?"

"Yes, of course. Dopey, Sleepy, Heppy, Doc . . ."

"There will be seven of them."

"No, Garv, penguins six. Dopey, Sleepy, Heppy, Doc . . . Oh my Got, eet very bad Sneezy *pizdyets.*"

"Otto, we have a new penguin. He's a dead penguin. Penguin *pizdyets.*"

"Yes, Sneezy dead. *Someday my print wheels come, someday wheels meets a can . . .*"

"Stop singing and listen to me, Otto."

"Otto sad, sing sad song of wheel very lonely."

"This is not Sneezy. This is a new penguin, a new dead penguin that was alive yesterday but is dead today. We are going to have him be our new Sneezy."

"Ahh! Yes, yes, yes. New dead Sneezy, I understand. My Got! But, lookink, eh? *High low, High low! A working wheel will go . . .*"

"Otto, please do not sing on the telephone!"

"Garv, why songs about wheels? Very nice, but—"

"Shut up and listen to me. The new Sneezy is frozen. Put him in the chest freezer."

"In chest? But—"

"Otto, put him in the chest freezer."

He sighed. "How you want. But I dunno. Not lookink."

"The new Sneezy needs to be kept frozen. On ice. Very cold."

"Yes, my friend."

"Also, there's a rental slip from the Elks, at the Sheraton. Go to that address, pick up the elk."

"Elk, up pick, Sheraton. I clean and make all very nice."

"Go to the U-Van down the block, rent a van to make the pickups. Tell them to put it on my account."

"Rent van, eets okay."

"Did you see the zebra pelts on the workbench?"

"Otto make all good, eh?"

"You cleaned them already?"

"*Pizdyets,*" he barked. Suffice to say, *pizdyets* is a Russian profanity that means *finished.* Use your imagination.

"And the caribou racks . . ."

"Yes, of course!"

"Good boy, Otto. Now, you'll pick up the penguins and the elk, yes?"

"Garv, I know, I know . . . Otto is very good up to pick."

"And you have our address here in Vermont?"

"Ah! Garv, I very much to see you."

"Yes, I'll see you soon. You can hang up now."

"Someday my print wheels come . . . Why wheels come, Garv?"

Next I checked my messages. Maybe Angie had lost the number of the hotel and left a message at home?

I was greatly disappointed.

"So, Carson . . ." Walker's voice chuckled. "I hear you got in some hot water up there in Vermont. Sorry it wasn't me that busted you but just wanted to reassure you that if you manage to wriggle out of it, *I'll be here waiting.*"

I hung up. Walker really had it in for me. As if I didn't have enough troubles, I had him stalking me too. I gave both Ma Bell and me a rest from that exhausting string of calls. But I was also giving it a break hoping Angie would ring.

Now, let's see . . . wasn't I just talking to a woman in Seattle about a gorilla funeral and a guy named MacTeague? I had an idea there was something crooked going on with the gorilla—they're inherently valuable for parts. But I still couldn't draw a bead on the crow or how I was going to find Slim and Angus, a.k.a. MacTeague, unless I was mistaken.

A flock of birds were flapping around my noggin and wouldn't roost on the same branch.

With any luck, Angie would call before long and ID the bird from Mallard Island as our white crow.

I picked up the car keys, figuring I'd grab a Lil' Anthony's Pizza and some Looney Bread from across the way, bring 'em back to the room, wait for Angie's call.

But I didn't figure on Slim sucking a toothpick on my doorstep.

Chapter 15

Like a crocodile's smile, Slim's wasn't so much a function of good humor as of accommodating all those big teeth—and, of course, of the self-satisfaction that comes with being the baddest beast on the beach. He'd taken the precaution of ditching his hat, which exposed the graying brown hair swirled around a thin patch on top. The skin on his face and neck was red, thick, and creased, elephantine from way too much exposure to the sun. On his ropy upper arms, I could see blurry tattoos peeking out from under his T-shirt.

In my usual cool, danger-be-damned demeanor, I think I said something akin to "Gleck!" James Bond, eat your heart out.

His smile wavered slightly, probably because he wasn't sure what I might do or what *gleck* meant. He probably wrote it off as some New York City phrase like *schmear* or *oy vey*.

"I think," he rasped, "you'n me got somethin' to discuss."

I stepped out of the room and closed the door, composing myself.

"Like about the crow?"

He looked mildly puzzled and hitched his pants up a notch.

"The white raven, remember? You and MacTeague and Bret Fletcher stealing all my best stuff just to get at that lousy crow. It's a crow, by the way, not a raven."

His smile remained fixed, but his eyes tightened when I said MacTeague's name. His toothpick waggled, which prompted me to walk out toward the parking lot, into the waning sunlight. I leaned on the hood of a car and waited for him to catch up. Slim checked the perimeter nervously and smiled harder.

"S'at all?"

"No, that's not all. Then you send Fletcher to kill me, and when he fouls up, you run him down with a truck."

"Pretty story, mister," he snorted, spitting a black pearl of tobacco juice to his left. "Kinda hard t' substantiate, don'tcha think?"

"Mister?" I scowled. "Where do you get off calling me *mister*? Do I look like a *mister* to you?"

He froze, his eyes darting in confusion.

"Forget it. Look, what do you want, Slim?"

His shoulders hunched. I don't think he cottoned to the moniker Slim. He reached a hand up to his mouth, plucked the toothpick from his teeth, and pointed it at me.

"Dang, Scarecrow, what's all this got to do with you anyhow? I mean, there's a world of trouble in this rodeo, if that's what you're lookin' for. Already seen some of it. Think you'd best cut n' run." Slim winked.

Well, at least he didn't call me *mister*.

"No can do. The police want to know what I have to do with Bret Fletcher's murder."

With the tip of his pointy boot, Slim stirred some dirt around a moment and drew a fresh smile from the deck. "Sometimes these things are never solved." He squinted. "Carson, you got your stuff back. You don't give a damn about that ol' crow. The rest—well, it's none of your bidness, is all."

Slim winked again, turned. "Be a shame to see that purdy woman of yours get hurt," he chuckled. "You know, on accident."

"*On* accident?" What was it with Westerners and the word *by*?

I was suddenly very itchy, and it was all I could do not to jump on that son of a bitch and beat him senseless. Of course, I've no doubt I would have tangled with the business end of a boot razor for my trouble.

He ambled over to a green Escort rust bucket with a license plate sporting a big red lobster. He pulled a screwdriver from his pocket, got in, started her up, and chugged off.

I dashed for my glove compartment, scrounged a pen, and jotted the Maine license number on my hand. Halfway to my room I was stopped by a sudden realization. Slim had started his car with a screwdriver—the tool of choice for hot-wiring cars—instead of a key. His plate number would be a dead end, and once again I'd be stuck with what sounded like so many more cowboy fantasies.

I cranked up the Lincoln and roared out after Slim. Happy Jim would be disappointed, but clearly he wasn't as on top of things as he claimed. One thing was for sure: If he and Slim were in cahoots, Slim wouldn't have dropped by to give me a second threat on the same day. And if he couldn't control Slim, could Kim really influence the DA's office?

I guess my idea was to follow Slim, though the Lincoln would be pretty obvious in his rearview mirror. But he didn't know that I drove a Lincoln, did he? Unless, of course, Bret had happened to mention that it was some guy in a Lincoln with New York plates who had stolen the bird. But at that particular moment of pursuit, I was fixated, determined to prove to Public Defender Phil that I wasn't loco. I had zero intention of bringing Slim in myself. No way. I just figured if I saw where he went, or maybe even where he was holed up, I could direct the cops there. Once they had him, I'd be in the clear.

Flying over a rise a couple miles down the road, I

caught sight of the green Escort making a hairpin turn off the main road and up a hill on the right. After maneuvering the Lincoln in a four-point turn, I followed the dust trail up the narrow dirt road.

"Follow, Garth, not catch," I reminded myself aloud, and eased up on the accelerator. The road was cut out of a rocky hillside, and a cliff grew on the left as a chasm deepened on my right. The hill's rocky wall glowed orange with the setting sun and made the dust trail even more blinding. I slowed down, conscious that I might just drive off the embankment if I wasn't careful. Surprised by an abrupt jog to the left at the hill's summit, I jerked the steering wheel and swerved the Lincoln into a shadowy alley through the rock at the hill's crest. I paused to let the dust clear, and when it did I saw the road dip steeply away into a hillside hollow.

I was suddenly aware of how confining the road was. If confronted, I'd have to back all the way to the paved road. Not a good way to make a hasty retreat should I need to hightail it outta there. However, there was some room to one side of the rock cleft for me to stash the Lincoln pointing back toward the road. So I crammed my boat there and started down the road into the mountain hollow.

All I needed to see was the kelly-green Escort parked next to a shanty, a whiff of smoke from the shack's stovepipe, and I'd be out of there and at the police station lickety-split.

The road was a switchback, and it wasn't long before I made out some bright colors down in the hollow. Descending further, I decided staying off the road would be best and walked directly downhill among the trees for better camouflage. I stopped and listened every now and then and heard nothing but a gentle whistle of the breeze through the tree buds.

As I approached the clearing, the colors took the form of large pictures, cartoons. I could see an alligator's head, a woman's body with lighting coming out of her head, a car in flames, a hand holding a sword. There were words, slogan fragments. *Gavoona the . . . Darkest Africa . . . Spiders and . . .* Old tires, trailer wheels, and multicolored plastic flag bunting, the kind you see at used-car lots, littered the ground. What the hell was I looking at?

When I was perhaps fifty feet from the clearing, I recognized it for what it was: a sideshow. But that didn't keep me from rubbing my eyes and giving myself a good pinch. Yup, the sideshow was still there.

It was the kind I used to see as a kid at the county fair with my little brother, Nicholas, the air thick with diesel fumes, the spike of cotton candy, and a child's wonder. A dream's echo, I could almost feel the bustle of the midway and touch the edgy glare of carnies eyeing their prey. Goose bumps chilled me, the lurid, intense curiosity of the freak-show spectacle rippling under my skin. Both alluring and repugnant, it was a false reality, a dimension of lost innocence and prickly memories. A specter. A hallucination. A nightmare.

There were two rows of trailers, four on one side, three on the other, the front of each rigged with a large canvas touting the spectacle within.

Electra, the 100,000 Volt Woman! SEE her IN PERSON. Lightbulbs! Fans! Appliances! JUMP STARTS A CAR! SHOCKING. Accompanying the red and green text were pictures of a buxom woman in a bathing suit and cape (strikingly similar to Wonder Woman) standing before a sky of blue thunderbolts and demonstrating her miraculous talents by putting things in her mouth.

GATOR MAN. Half-Reptile half "HUMAN"? $100,000 if you can prove he's not real! The Bayou's Most Hideous Secret!!! ALIVE.

PYGMY WARRIORS! ARMY ANTS! SHRUNKEN HEADS! GIANT SERPENTS! 100 lb. GUINEA PIGS! Fear for your life—The Amazon's Ungodly Hell! SEE IT NOW.

Goonah the "Ape" A-Go-Go! ROCK AND ROLL SENDS HER BACK IN TIME. Behold the Result of our Sinful Age. Must be 18 to Enter!!! SEE NOW— NEVER FORGET.

FONJON—Human Pincushion. NAILS—KNIVES— SHOOTS HIMSELF IN THE HEAD!!! The Cursed Mongolian. CANNOT DIE.

Science Gone Mad? TWO-HEADED COW—POL-LYWOG BABY—DOG CAT—EAGLE FISH— CLAM RAT. What Hope is there for Us? Dr. Abdul Reveals Shocking Truth. AUTHENTIC.

There is nothing wrong with your television set. . . . We repeat: There is nothing wrong with your television

*set. . . . You are about to experience the awe and mystery
which reaches from the inner mind . . . to the Outer
Limits.*

A clam rat?

The last trailer's canvas was half torn down, the
shabby white carny trailer behind it partially exposed. On one side, the canvas rolled back and
forth in the breeze, and the image of two beady blue
eyes on a bald head—part of an illustration—stared
at me, vanished, stared again, vanished. . . . It was as
if this figure was lurking behind the trailer, peeking,
taunting.

On the other half of the canvas there was a blue
arctic landscape against an orange sky emblazoned
with the words *THE PENGUIN BOY* and *A Living
Legend!*

No blinking lights stung my eyes, no barkers
garbled in my ears, and no throngs blocked my
view. This memory incarnate was barren, stripped
of the animate like an old photograph, people long
dead, places long gone.

Canvases were torn, mildewed, and faded.
Bunting was loosely piled in shopping carts. The
ground was strewn with cans, cups, bottles, and
plastic bags. The trailers were up on blocks, the
wheels piled to one side with dead grass grown between them. Ghost town.

As you might extrapolate from my boyhood fasci-
nation with bug collecting, taxidermy, and horror
movies, my attention at county fairs was drawn
toward the freak shows. Now seen as exploitive, the

traveling "back end" shows are all but gone, the community of the disfigured in retirement. "Back end" referred to where the freak shows were relegated on the midway. For me as a kid, you could keep your fat men, blockheads, lobster guys, and bearded women. What I wanted to see was the Bimini Mermaid, Vampire Frog, Double-Bodied Duck, Horned Skull, Pygmy Rock Man, Macedonian Crocodile Mummy, Saber-Toothed Flounder, or Fossilized Elf. Or the Clam Rat, if only they'd had one back then. (Okay, I'll admit I had a weakness for Gila the Gorilla Girl, but that was as much to ogle the bikini-clad woman as to see her turn into a gorilla.)

I have a fair knowledge of these oddities because I see some of them come up for sale among traditional taxidermy at auctions and estate sales. Carnies and showmen refer to these as *gaffs*. I don't buy gaffs, which I can tell you on authority are all one hundred percent completely and utterly fake. Not that there aren't some talented people out there who made Bimini mermaids out of old fish mounts, roadkill deer, PoxieSculp, and horse tails. There are even some contemporary artists in Minnesota who sell gaffs as art, or "cryptozoological creations." And you'd be surprised how realistic they can be. They are all mixtures of taxidermy craft and/or the sculptor's keen eye for the bizarre. I've heard there's a guy in Fresno who used to make ends meet by sculpting alien fetuses for sideshows.

I can't help but appreciate the imagination and craftsmanship that go into the better gaffs, but I don't own any—mainly because I have no market for them. Show people usually bought them directly from the artists. And while I still appreciate their bizarre charms, gaffs aren't something I necessarily want around the house. Let's face it: Were I to bring home a vampire mummy, no matter how fake, Angie would freak. Most people would.

I did once supply some parts to a guy who made gaffs. I was told carnies called him King of Gaff because his creations were so realistic. I remembered he was in the market for goat hides and skulls, and when I asked what kind of goat (ask the 4-H, there are many), he said it didn't matter because he was making centaurs. That took me back a bit, but it made filling his order a lot easier. He offered to barter one of his "creations" for the goat products, and I think he was offended when I demurred in favor of cash. Never heard from him again. Artists can be so temperamental.

Memories of those wonderfully creepy displays didn't help my unease as I looked down at this derelict freak-o-rama. Sideshows have to go somewhere to die, I guessed.

The clearing had a Porta-Head at one end, and nothing else. The green Escort was nowhere to be seen. A dirt road led out the other side of the clearing—if he went down there, I wasn't going to follow. Too isolated. It didn't help that the light was still fading and I was getting chilly. I turned to go.

"Hello?"

Startled? It was as if Electra the 100,000 Volt Woman had hit me with her jumper cables.

I wheeled around, but there was nobody there. My skin rippled with fresh goose bumps, and I willed my heart and lungs to start functioning again. I was going to start running and I needed their help.

"Please, help me, please!"

It was a girl's voice, very weak, and it was coming from one of the trailers. Chivalry was dead as far as I was concerned—the needle on the strange meter was pinned in the red zone. I'd get the cops and they could save her.

"They'll be back soon. . . . I want to go home." I detected faint sobs.

One part of my mind had me halfway up that hill to the safety of the Lincoln, smoke pouring out of my running shoes, Speedy Gonzales put to shame.

Another part of my mind was becoming fixated on the plight of this girl.

And still another part of my mind said, *IT'S A TRAP, YOU IDIOT. FLEE!* It was like I was watching myself in a drive-in horror show.

You'd think those two parts sandwiching the middle one would have won hands down, and they were very near to quashing my burgeoning guilt for being a heartless bastard. I'll admit there was still another part of me that imagined a zombie girl like from *Night of the Living Dead*, her arms clawing the air, her bloody fangs bared. Sure, she was saying "Help me!" now, but when I was within arm's reach it'd be

"MORE BRAINS. NEED MORE BRAINS!" Perhaps the lingering, grisly image of Bret Fletcher's crushed body and wriggly fingers had left me more squeamish than I might have been otherwise.

I scanned my surroundings. Nothing stirred. I stepped out from behind my tree, took a step toward the clearing, and a piece of the tree exploded.

An arrow hummed, vibrating where it protruded from the tree, which only seconds earlier had been protected by my head. The arrow was a tiny thing, like a large toothpick, fletched with leaves instead of feathers.

A shriek bounced across the hollow. I'm pretty sure it was mine.

My next conscious sensation was pounding. My heart, my feet, my ears.

By the time I had visual to go with my audio, I found that I was doing an admirable Speedy Gonzales imitation on the switchback road. I now know why all that smoke comes out from behind the Road Runner and Speedy. It's not the friction from their feet on the dusty southwestern roads. It's burning calf muscles. Mine felt like Kingsford briquettes ready for the chops.

I heard another arrow whistle by my ear, thwack a tree. I veered off the road and ran directly up hill through the woods. I was beelining for the top of the hill and the Lincoln.

Flight instinct was fully engaged; there was no stopping. For all I knew I was running toward the archer. Believe me, I'm no athlete, but under those kinds of circumstances you'd be surprised what you can do. My legs were about to leave my torso behind.

MANLESS LEGS. Behold World's Fastest Feet that Left Their Master Behind! Free Deodorizing Insole if You Can Prove They're Not Real! ALIVE and KICKING!

I could see the hill's rocky summit, trees silhouetted against the growing twilight. The niche where the Lincoln would be, it was up there, to the left. I saw a glint of the chrome bumper.

Voices, squeaky voices behind me, cursed, as I closed in on the Lincoln.

Unable to resist, I looked back down the hill. I wish I hadn't.

Charging up behind me was a squad of . . . well, pygmies. I don't know, they could have just been black midgets or dwarfs, but they were small dark men carrying bows and arrows, and they were screaming at me.

I vaulted over the passenger-side door. My knee slammed the steering wheel but I cranked the key, pushed the pedal to the floor, and shoved the gearshift down in one smooth motion.

An arrow hit the inside of my windshield, bounced back out of the car.

My tires churned, shuddered, looking for good traction. The Lincoln lurched forward.

Looming just ahead was the rock cleft.

Something moved.

I looked up.

It was the second time in two days that I saw something that made absolutely no sense. There was a silhouette against the sky, atop the rocks, that was too smooth to be part of the stone. It was like some oddball bedevilment from Zeus, a Colossus, Harpy, or Cyclops—or even Symplegades of the Clashing Rocks. It looked vaguely human at first, and then part of it detached and spun end over end down at me. What was left atop the rocks had no arms or legs, was rounded and slightly bulbous. A giant thumb?

I ducked, pedal to the metal.

Something slammed the Lincoln. Hard. From what direction I wasn't sure. All I knew was that the impact tossed me into the air. I landed sideways across the seats and struggled to right myself as the Lincoln swerved for the embankment.

I wrenched the wheel right and plowed the Lincoln into the dead weeds and saplings on the uphill side. As the car fishtailed, I reached my feet back to the pedals, righted myself, and tapped the brakes. The Lincoln came to, gravel churning in my wheel wells.

I shot right out onto the highway without looking—knock wood, nobody was coming.

Back on pavement, my exhaust system started to rattle. So I pulled on the headlights and saw I was doing a hundred miles an hour away from Brattleboro. The dashed roadway stripes looked like a solid line. Next to me, on the driver's seat, were a bunch of twigs and leaves I'd picked up when I scraped the hillside. I glanced in the rearview mirror—no lights following. I took my foot off the accelerator and tapped the brakes. The exhaust system quieted. My knee throbbed where it had hit the steering wheel.

From the red glow of my brake lights, in my rearview mirror, I saw the silhouette of something on the trunk lid, a lump of some kind. I swerved onto the shoulder and stopped. *Please tell me the giant thumb didn't jump onto the back of my car.*

It was a rock. Or maybe a boulder. Anyway, this one was the size of a microwave. The impact had destroyed the trunk lid, but otherwise the Lincoln seemed unfazed. Two points for the old battleship. Fixing that was going to cost me plenty.

Then I noticed the pygmy arrows sticking out of my upholstery.

I put my shaking hands back on the steering wheel and made tracks away from Brattleboro. I'd be damned if I was going back that way. It took me a half hour to loop around and find my way back to town. I didn't even want to take the time to try to remove the boulder.

Clam rats and pygmies—eat my dust.

Chapter 16

Pygmies." Phil eyed the Lincoln hesitantly. "In Vermont."

Clearly, he was mulling over ways to explain it to a jury and make them believe it. I could tell by the way he'd bitten a pencil in half that the boulder on my trunk didn't bolster my case, though the small crowd gathered in the spring twilight on the courthouse steps seemed impressed by the spectacle. The Lincoln's backseat was stuck like a pincushion with little arrows.

"Well, they were little, and dark, with bows and arrows. What would you call them?"

"And the pygmies . . . did they throw this rock at you?"

"C'mon, how could pygmies lift a big rock like that?" I felt myself redden as the crowd's attention turned from the Boulder Mobile to me. "This came from atop the cleft. The pygmies were charging up the hill behind me."

After I told my absurd story, Phil led me inside, where I was compelled to repeat this yarn to Danny DA. When I got to the end, I summarized:

"So there's these three: one who I think is a funeral director named MacTeague from Oregon, Bret, and then this cowboy and—" I quickly decided to leave Jimmy out of the picture—he didn't fit. "Bret worked carnivals, and then there's this sideshow in the woods where they shot little arrows at me. . . . Look, I may be going out on a limb here, but I think these carnies grabbed a dead gorilla from an Oregon zoo, maybe to make a gaff, I dunno."

Danny squinted at the floor, a paper cup dangling from one hand and his tie undone.

"Pygmies. In Vermont."

Phil was standing at the window, staring at the meager city lights of Brattleboro.

Then Danny asked, "What's a gaff?"

"Yeah, you know, a carnival attraction, like a saber-toothed bass, alien fetus, mummified mermaid . . . or a clam rat. They don't make them anymore because the traveling freak shows are extinct. Not PC."

"Clam rat?" Danny shook his head in bewilderment. "So you're saying that Fletcher and some carnies and a tribe of pygmy warriors and a giant thumb have stolen a dead gorilla for a sideshow attraction. For a gaff. Even though freak shows no longer exist."

"Maybe they were going to make a yeti or something." I shrugged. "They usually make them out of bears, but . . . anyway, that's the way I figure it."

Phil didn't flinch. "Yeti?"

"*Abominable Snowman.*"

"Ah." Danny pursed his lips. "So now we have Big Foot. Does Bat Boy enter into this anywhere?"

I reiterated: "It's about the white crow."

Phil sighed before I did.

I continued: "What this has to do with the crow is anybody's guess, but they wanted it enough to come all the way to Manhattan to steal it and dump a lot of very valuable taxidermy in the river."

Danny stood next to the blue cigarette-burned table, shaking his head at the floor. "I don't see any connection. But at the same time, I can't see why you would make up such a load of crap. Why would you drop a rock on your trunk and shoot arrows into your upholstery? The sheriff did go out there. They found that abandoned sideshow in the woods. Too dark to see much else, nobody around. *No pygmies.*"

"Yeah, but there was a banner for a sideshow featuring pygmy warriors," I retorted.

He looked up at Phil, took his turn at a sigh, and left the room. Detectives and DAs always do that, just walk out. Which almost always means they're going to talk to the people behind the big mirror to see what they think.

I cleared my throat. "So, Phil, am I getting anywhere near being able to go home?"

"Are you sure you're telling us everything?" He didn't turn. "You didn't forget anything?"

"All the news that's fit to print."

"You didn't see who rolled the rock down on you?"

"Is it a rock or a boulder?"

Phil almost turned to look at me. "What?"

"I mean, is the rock on my trunk big enough to be considered a boulder?"

Phil scratched his head but didn't say anything. You didn't really expect me to tell them a giant thumb threw that boulder, did you?

Danny came back in.

"We'll be willing to bargain on the manslaughter charge if Mr. Carson agrees to cooperate with an ongoing investigation."

Phil came to life. "Manslaughter? You'll be lucky if you get reckless endangerment, Danny. Frankly, I think my client has a very good—"

The door opened again, and Special Agent Renard of the NYSDEC strolled into the room, a little more awake than the last time I saw him. But just a little.

"We meet again, Mr. Carson." He dipped his head at the others before coming back to me. "Your white crow seems to be causing a bit of a ruckus."

"What's this?" I pointed at Renard.

"We're interested in your gorilla story." Renard suppressed a yawn. "And want your help in getting to the bottom of all this. About who dumped that boulder on your car."

I snorted at him. "Are you sure it's not a rock?"

"Hmm?"

"I mean, Phil thinks it's a rock, and you say it's a boulder. Anybody know when a rock becomes a boulder? How big does it have to be?"

I can get pretty trivial when I'm reaching the end of my rope.

Danny groaned. "Boulder, rock, what's the difference?"

"Exactly!" I added.

"A boulder"—Renard raised an eyebrow at me—"is too big to lift without aid of a machine. Look here, Mr. Carson, we're trying to help you, but you'll have to help us."

"I think I've done quite a lot already. Don't you think it's about time you people did something about all this? I'm a taxpayer, for God's sake. And a victim."

Renard exchanged glances with Danny, who opened a folder and dropped a photo in front of me.

"Your cowboy look like this?"

It was a black-and-white 8x10 of a man with a black eye, new stitches on his forehead, holding a mug-shot placard that said TAYLOR COUNTY CORRECTIONS, NC. The date was ten years earlier, and Slim looked like he'd been in one heck of a bar fight.

"That's him! He's older and wears a cowboy hat. How'd you find this?"

"We do this kind of thing for a living, Carson. What taxpayers pay us for. That's Tex Filbert, an independent showman who did travel with a carnival run by Faldo Amusements. He has a record, bar fights, check kiting, spent some time in county here and there, but nothing serious."

"Was he a showman?"

"He was a carny, if that's what you mean."

"What I meant was, did he operate a concession on the sideshow that featured gaffs?"

Danny took the picture back. "Yes."

I folded my arms, grinning. "See there, I was right."

"He's *not* a cowboy."

"Well, he's got the hat, and he's bowlegged."

Danny ignored me. "So, Renard, you want to take it from here?"

"It's that snipe of yours." Renard flashed a smile, but it wasn't friendly. "It's actually a *Limnodromus scolopaceus.*"

"You came up here to tell me that my snipe is—lemme guess—a woodcock? A Virginia rail?"

"Scolopaceus is a long-billed dowitcher."

My grin wearied. "It's a snipe, Renard. LBDs don't have the ruddy breast feathers."

He cleared his throat and folded his arms. "The males do when they're in breeding colors, Carson. And, as you're aware, long-billed dowitchers are a protected species."

"Fine, let's do a DNA test. What's this got to do with—"

"We're willing to overlook this irregularity, and Brattleboro County is willing to drop any charges—"

"Rescind the charge," Danny corrected.

"—your reckless endangerment—"

"Manslaughter," Danny corrected again.

"—if you assist the New York DEC with an investigation into—"

"Egad, fellahs, you don't have to beat me over the head with my snipe, or dowitcher, or whatever. If you look right outside you'll see a *boulder* on my trunk. Pygmy arrows in my backseat. Know what that means? It means that between you and them I can't stay out of this mess. So what's it going to be? Going to wire me up, night scopes in a van parked across the street, or what?"

Agent Renard was stroking his chin. "There's something amiss here, and the NYSDEC and the State of Vermont have agreed to cooperate in getting to the bottom of it. We have some jurisdictional complications, some technical problems. Because your pelts were stolen in New York and found in Massachusetts, we can't convince a Vermont judge that there's compelling evidence for the NYSDEC to conduct an investigation in this jurisdiction."

"Then what are you doing here, Renard? What is this?"

"And the Vermont State Fish and Game have neither the facilities, nor the manpower, nor the impetus from the FBI to conduct an investigation into what amounts to the interstate theft and transport of a dead crow. However, under a codicil in Vermont State law, another state's police force can conduct a limited investigation if approved by the district attorney's office—"

I stood as Detective Walker ambled into the room, looking decidedly unrural in his new plaid flannel jacket and mad-bomber cap. An airline ticket folder protruded from his jacket pocket. He smirked at me, and it felt like a poke to the sternum. His smirks are like dares, like drawing a line for me to cross. Walker would like nothing better than for me to take a swing at him. Or him at me.

"Detective Walker is going to work with you undercover. He's going to pose as your partner. You'll wait in your motel for MacTeague and his friends to contact you again. We figure if they tried to kill you once, they'll probably try again."

"Walker? I've got a tribe of angry pygmies after me, and I get Walker?" Jungle Jim he's not.

The subject of my disdain sneered. "You got a problem with that, Mr. Dead Things?"

Chapter 17

Well, the good news is that I finally got my Looney Bread and pizza. The bad news was that I had Walker for a roomie.

I managed to sleep fitfully for two hours, but by ten o'clock that evening, I was pacing the floor in what I'd packed for pajamas: red sweats and a white T-shirt. Where was Angie? Why hadn't she called? Walker's snoring was a growing annoyance. I was worried sick.

I picked up the phone and called my birdman, Dudley, back in Manhattan. He does bird taxidermy for me on occasion.

"Gawth, you ragpicker!"

"Dudley, I'm in a pickle. But I don't have time to explain. I'm in Vermont."

"Let me guess." He cleared his voice. "The

Deathmobile finally passed this mortal vale of tears."

"Nothing like that. . . . It's complicated and I can't stay on the phone long."

"Anything I can do?"

"You remember that guy Waldo?"

"Waldo . . ."

"The King of Gaff."

"Indeed! I do recall that I referred him to you."

"I need his number."

"At this hour? I can only imagine what kind of jam you might have found yourself in where—"

"The number? Do you have his number?"

"Hold the line." I heard him groan as he got up from his chair. He had the accent and build of Boss Hogg.

He was back within thirty seconds with the number.

"Gawth, do remember that Waldo is rather an odd fish, so handle him with kid gloves if you want any cooperation. Now, are you sure there's nothing else I can do? This effort was a trifle. The timbre of your voice suggests grave circumstance."

"Thanks, pal, I appreciate it, and if there's anything else—"

"You call Dudley, y'hear?" He hung up.

I dialed somewhere in Florida. A long series of scratchy rings followed. They sounded like they might be coming from a phone at the bottom of a dry well in Timbuktu. The ringing stopped, and I thought I was going to get a recording telling me the phone was out of service. Or that the well was full of water.

I didn't hear anything.

"Hello?" I looked at the receiver.

"Who is this?" shot back. The southern accent wasn't buttery like Dudley's, but deep and gravelly. And slurpy, like some kind of seething Klingon.

"Waldo? Garth Carson."

"Who?"

"Carson, Garth Carson, from New York. I sold you some taxidermy a while back."

There was a pause. "And?"

He was doing a very good job of making me feel uncomfortable. I didn't know whether he remembered me or not.

"Dudley gave me your number."

"If, as you say, you sold Waldo taxidermy, how come you don't have Waldo's number?"

"I lost it."

I heard a click on the other end. He'd hung up.

I tried redialing, but the line was busy. My mind's eye was picturing this Klingon as a mad scientist surrounded by bubbling vials, half-made mummies, little yellow fuzzy two-headed duckies in a freeze-dry chamber, and a Bimini mermaid on the operating table. Or maybe a bivalve and a rodent, strapped on gurneys, with little metal helmets and interconnecting wires, the intertranferencebifulminator shooting off sparks as it created yet another clam rat. He was a nut. And he probably wouldn't have been any help anyway. I was grabbing at straws, waiting for Angie to call.

I turned on the TV and started pacing again, chewing and popping bubblegum like a metronome. The cops, the DEC—I had them believing my story now, but I almost wished I didn't. Agent Renard had hatched a pretty loose plan. (Was this the kind of brain trust I could expect to join if I took a job at NYSDEC? Would every day on the job be like this one?)

I couldn't figure Renard out. He was so dry and nonchalant, while trying to bust my chops over a snipe. I guessed he wasn't too bright. Either that or he was trying to get me killed. Sure, there were two cops sleeping in an unmarked car across the road. Not much protection from a grease gun drive-by or a wad of dynamite. Of course, more than likely, Tex Filbert and MacTeague had left the state, figuring the heat would be on. How many days would I have to be imprisoned in this room with Walker before Renard figured this was a cockamamie plan?

Or was this the work of Jimmy Kim? I was off the hook, more or less, but I was also tucked safely out of the way, my nose against the back wall of a blind alley.

Anyway, at that moment I was more worried about Angie than my predicament, so I paced in front of the phone, watching the Late Nite Show with Buddy Fetterman and loathing bunky Walker, who, despite the flannel getup, still reeked of cop. I guessed he needed the undercover work to make detective sergeant.

And out came Aunt Jilly onto the stage of the Network Theater. Seems the writers had a gag whereby every time one of Buddy's jokes bombed, Aunt Jilly was wheeled across the stage holding a Buttergut turkey. It was funnier than it sounds.

The phone rang and I pounced on it.

"Angie?"

"Waldo is calling."

"Waldo? Is that you?"

"Waldo checked you out with Dudley. He asked Waldo to talk to you. What do you want?"

"Let me start by saying, Waldo, that I've admired your work for many years. Really top notch. Your artistry is first rate."

Silence.

"Yes, well . . . look, I'm in Vermont. And I've got a situation here involving gaffs. I think."

Silence.

I hadn't heard a click, so I kept talking but tried to elicit a response. "Are you familiar with any of the showmen who traveled with the Faldo carnival?"

He paused so long I thought he had hung up. "What kind of showmen would they be if Waldo didn't know of them?"

"Exactly, right, right . . . so, there's a guy named Tex Filbert. Have you heard of him?"

"Waldo knows."

"Can you, I mean, tell me anything about him, what he may have bought recently?"

He let another long pause sink in. "Why?"

I wondered if Waldo might be mixed up in this somehow. But if he were, what would he be doing down in Florida when the rest of the gang was here?

"I think he may have been planning to steal a gorilla carcass and make a Sasquatch gaff."

"*Swamp Demon.*"

"Eh?"

"Swamp Demon. Waldo creates a Swamp Demon, not a Sasquatch."

"Well, I wasn't suggesting he bought this from you. He was trying to make it himself."

He loosed a protracted growl. "And if someone had a gorilla carcass, why would he bother to make a gaff? It's worth much more just for the hands and organs than a gaff could make in two years."

"I know, that's what's so strange about it. Tex Filbert is working with a man named MacTeague."

"MacTeague? Ha!" He came back fast that time, and with force. I'd obviously hit a nerve.

"You know MacTeague?"

"Waldo would not sully his reputation!" he exploded. "MacTeague is a hack! His Bimini mermaids are junk! You hear? Junk! Trash! Garbage!"

Man, these Klingons are so tightly wound.

"So MacTeague made gaffs?"

"Those are not gaffs!" His flying spittle reached me all the way from Florida. "MacTeague couldn't make a true gaff if his life depended on it. He shames himself and the showmen who buy his road-kill!"

"Who could possibly come close to Waldo's perfection?" I was pushing it, but I'd got pretty much what I was looking for already.

"You are a man of discernment!" he hissed, like a campfire hit with a bucket of water.

Discernment? Is that a word? Whatever—he was finally warming to me, at least a little, I hoped.

"What can I say? I appreciate fine art, fine craftsmanship. Waldo is a master, everybody knows that. Did Tex or MacTeague come to Waldo for any parts, any help with making a Sasquatch?"

"Waldo has not communicated with either in years," he spat. "But know this: If MacTeague was involved, this atrocity he would call *gaff* would look like the work of a child. There would be no suspension of disbelief."

"Look pretty fakey?"

"Very, very *fakey.*"

A light on my phone lit up. Another call. Angie?

"Waldo has been very helpful, and Garth is extremely thankful for Waldo taking time out of his busy day to consult with him."

He hung up without a word.

I pushed the blinking button.

"Angie?"

"Hi, sugar lips!"

"I was worried out of my mind." Angie sounded great, and I groaned with relief. "Where are you?"

"Sea Bass Motel, in beautiful downtown Mallard Island. Guess what?"

"What?"

"We know who Guy Partridge is."

"Who?"

"You know, Guy Partridge, the one who bought the crow?"

That was in the morning, and this was night, but it seemed like a million years ago. "Yes, I remember—so who is he?"

"Think. He's been on television."

"We've got a vintage thirteen-inch TV that gets all of three stations."

"Partridge was the guy who had those specials on TV where he went looking for the Loch Ness Monster, or that dinosaur in the Congo. A real eccentric, rich, an adventurer into the unknown."

"Yeah, right, okay. So is our crow his crow?"

"Get this. He collected all sorts of spooky stuff in his mansion here, including taxidermy. He was robbed of a bunch of skins just the way we were. Except he was killed."

"Killed?"

"Stabbed. And one of the things they took was a white crow in a bell jar. Got the scoop down at the station hall. The local police are real helpful. They seem kind of bored."

And probably deferential to cute blondes, I mused. My cute blonde. "But we don't know for sure it's the same crow?"

"Well, I mean it was in a bell jar and all. . . . Oh,

and listen to this. It says here that when Partridge died, they found out he didn't have five million dollars to pay for a Big Foot. In fact, he was practically broke from throwing money at his expeditions and publicity. He still lived in a mansion near here but all alone because he couldn't pay his household staff. That's sad."

"Back up. What about Big Foot?"

"Let's see. I got some clippings from the library. . . ." I could hear her shuffling papers, then she cleared her throat. *"Guy Partridge, Mallard Island's wealthiest . . .* blah blah blah . . . *was apparently stabbed to death with a carving knife during a daylight robbery. He was known for his exploration into the unknown, the occult, UFOs . . .* blah blah blah . . . *He used a submersible to fathom Loch Ness's mysterious . . .* blah blah blah . . . *his recent special taped in the Pacific Northwest in which he challenged America to prove the existence of Big Foot . . .* blah blah . . . *He'd just flown back from research in Korea, where he claimed to have physical proof of a kving-kie, a mythical wild cow with magic horns—"*

"Whoa—again, what about Big Foot?"

"What do you mean?"

"What does it say about Big Foot, exactly?"

"Oh, well, like I said . . . *Typical of Mr. Partridge's style was his recent special taped in the Pacific Northwest in which he challenged America to prove the existence of Big Foot. This quest gained him widespread media attention and legal troubles when he offered a 'dead or alive' reward for the capture of an actual Big Foot. State game officials arrested him for conspiring to kill pro-*

tected species. Under Washington game laws, it is illegal to shoot or conspire to kill any bird, mammal, or reptile not listed as a game species. After paying a fine, Mr. Partridge altered his offer to read 'alive or any mortal remains.' Mr. Partridge's five-million-dollar reward went uncollected, although a number of hunting accidents were blamed on those trying to cash in on his offer. His seaside Maine estate was besieged for a time by hoaxsters with photographs and plaster footprint casts, but none with physical proof. That's all there is about Big Foot, sweetie."

"Wait a second." I rummaged through my wallet and came up with piece of paper. "Remember that ad Durban gave me? *WANT MY WHITE CROW BACK. No questions asked, finder's fee. P.O. Box 34, Wells ME 04090.* But Partridge lived on Mallard Island."

"Oh my gosh, Garth. That's right. The ad! Mallard Island is just down the road from Wells. You have some idea about what's going on, don't you?"

"To make a long story short, I think carnies tried to pass off a sideshow Big Foot on Partridge for the five million and then for whatever reason ended up killing him for the crow. So now we know where they got the crow, more or less how, but not why. Dammit." My stomach went sour. Angie was too close to the source of this imbroglio.

"Partridge is trying to get it back?" Angie snorted. "But he's dead. I don't get it, Garth."

"I don't get it either." I tried to avoid any suspicious pauses. "Somebody else must be trying to get it back. Look, you didn't go up to his house, did you?"

"I went up to the gatehouse and partway up the drive before I noticed a dented green car, probably a caretaker or something. It kind of blended with the bushes. I decided to walk back to my car rather than get kicked out. Maybe I'll try again in the morning. Too dark now."

My jaw tightened. "A green car? Like an Escort?" MacTeague had a flight leaving from Maine the next day and Tex was cruising around in a green heap with Maine license plates. Tex could have gotten there in the hours since he dropped a boulder on the Lincoln. Might he and MacTeague have a rendezvous on Mallard Island to sell the crow back? Might they have recognized Angie at the gatehouse? If they knew she was around asking questions, what would they do? And who was the joker in the deck with the Wells P.O. box?

All sorts of leads were pointing—shoving—me toward Maine. I've since learned that such compulsions are like being worked over by a pushy car salesman. He makes you want to buy the clunker with the CHERRY! sign on the windshield, when all the while there's a strangled voice deep inside telling you to kick him in the shin and make for the hills. I should have told her to get the hell out of there.

"An Escort? Why?"

"Look, Angie, a lot happened here today, too much to go into. But that may be Slim's car. If he saw you or knows you're there—look, it could be they're back there at Mallard Island right now with the crow, selling it to the guy in the ad."

"Here?"

"And I'm on my way," I gulped, "leaving now. Listen, Angie: Stay in your room, lock the door, and don't open it for anybody. They may know you're around. I'll be there in a couple hours."

"Should I do anything? Call anybody?"

"Just sit tight."

I hung up and looked over at Walker lying on the other bed. He had one bloodshot eye and his smirk trained on me.

"Just where do you think you're going, Carson?"

"I gotta go meet Angie." I sat up. "I think she may be in over her head."

"Where's she at, Carson?"

"Maine, somewhere."

Walker got up casually and stretched. "Maine, huhn?" I heard a click and felt something hard and cold hit my wrist, namely a handcuff. "That's a long ways from here. What would happen if our friend the cowboy showed up and we weren't here?"

"Take this thing off, Walker!"

He snapped the other end to the bed before I could jerk it away. "You're the bait, and you're staying right here."

"Look, Walker, wanna get your sergeant's stripes? Want to solve this case single-handedly? Come with me to Maine. Angie called, and she's found something that leads me to believe what these characters are after is in Maine. See this note, this ad? Somebody there is looking for the crow."

"We're after a monkey, Carson."

"But the crow . . ."

Walker sauntered off to the bathroom with a *Sports Illustrious*, turned on the fan, and closed the door. I was furious but knew that splitting a gut would only give him perverse satisfaction. So while Walker caught up on a little light reading, I started fumbling around in my pockets, then my bag, then the desk drawer looking for something—anything—that might work as a lock pick.

The only thing handy was a red ballpoint pen, which I promptly jammed into the lock and deftly got it stuck in there. So I grabbed the pen with my teeth and yanked it free, only to find the front part was still in the lock. I also discovered a sour taste in my mouth: ink. A handy pillow became smeared in red ink as I used it like a salt lick to hastily wipe my tongue.

My frantic tongue-scraping came to an abrupt, chilling halt: The front doorknob was turning, the door pushing slowly open.

I was trying to formulate some intelligible yell to my protector on the throne when Otto popped his grinning, satyrlike face around the door frame. He was dressed in what I guess he considered vacation-wear: a garish, wide-striped sport coat, white slacks, two-tone shoes, and a white dress shirt with stiff collar points that reached halfway to his navel.

Must be what Russians wear when making the swinging beach scene on the Baltic.

He threw the door open and splayed his arms apart, a robust greeting welling up from inside. A finger to my lips managed to shut him up. Or maybe it was the handcuffs. He dropped his bag and tiptoed up next to me, his stinky tobacco breath never so welcome.

"What are you doing here?" I rasped.

"Garv say to Otto: Please, come to me! Vac-ate-ton! I see you soon."

I rolled my eyes. "I didn't mean for you to come on vacation. . . . Okay, look, KGB on toilet," I whispered, nodding toward the bathroom. "Angie, she's in trouble. Angie not looking, Otto. We must go help Angie."

Otto studied me a moment. "Garv, I dunno." He studied me for another moment. "Lookink like circus."

"What?"

He pointed at my face. "Circus man, lips to red, poke a darts, pants much big . . . amusink very much."

I paused. *Circus man, red lips, polka dots, big pants . . .*

I glanced at my visage in the mirror over the dresser. Red ink was smeared all around my lips, and there was a smudge of it on the end of my nose. My frantic tussle with the pillow had broken the shackles of my styling gel—my hair was standing straight up. And I was wearing baggy red sweats.

Sure enough, I looked like a clown. And felt like a bozo.

"There was a pen, with red ink—oh, never mind. Otto, get me out of this!"

I'll never say another deprecating thing about the little imp. Well, I will, but I'll feel an eentsy weentsy bit guilty every time.

Otto went into action. Cutting off the curtain pull strings, he made several big loops out of them. Tying one end carefully to the bathroom doorknob, he tied the other end to the closet doorknob opposite. He put a coat hanger between the multiple strands and turned the hanger until the cords doubled up on themselves and twanged to the touch. Then he used a handkerchief to tie the hanger to the back of a chair so the cord wouldn't unwind.

Next Otto tiptoed back over to examine my handcuffs. Stroking his pointy beard, he considered the problem from all angles: my wrist, the chain, the locks, the bedstead.

"Hurry!"

"Eetz interesting, eh?" He tapped the cuff on my wrist. "Much very Moscova Police. Same. Gear, shackle, spring. Key, eet push on spring, gear turn, shackle—"

"Hurry!"

"Yes, of course." Otto took out his penknife, opened a blade, but decided it was too thick. He thought a moment, then sliced the collar off his shirt. "*Ahoyatilne!*"

The toilet flushed.

Otto pulled the white plastic insert out of his shirt collar and fed it gently into the cuff where the male part joined the female part. His tongue peeked out between stained teeth.

Water began to run in the bathroom sink.

Then the water in the bathroom shut off, the vent fan stopped, and a hand landed heavily on the bathroom doorknob. "What the—"

"Eh?" The cuff slipped open. "Eetz looking!"

"Carson!" Walker yelled, the bathroom door convulsing. "Carson!"

I slapped Otto on the back. "Ve go!"

When my bare feet hit the gravel, I turned back to the room for shoes but saw the bathroom door about to burst open. I stepped into the shoes nearest the door—Walker's. They were about a size fourteen, and I had to clench my toes to keep them from falling off my feet.

Otto stared, giggling. "Garv . . . Bozo shoes amusink."

"Hurry, you idiot!"

We gathered up the plastic bags full of my valuable skins and shut the door on the growing racket in my room. Otto had a van out front.

"We'll take the Lincoln," I said, opening the back door and shoving my bags in. "It's faster than the van." Otto shoved his bags in the opposite side and went toward the van.

"Otto! This car!"

"Yes, of course." From the van, he heaved a large cooler toward the Lincoln.

"Otto, what the hell is that? Come on, hurry!" I could hear banging in the room. Those bathroom doors aren't exactly solid oak.

He approached the trunk and I quickly popped open the dented lid.

"I dunno." Otto dropped it in the trunk, smiling. "You tell to Otto bring chest freezer."

I flipped the top of the cooler, and my jaw dropped.

Dry-ice vapor cleared, and by the motel porch light I saw a fat beak.

"Eetz good, eh?" Otto folded his arms. "Sneezy *pizdyets.*"

Chapter 18

The cops in the un-marked car across from the motel *were* sleeping. Can you believe it? Making small-town cops everywhere look bad. Of course, even if they had been awake, I think my ad hoc Clarabell disguise would have fooled them.

Blasting east on Route 9, we made the New Hampshire border in six minutes ten seconds. But who's counting?

Beside me, I had an erratic Russian gnome. In the backseat, $50,000 worth of protected species' pelts. The day wasn't over yet, and I'd been shot at, had a boulder dropped on my car, been used by the police as bait, handcuffed to a bed, and effected an escape. My girlfriend was likely in mortal danger. Carnies had stolen my white crow, and there was probably a missing gorilla corpse out there somewhere. A mysterious guy named Jim Kim claimed he was trying to help me but wasn't. The police and the NYS-DEC claimed to be trying to help me but weren't. My destiny was perched on the sharp edge of a job offer I was deathly afraid of accepting and deathly afraid of not accepting.

And as if that weren't enough, I had a frozen penguin in the trunk. His name was Reggie. RIP.

Rural New Hampshire ghosted by in the periphery of my headlights, my eyes trained on the white line that would lead me to Angie.

There was no sense asking Otto how he could possibly have misunderstood my instructions, if for no other reason than I was so happy he had.

"Otto, where did you learn to open handcuffs?"

Otto sighed heavily and flashed steel dental work. "Garv, many things Russia men must know. To live life, men must make smart."

"Thank you, Otto."

"Yes, of course. But tell to me, Garv. Where Yangie? Why we go?"

"She went to Maine, to a place called Mallard Island. The men who stole from us, who attacked Angie and me? We followed them to Brattleboro. They tried to kill me today."

"*Yob tvoyu mat!*"

"Now I think they've gone to Maine. To Mallard Island."

"*Poshol v pizdu!* Garv, men, ve maybe must killed. Eh?"

"I'm hoping nothing bad has happened, Otto."

"But if men—"

"Don't say it."

"Hmm."

I looked over at him and saw a metallic glint, which I thought was from his steel-capped teeth. But in his hand was a large, nickel-plated revolver. "Garv, men, ve maybe must killed."

I practically ran off the road.

"*Poshol ty na khuy!*" Now he had me doing it. "What the hell is that?"

"Eetz important. Otto travel, he takes beeg gun. Mother tell to me: *Otto, you to take beeg gun, to you always make safe.*"

"*Eetz* dangerous, and probably very illegal."

He gave me a withering look. "Vhat illegal when bad men to Yangie!"

"I told you, don't go there. . . ."

He made the gun disappear. "Make to Yangie destination very fast."

I seem to remember promising myself just the night before that I was going to get myself a big Dirty Harry gun. Yet the sight of that revolver brought me anything but peace of mind. If anything had happened to Angie, I *would* kill them, given the chance. And Otto's mother's gun suddenly made that possible. I'd fired a gun once or twice, knew how to work one, but didn't own one and didn't much care for them. Chalk that up to being a New Yorker. The less you see of guns in Manhattan, the better.

My vision swam. I felt sick. The pedal went closer to the floor.

I felt better once I saw a sign for Concord. I knew this route. I'd driven it a number of times on my taxidermy safaris. At Concord, I could pick up I-93, to I-393, cross the Merrimack, and beeline on Route 4 to Portsmouth and I-95. I looked down at the speedometer and edged the needle up past eighty-five. I figured I might make it in three hours.

I didn't feel like talking, not even to ask Otto to quit smoking, which he did continuously across New Hampshire. I fumbled around through my 8-tracks. There's a guy at the 26th Street flea markets who still sells the cartridges. Of course, I don't exactly have my choice of any music post-1982, but there was no shortage of good music up to that point in man's evolution—Supertramp and Foreigner notwithstanding. Hank Williams started twanging and moaning through my dash speaker—perfect.

My thoughts were focused on Angie, and it was all I could do to keep from slipping into a stupor of dread. Was I letting my imagination go a little wild, picturing Tex and MacTeague closing in on Angie after seeing her poking around town? Could I even be sure they were in Mallard Island to take delivery of the crow? The thought of Angie being victimized kept surging to the fore. I'd already had my fill of that, and in person. I was determined not to let it happen again.

I could picture Tex winking. *Be a shame to see that purdy woman of yours get hurt.*

Can't think about that. Better think about something else.

Gee, what about that job offer? There was a subject I really didn't want to think about, yet it was consuming enough to force the other from my mind, at least for a little while.

So why was I *deathly afraid* of this thing? Why not take the job, and if I didn't like it, go back to brokering taxidermy?

Well, for one thing, after traveling around ratting out antiques dealers up and down the East Coast, my name would be mud. It's not like I saw that many protected and endangered species around. But there were some. I saw songbirds, for example, but not whole slews of them. Most were probably killed by cars, ran into plate glass, or died from parasites. I doubt that people are shooting them for trophies in numbers even mildly comparable to the damage that domestic and feral cats do. Songbirds are exquisite creatures, and I can't fault someone who—like me—sees a dead blue jay as art too beautiful to discard. I see ducks, which can be mounted for the hunter who shoots them but cannot be resold, and the heads from old rugs, like lion and cheetah and leopard and polar bear. They're pre-CITES, obtained legally, but without permits it is illegal to sell them.

This is at Mom n' Pop stores, largely. Sure, they're technically breaking the law, and maybe some of them even know it, but from my perspective, Mom n' Pop antiques dealers are not the enemy. It's people like Smiler, the chop-shop gangs, that need to be taken down. And that's the job of someone like Pete Durban, who thrives on danger.

So that's that: I'm turning down the job.

Then again, what about Angie? Didn't she deserve someone better than a dealer, a taxidermy bum, for a consort? Someone who could provide better insurance, some financial security for retirement, maybe even vacations, a trip to Europe? One of these days, she might just meet a guy who could rescue her from contract jewelry work, a man who would afford her the ability to spend time making her own art jewelry. I'd always harbored some guilt about holding Angie back from making it in the art world. There had been times when we first joined forces when things were slow for me, and she footed the bills. It had never been the other way around. With a steady job, and raises, and if I made some money on the side brokering taxidermy, I could fulfill my obligations as partner. I might not amount to much, but at least she could reach her potential.

That settles it. I'm taking the job.

A gas station loomed, and signs announced the I-89 interchange just ahead. I roared into the station, showed the attendant where the gas cap was, and asked him to fill it with premium. Otto went into the QwixMart. I went to the phone booth, whipped out my calling card, and tried Angie. I wanted to make sure she was still snug in her motel. And I was going to tell her about the job and that I was going to take it.

No answer.

No answer again.

No answer again.

"Otto! Let's go!"

He came trotting out of the market with two coffees and a small shopping bag of jerky. "Yes, of course, Garv. How Yangie?"

"She didn't answer."

His face darkened. But he didn't say anything. For a change.

Chapter 19

It was after midnight and raining by the time we exited I-95 and passed through the tollbooth.

The elderly toll collector looked at me over his reading glasses, pausing before giving me the change.

"The Big Top in town, is it?"

I glanced at myself in the rearview mirror. Totally forgot about the ink and my harlequin's disguise.

"Sure, Pops." I held my hand out for the change. "I've got the elephants in my trunk."

"Aw haw haw." He handed me the change, chuckling. "Elephants, trunks . . . you fellahs know all the rib ticklers."

I sped away and soon found myself on Route 1. The sloshing pond of rainwater collecting in my dented trunk distracted me; I missed the modest *Mallard Is.* sign and had to make a U-turn at a donut shop. Peering through the slap and smear of the windshield wipers, I wended the Lincoln over a rickety causeway and into a narrow cottage-lined lane where a painted cast-iron sign read *Mallard Island Est. 1701.* At a T-intersection, I found my headlights shining on the ocean, the white foam of breakers visible through the downpour.

"Ah, beach." Otto awoke. "Very nice."

Cottages overlooked either side, but larger ones. No hotels, no shops, no nothing. I made a left. About a mile up I saw a sign with flood lamps splashed over it. I pulled up to the office of the Sea Bass Motel.

"Excuse me, is there an Angie staying here?" I looked hopefully at the porker behind the counter, whose day job was probably at the nearby donut shop.

Chubsy stared at the clown before him, wide-eyed. I hadn't had any luck getting that ink off my face or matting down my hair.

"Hello?" I snapped my fingers, and he emerged from his reverie, probably a fantasy about caramel apples and circus peanuts.

"Wan' that I should buzz her room?" He picked up the phone like it was something to eat.

"I'll just stop in."

"I gotta buzz her first, mister. Oh, wait, she went out anyhow."

"Out? Out?"

"Yeah. I seen her. With her dad."

"Dad?"

"Yeah. Came by the office, said he was here on a surprise like."

"Did he have black hair and a mustache?"

"Nah, red hair this fellah has."

"Where's the police station?"

"Police? Down the end the road, thataway. Why?"

"Where's Partridge's house?"

"What?"

"The place where that guy Partridge lived."

"Why you wanna—"

"It's an emergency, I—"

"I better call the police."

"You call the police." I grabbed Lard Butt by the collar and put my angry red eye up against his scared white peeper. "But first you tell me where Partridge's place is."

"J-just keep up this road. The manor is at the end. C-can't miss it."

Dashing out the door, I screeched the Lincoln out of the Sea Bass parking lot, setting a new land speed record for the State of Maine, my exhaust pipe rattling so loud I thought this time it would fall off for sure. The blur of wet cottages was soon replaced with the smear of scrub and dunes.

"Fast, yes?" Otto sucked casually on a cigarette. "Yangie?"

"Up ahead, I think."

"KGB has veapons, eh?"

"You have that gun your mother gave you?"

I glanced over and saw he already had it out. It looked like a friggin' cannon in his little hands. He flipped the cylinder open, held it up to the light. I looked away and heard it clack back into place.

"Garv, men you have killed?"

The tone of his voice was devoid of the usual impish lilt. To look over at him at the speed I was going could have been fatal.

"None. But it's early yet."

"Mebbe, please to let Otto killed men who take Yangie."

"There's not going to be any killing," I said, with little conviction. It occurred to me briefly that if I did kill them, they might just chalk it up to a John Wayne Gacy copycat.

"Garv, very important: must to always shoot gun fast. Mother tell to me: *Shoot, shoot, shoot.* When gun is *pizdyets,* yes?"

"I told you, there's not going to be any killing."

"She tell to me: *Otisha . . . today is to kill, tomorrow is to interrogate.*"

"Please, Otto—"

"She tell me: *Otisha, to take gun, they must to dig hole at grave, remove my smelly hand.*"

"Otto!"

"She tell to me: *Otisha, it is to make them meal on your projectiles.* Ah, Mother very beautiful woman. Cookies very nice when to kitchen make."

No doubt Mother's brownies were made from chocolate, flour, and C4. I'd hate to be the one to blow out the candles on one of her birthday cakes. Better to submerge it in a bucket of water.

I pushed the gas pedal to the floorboard, and the speedometer surged far to the right, I guess around 120 miles per hour. I wasn't counting.

"Ve careful. KGB very dangerous. Yangie maybe good. Garv—" Otto poked me in the shoulder with the gun barrel. "Careful, eh? Very important."

"Otto, didn't your mother say anything about not pointing a gun at your friends? It's not a toy, for Pete's sake! Point that away from me!"

"Mother say to Otto: *Otisha, gun not toy, but much fun.*"

Ahead was a rocky bluff where waves crashed and lightning shimmered on the horizon beyond. The dune scrub cleared, and I could see the manor silhouetted ahead. It was perched alone at the top of the bluff like it wanted to take a dive off into the sea.

The rain had passed, suddenly, and a quarter moon was veiled in clouds above as I raced the Lincoln past a vacant gatehouse, over a downed chain and a stone bridge, and toward the spooky mansion. *Dark Shadows* meets the Indy 500.

I took my foot off the accelerator and pumped the brakes. The exhaust stopped rattling. Dousing my headlights, I snaked the Lincoln up the winding drive through tall hedges, the kind of bushes from which they make mazes. That gave way to cypresses, and I could see the manor's cupolas above them. Close enough. Grinding to a stop, I threw the Lincoln into reverse and backed her between two cypresses, the car's bumper hitting a statue, one of those knockoff Greek nudes. The white goddess gyrated and glowed in the dark like a Finnish belly dancer, but wobbled back into place without falling over.

We got out, closing the doors quietly.

We listened.

The only sound was the crashing ocean to our right.

"I stay, lookink." Otto gestured with the gun, for me to take it. "Otto come to help, mebbe."

I couldn't read his face in that light but didn't much care what he did. For me, it was all about finding Angie, making Angie safe. It's at a time like that when you really come to understand how much your own life is intertwined with your mate's. It's not just about companionship, about eating and sleeping together. And it's not so much about being *in love*. There's something about loving someone deeply for a long time, where the love becomes part and parcel of your own consciousness, of your being. Your sense of self is no longer *me*. It's *us*. Perhaps the most apt expression for this is *raison d'être*. Roughly translated: If she dies, I die. We die.

I waved away the gun and trotted toward the circular driveway. The crunch of my oversize shoes on the gravel made me wish the weather was still stormy to cover the sound of my approach.

Partridge's darkened manor loomed before me like a sleeping dragon, the row of peaks on the roof so many scales on the giant lizard's back. It was a hulking and ominous shadow that a sneeze might awaken into a fire-breathing mood. Where the house hung over the cliff, dimly lit windows looked like the monster's sleepy eye.

It was like being faced with a house designed by J.R.R. Tolkien, though I was afraid any hobbits I ran into were likely to be pygmies.

Gripping the ten-pound iron ring that passed for the front doorknob, I gave it a push and the massive oak door swung in.

Hands sprang from the darkness and latched on to my lapels.

I fell to the side, pulling my attacker with me, kicking frantically. I tried to hit some kind of soft spot. My thrashing quickly unseated the assailant and I found myself perched on top of MacTeague. By the light of the quarter moon, and my wet sticky hands, I realized he was covered in blood.

"Stop, clown, stop!" he rasped piteously. "Help me, an ambulance, help me!"

"Gack!" His chest was spongy with blood. Did my pseudo-bozo judo do that? Who'da thought my hands could be lethal weapons just from watching all those Bruce Lee films?

"Anything, jes' 'elp me. I don't want t'die," he whined.

"Where's Angie? The girl?"

"Inside, with Tex, with the raven..." MacTeague jackknifed in pain and I jumped off him. I could see dozens of small arrows sticking out of the Scotsman's flank.

"Is she all right?"

"I've been stabbed, shot with arrows, man! That double-dealin' freak . . . Help me . . ."

"Where's Angie? Is she all right?"

"Flip . . . stabbed me. Wanted the finder's fee to himself. Please . . ." he sobbed. "I'm . . . I'm bleedin' t'death, can't ya see? An' the wee devils got me with poison. . . ."

"Police are on the way." Car 54, where are you? I sure hoped the local constabulary had tossed aside their claw crackers and lobster bibs and scrambled for their squad cars when Blimpo at the motel buzzed.

I left him groaning in the flower bed and slipped past the front door into the manor, my hands cocked like fists of fury. Steven Seagal had nothing on me, except, well, most of the guys he subdues haven't already been stabbed. Hey, even golfers get handicaps, don't they? I was ready to kick some more butt. Specifically, Tex's. My raison d'être was in there somewhere, and I was trying to hold on to the idea that she hadn't been harmed. If she had— my brain churned with adrenaline, and the very idea that they'd so much as touched her made me feel superhuman, ready to throw lightning, rend limbs, crush cars. Pummel pygmies, if need be.

I couldn't see a thing at first. Feeling along the wall to the right, I came to a door and hallway. Dimly lit windows on one side, large oil paintings of ships on the other. Yellow light leaked from a room at the end of the hall. I jogged along the carpet as quietly as I could.

It was a cavernous, oak-vaulted room overflowing with head mounts of every conceivable exotic deer, antelope, and goat. For Garth the collector, it was like finding a secret grotto piled high with gold booty. A truly awe-inspiring collection of museum-quality taxidermy, and for a millisecond I was Ali Baba. Hartebeest, nyala, blackbuck, kudu, impala, gerenuk, steinbok, springbok, waterbuck, aoudad, axis, suni, fallow, mouflon, muntjac, gobi, chamois, tahr, roe, gray duiker, blue duiker, red duiker, bushbuck, eland, grysbok, dik-dik . . . Every twinkling glass eye seemed trained on me as I gradually brought my face around the door frame. Keep those eyes peeled, fellahs, Ali Baba is gonna do some serious kung fu fighting.

The flicker of lamplight shone from behind the door, shadows of antlers cast black snakes on the ceiling. My giant shoes seemed to sink into the rug as if it were new-fallen snow, my gentle footfalls an audible hush as I rounded the door.

"Don't do nothin' dumb, Scarecrow."

I pivoted left. Tex was sitting on the edge of a desk holding a large whaler's lantern in one hand, a hefty revolver in the other. Next to him was my crow, the lamp glow on the white feathers lighting up the bell jar like a hundred-watt bulb.

I froze when I saw Angie. She was behind Tex, to the right, gagged and duct-taped to a thronelike chair. Her eyes bulged and watered at the sight of me. This was her knight in shining armor, come to the rescue? I glanced down at my absurd costume apologetically. Where were the lightning bolts when I needed them? My heart and brain were aflame with the urge to destroy. Monster clown!

"C'mon in, hava seat right over here, nice an' easy, that's it." His toothpick waggled nervously as he motioned me toward the chair next to Angie's. "What're you supposed to be? Some kinda clown? Well, come on in, Bozo. Been an excitin' night, what with everybody gettin' jumpy. We could use some laughs."

I sat dumbly in the chair, Angie blinking anxiously next to me. I suppose I should have attempted a reassuring gesture of some kind, but I didn't want to get shot patting her knee.

My throat was all sand, but I managed to croak "Whatever it is you want here, it's all yours. All I want is Angie."

"Aw, that's sweet." Tex drew a forearm across his brow, checking his perimeter. I noticed that he was favoring one leg—the other had one of those pygmy arrows stuck in it and was matted with blood. "But you can't tell me that you didn't have some kinda deal, some kinda angle on the raven. I mean, why else you been so keen on that ol' bird? MacTeague an' me wasn't stupid neither. Think we din't know you'n Bret had some kinda deal in the makin'? Just too much coincidence, is all."

"Fletcher? He tried to kill me. I don't even know what all this is about."

"If you din't know nothin', then just why did

your li'l missy come to Mallard Island? We know Fletcher tol' you somethin', tryin' to cheat us outta the prize."

"Prize?"

"Pay dirt," he mocked, spitting his toothpick on the floor. His face welled up with a mass of mean-spirited squinty wrinkles. "Buyers comin to take that ol' bird offa our hands to the tune of three hundred grand. Be surprised what folk'll pay good money for."

"You stabbed MacTeague over a couple hundred grand?"

He checked his perimeter again. I looked around too, for the first time. The room was a library. Tex was backed up against a stately desk, beyond which was a wall of hanging tapestries. Right and left, walls were filled with bookshelves and another array of taxidermy. You don't suppose any of the shelves concealed a hidden staircase? There was a chandelier overhead, a vaulted wood ceiling above that—way up in the stratosphere. Behind Angie and me, opposite the desk and entrance to the room, large multipaned windows covered almost a whole wall. I could hear the ocean through them.

I sat rigidly like I was in the dean's office at some exclusive university, about to be expelled for being the class clown. Or maybe this was Clown College? But it was no laughing matter.

"T'wasn't me killed him," he hissed, wiping his brow. "It's that fool. *Flip*. And the little fellers. They're around here somewhere too."

"*Flip?*" I ventured. "Who . . . who is *Flip?* And the pygmies? What's up with that?"

Tex paled.

"He killed MacTeague, now he's a-tryin' to kill me. A double-cross. No three-way split. This whole thing? It was Flip's idea. Yeah huhn. He seen Partridge on TV. Good idea too. Collect the reward for the Big Foot with a gaff. Little fellahs jes' do whatever Flip sez, is all. They got thrown outta work too. We all did. Back end shows jes' aren't PC."

I stared at him as he waved his gun around the room, ready to shoot anything that moved. Wasn't going to be me—I sat rigid as a truant freshman. Angie, of course, had little choice but to sit still, though I could hear her breath coming fast and nervous through her nose.

Lamplight glittered on Tex's sweaty face, his eyes wide and trying not to blink lest his guard be compromised. I wasn't stalling by talking to him—he seemed content to let us wait with him for whatever was lurking beyond the door. Of course, having him distracted by conversation posed the possibility that his guard might be down at the crucial moment. I didn't have much at my disposal under the circumstances. So I clung to the hope that when Flip, or the pygmies or the Werewolf or The Mummy or whoever, came at him, Tex would get into a struggle. The gun would be trained elsewhere, possibly affording a window of escape for Angie and me. Possibly.

I had to ask.

"So how did you come to take the crow from Partridge? You were here to sell him a gaff Sasquatch."

He spat derisively. "We gets here, an' ol' Partridge sees through MacTeague's gaff. He sez he ain't no fool. But Flip, he sees the crow and sez, *We gotta have that. It's valuable. Real valuable.*"

"Valuable? What made Flip think it was valuable?" I shrugged, my eyes scanning the room for something, anything that might get us out of the dean's office.

"I guess you'd have to say Flip has a special sense about things, about people." He winked at me. "Could use that crow to make things happen. So Flip takes out this ol' carvin' knife and does Partridge. We take the crow. Didn't know Flip was gonna stick Partridge, he was gonna die. Fletcher took the bird back to Vermont for safekeepin' until we could figure out what to do with it. I thought the whole thing was crazy, but Flip said a buyer would find us. The freak was right, all right. But thing is, ol' Flip has prob'ly screwed the pooch this time. Buyer won't show up now!" he shouted. This statement was obviously meant for Flip, wherever he was hiding.

"Flip . . . is he Korean?"

"Whut?" He looked at me in disgust. "Shut yer trap, clown!"

That was all I was going to get out of Tex. He began yelling at the walls instead of me.

"C'mon, now, Flip! Let's put an end to this, call off the little fellers. I don't wanna hafta shoot another one. MacTeague is dead, an' that's okay with me. But half is better than nothin'. You don't cut this out, we ain't gonna see any of that money."

The heavy oak door creaked and Tex swung the gun on it. I could see sweat was stinging his eyes. His thumb slid forward to make sure the revolver's hammer was back and cocked.

There was a coo. I scanned the ceiling to see if there was a dove in the rafters. It built into a sweet crescendo, a giggle that seemed to come from beyond the door. Then there was a breathy pause, like Shirley Temple being presented with a lollipop.

"How do I know you won't shoot me, Tex?" It was a little girl's voice. The distant voice I'd heard at the mothballed sideshow.

Angie and I exchanged glances, pupils dilated. Those goose bumps were back, surging across my arms like the ocean swells outside. Creepy? I didn't know the half of it. Yet.

"I promise, on a stack of Gideons, Flip." Tex grinned. But he kept his gun pointed at the door. "You just come on out and we'll get that money. Not two o'clock yet. We still have time to make the deal go down."

Not two yet. Was the buyer showing up at two? Tex, MacTeague, and Flip had arrived early, and this cat-and-mouse erupted?

The little girl began to sing:

> *"Watch me, swingers, and let's all strive*
> *To do the Mambo Rumba Two-Hand Jive*

Get down low, and back up high
Shimmy those hips, give it a try."

Her high, mildly nasal voice was a dead ringer for Belle Beverly, that early sixties' pop singer. Uncanny.

"Stop playin' games, Flip. C'mon out and let's get back on track."

"How can I be sure?" the girl's voice said.

Tex took a step toward the door. He meant to shoot her, all right, and was trying to make sure he didn't miss. How could this little girl—*Flip?*—have killed MacTeague?

"You know, Tex, the white crow is very powerful," the little girl's voice chimed. "I think maybe we should use the New York buyer. It's a lot more money."

"We already talked about that. Ain't goin' back to New York and dealin' with those slanty-eyed sleazeballs. We voted to sell it here. Tonight. 'Sides, I'm thinking you like that crow too much." Tex took another step, his lantern held out toward the door. "I don't think you have any notion of selling it at all."

"Feel the music in your feet
The gang on the beach has the beat
Let your hands show your honey
You're no square, on the money."

More Belle Beverly. And there I was without my surfboard—not exactly the set of *Beach Blanket Bingo.*

Tex's neck muscles flexed, and he looked a little unsteady on his feet, possibly from the poison on those wicked little pygmy arrows. "Now, that's enough of that."

"It was a three-way vote." She chuckled. "Before I made MacTeague a bloody mess. Now the vote is fifty–fifty. So who wins?"

"Stop the tomfoolery, Flip. We got these two New Yorkers we gotta take care of. Soon as they go missing, I wanna be long gone."

I heard myself gulp and purposely didn't exchange glances with Angie. My eyes were glued on Tex, my reflexes keyed to what was going to happen next. I had a move of my own to make. The window of opportunity would be small, the chance for escaping unscathed smaller. Timing would be essential. I knew my first move was to knock Angie back with my right arm onto the floor, hopefully under the line of fire. After that? I guessed I'd go for Tex and the gun. The little girl, I reasoned, would be easier to subdue. One knuckle sandwich to the face and she would go down and stay there. Hey, it's not like she was peddling Minty Melties for a new scout camp. Tex said she had a carving knife, and by the looks of MacTeague, she wasn't afraid to use it.

I registered motion in my right peripheral vision. Turning, I saw the tapestries behind Tex bulge. He saw my head swivel and started to spin. But Flip was already upon him, shrieking, knife in the air.

Flip was tall. Wide. Not little. A girl? There was no way of telling. There were denim coveralls, bare shoulders, a bare head. She, or it, looked like a giant thumb. But the voice had seemed to come from the doorway.

I flung my arm out and knocked Angie back, and heard her tape-muffled scream as the high-back chair clunked heavily to the carpet. Spilling out of my chair and onto the floor next to her, I ripped the tape from her mouth and frantically went to work on the tape around her arms.

"Angie, are you okay?"

"Garth, why are you dressed like a clown?" she shouted over the ruckus between Tex and Flip.

"It was on accident—I mean, by accident—with a pen and some handcuffs and Detective Walker." I growled. "Just hurry!"

Tex and Flip still struggled against the desk, cursing. It was all I could do to concentrate on the tape. *A giant thumb? In coveralls?*

I wanted to look, to make sense of it, but was busy trying to free Angie. I heard the lamp hit the floor and glanced up to see kerosene gushing onto the carpet and back toward the wall. The whole area burst into flame. The flickering shadows of the two combatants danced across the windows.

To one side, the elongated shadow of the crow shimmered on the bookcases, a seemingly sinister observer of the fiery mayhem.

I felt the growing heat on my face and saw the curtains swirled in flames.

That's when Otto kicked open the door and charged into the room, his mother's gun and steel dental work flashing like the Frito Bandito. He squinted in our direction before spinning his pistol toward Tex and Flip, who were still doing their tango. Otto's mother would have been proud. Gun at his hip, he fanned the trigger like he'd just hit Dodge City. Fire spiked from the barrel, dealing a deafening roar and tumult of gunfire. Take it from me, kids, don't fire a gun in the house—it's so loud you'd swear someone was clonking your ears with ball-peen hammers.

Books exploded behind Flip and Tex. Glass shattered. Splinters jumped like grasshoppers off the desk. His aim was all over the place. I guess Mama neglected to admonish him about hitting his mark.

Then Tex's gun fired two shots.

Otto shouted, *"Khuy!"* His gun dropped to the floor, and he staggered to the wall. He was hit.

Angie had one hand free and we were both clawing at the tape on the other.

Tex's gun went off again, and an antelope head fell from the wall. Flip shrieked with glee. Something cracked, like a tree branch snapping.

Angie was free. She rolled to one side, away from the chair.

I looked up, my ears ringing from the gunfire. The bell jar, the crow, was nowhere to be seen. In its place was broken glass.

Tex was half sitting, half leaning on the desk. Flip was gone. White feathers floated to the floor. Off toward the bookcases, on the carpet, I could see the headless white crow lying on its side, still clutching its little branch. Next year's birthday? Angie is getting a vacuum cleaner.

Tex slid from the desk onto his knees. His eyes were just white, no pupils. He fell forward, face flat down, onto a bed of the feathers. I heard his nose snap. His body rolled in one direction, his head the other, in a way that didn't look possible. Not without a broken neck.

I grabbed Angie's hand and pulled her toward me. The flaming tapestries had touched off the bookcases, and the temperature in the room was rising rapidly. There was no dousing this fire—it was hungry, and you just knew it was going to devour the whole house.

My eyes stung with the heat and smoke, but I found Otto, still crumpled against the wall, rocking slightly.

I pushed Angie toward him and paused, scanning the room for Flip, Frankenstein, the Wolfman, Dracula, or any other monsters, but saw only Tex twitching on the floor. Then my eye caught cinders falling like flaming snow around the headless crow.

Don't ask me why, but I darted over and grabbed the crow by the branch it was attached to before joining Angie and Otto. There was blood on Otto's arm, on the wall, on the floor. Not a lot. But that didn't mean anything. He could be dying. I looked at the door. There were no flames blocking our escape.

It was open.

And then it wasn't.

Standing before the closed door was the giant thumb.

I can't say that I've ever—before or since—found myself so utterly terrified, my veins all ice. If for no other reason than understanding the full freakish menace of what stood before me took me a good ten seconds. And then some.

Way at the top of the thumb, set preternaturally high in a bald head, were little blue eyes; not just any eyes, but the kind that glow in the slightest light. Flames danced in those tiny blue eyes. I knew those eyes. They had flapped at me from the torn canvas at the abandoned sideshow.

Below the eyes was the rest of the thick, meaty, and expansive head. The nose was tiny, shaped like a peanut; the mouth was a red bud, kewpie-doll lips.

It looked sort of like Tweety Bird with a thyroid problem. Sylvester the Cat would have had his hands full with this canary. So would the bulldog, for that matter.

The ice in my veins hardened and cracked. What the hell was this thing? Could it be real? I was still trying to take it all in.

The neck and chin were indistinguishable from the shoulders, which sat like a rotting pumpkin atop a wide chest. Past a prodigious belly, at the bottom where the coveralls ended, were some orthopedic shoes, each different. Black. Ugly. The kind with lifts and shunts. The feet were huge and splay-footed.

At the top of the coveralls, to the sides of the hideous head and neck, where the arms should have been, were flippers. Big, pimply-looking flippers that came down to the giant thumb's waist. They were thick but flexuous, the ends curling like a squid's tentacles.

One was wrapped around a carving knife. One part Tweety, one part octopus, both parts psychotic killer.

I heard Angie catch sight of Flip. She yelped like she'd just gotten a paper cut.

Flip was no girl, big or little. Add a tuxedo . . . I suddenly thought about Reggie in my trunk.

This was *FLIP THE PENGUIN BOY. A Living Legend!* This was the Reaper in our apartment. This was the shadow in the truck that smooshed Bret. This is what threw the boulder at me. This is what called for help at the sideshow, luring me into range of the pygmies' arrows.

I'd seen my share of deformed sideshow freaks as a kid. This was probably an extreme example of phocomelia—prenatal exposure to thalidomide. But instead of short flippers for appendages, these suckers were long, almost like scaly wings. In a strong breeze, Flip might have flown circles around the Flying Nun. I'd also heard about "lobster claw" syndrome, where the embryonic hands and feet split to form "claws." They say some freaks actually sought to have freaks as children, to effectively usher them into the family business. If so, Mom and Pop must have been very proud of Sonny Boy. He was twice blessed. So much for wanting Junior to be a dentist.

I realized my jaw was hanging open, because I began to cough from the smoke. If we ran from Flip, he would have Otto. If we stayed, Flip would probably kill all three of us. Tweety or not—this was one mean-looking bird.

My eyes darted, looking for something, any-thing, to use as a weapon. Otto's gun was engulfed in flames by the desk. Probably empty anyhow. The chairs were too heavy, and too far. Books on the shelves were useless.

Above, the fire glittered in the eyes of an audi-ence. I'd never before thought taxidermy looked sinister, but this bunch did. A gnu seemed to grin, a hartebeest to sneer, a blackbuck to smirk, a duiker to wink. Hell's gallery of horned fiends greedy for mayhem.

I pushed Angie back, trying to signal her to get away.

Flip took a step forward, the fins rippling, squirming. From the kewpie-doll lips came the little-girl voice:

"The kving-kie is mine! Not yours, clown."

I slid sideways toward the giant windows, and Flip stayed with me. Those tiny blue eyes were fixed on the headless crow in my hand. I kept mov-ing, and Flip kept following. This was progress.

Through the smoke and wafting ashes I glimpsed Angie usher Otto to his feet and toward the door. But my eyes were trained on Flip, those sparkling little blue eyes, the rippling flippers.

Flip pointed the knife in my direction, weaving it through the smoke like a snake, coiled and ready to strike. He began to sway as he crept forward. The rosebud lips parted, and Belle Beverly came out:

> "Watch me, swingers, and let's all strive
> To do the Mambo Rumba Two-Hand Jive
> Get down low, and back up high
> Shimmy those hips, give it a try."

My mind flashed to Belle Beverly in a sixties' beach flick, her beehive hairdo, her fringed one-piece swimsuit, and her hands doing an early version of the Macarena—except Flip was doing it with a carving knife.

My back was suddenly up against the window, seemingly much too soon. My thoughts scurried around my skull like manic rodents looking for cheese in a maze, for options, for escape. I glanced at the headless crow in my hand. He still wanted the damn crow even though there was nothing left of it. I was suddenly furious that all this was happening, that I'd bought the crow in the first place. That I'd followed it up here. That it was in my hand now. Why did I pick it up? And why was I even hesitating to hand it over to this knife-wielding proto-penguin freak?

Perdition, thy name is Belle Beverly:

> *"C'mon, Cats, work those mittens*
> *These ginchy girls are all but kittens*
> *Doin' the Mambo Rumba Two-Hand Jive*
> *Way out, Daddy-o, it's a dance alive."*

Let's face it—it's this kind of thing that sends people to asylums. You know, like when the evening news follows a report on Third World genocide with a story on barbecue safety tips. My brain, while fraying around the edges, managed to find footing in the form of an impulse. An overwhelming, consuming, volcanic loathing. Hatred and rage. Not of Flip so much but of my predicament.

Roaring white flames framed Flip as he danced the Mambo Rumba Two-Hand Jive, the flickering knife point drawing closer to my chest. I could smell the taxidermy cooking, the acrid smell of burning fur and hide. The eyes from above twinkled with satanic glee.

The impulse surged. I couldn't hear my heart, and I didn't seem to be breathing. Was I dead? Had something happened that I missed? I was looking at myself, at Flip doing his little Penguin Dance of Death in front of me. A sashay of slaughter. A Macarena of murder. A veritable Watusi of knife-wielding.

Glass cracked and splintered. With a whoosh, the giant windows exploded.

The entire array.

It played out like a silent movie; I couldn't hear a thing. A wave of flame-licked shards billowed outward into the night, the manor dragon enraged and vomiting flame over the sea.

The flood of fire carried the Penguin Boy with it, his flippers flapping wildly like he was trying to take flight. Tumbling head over heels toward the crashing waves, the flicker of the knife wobbled after him. In a wink he and the knife slipped from view, consumed by night's black gullet.

Too bad penguins can't fly. He was in for a pretty rocky landing.

Through the smoke I could make out the open door at the far end of the room. Angie and Otto were gone, escaped, and I aimed to be right on their heels.

My mind zapped back into my head as if awakening from a nightmare.

The torrent of heat and flames that had burst the windows had ceased. The floor was clear of smoke, but the whole room was humming from the ferociousness of the fire, like a woodstove on a winter morning. I could still make out my malevolent spectators, now just fire with eyes, Hades portent working its will.

I began to crawl, my vision swimming with black jigsaw pieces that I knew meant imminent unconsciousness. I felt myself crumple against the side of the desk. The puzzle of unconsciousness and death crowded in, and I remember thinking:

> *"Watch me, swingers, and let's all strive*
> *To do the Mambo Rumba Two-Hand Jive*
> *Get down low, and back up high*
> *Shimmy those hips, give it a try."*

I've never been so ready to die. Overcome by smoke and heat, I lay there in a half-conscious state, waiting, almost hoping for the Reaper's guiding hand. *Come on, take me. I'm through.*

But I was uncomfortable, the floor was lumpy, and my body was moving. My head thumped against something a couple times, and it hurt. I smelled a familiar odor through the smoke, not exactly cologne. . . . Why wasn't I out of my body yet?

I was cold, and it was suddenly dark. The bumping had stopped. *Now I must be dead.*

My face was wet.

"Garth!"

It was Angie's voice. I hoped she wasn't dead too. Though I have to confess—I was glad she was with me, wherever I was.

"Garth!"

I could feel her touch. That was nice. They think of everything in heaven.

"Garth!"

Visual sensation, light, and then flashing red lights. I was moving, and there were some metallic clunks as I was jostled onto a stretcher. I opened my eyes and I was in an ambulance, tubes and things overhead swinging to the sway of the vehicle.

Angie was stroking my forehead. Her eyes were red, her soot-smeared face streaked by tears. Here I was again, just like that shoot-out in West Harlem with Smiler.

"Let go of it," she said.

Let go of what? I could feel my arm moving.

I tried to say something but couldn't speak. Devil hadn't got me, only my tongue.

Angie held up my hand in hers. Doggedly clenched in my hand was what was left of the crow: singed legs and a sooty white belly and tail. I was gripping it by the branch, which was humming hot in my hand but undamaged. Figures that the least valuable part went unscathed.

And to think they could have had this for five hundred dollars. It's sad to see taxidermy destroyed. Nobody should have to die twice, not even an albino crow.

I relaxed my hand. Angie tossed the crow aside and threw her arms around my neck, sobbing.

I was pretty sure I wasn't dead.

Chapter 20

As much as I'd rather Angie had not been caught up in that deal at Partridge's spook house, I'll admit I was relieved someone else got to tell the bizarre story to the cops for a change. It's my guess that blond-haired, green-eyed Angie comes across as a heck of a lot more credible than I do.

And as much as I'd just as soon stay out of hospitals, I have to admit that being flat out with your face and hands bandaged is a better vantage point than an interrogation room from which to explain your story. I looked a lot worse off than I was: mainly first-degree burns on my face, scalp, forearms, and hands accounted for the mummy wrap. It was about as bad as a sunburn. My hair was a tad crispy—the horror of split ends. I also had a few choice bruises from being dragged out of the inferno. Mainly I was there under observation, for smoke inhalation.

Dragged? Well, here's the thing. I know I passed out, that I couldn't go any farther once I reached that desk. Ergo, somebody must have dragged me out. Angie had hidden Otto behind a hedge and raced back to find me, which she did, on the door stoop. My shirt and jacket were hiked up almost over my head from whoever had latched hold of them and pulled. Ah, yes, but who? The band of brown midgets? Doubtful. There was only one person from the guest list not accounted for, the one who was supposed to show at 2:00 P.M. The buyer. Whoever that was. But why did he bother to risk his neck for me? My brain hurt just thinking about it.

Anyway, turns out the kid at the motel did call the cops, complaining about an abusive clown, and when Angie found me on the stoop next to MacTeague's dead body, the fuzz had just pulled up. An ambulance arrived a short time later to find me slipping into shock, and Otto with a gunshot wound to the left hand. The slug had passed cleanly through the meaty part between his thumb and forefinger, missing bone and any vital muscles or nerves.

While Angie had given the police her version of the events of that night at Partridge's, they of course wanted my version, which I gave them on the second day I was laid up. (They couldn't make heads or tails of Otto's description.) I chose to leave out the Belle Beverly moments, as much to spare myself the horror of that delightful encounter as to keep the story as plausible as possible. Hey, they already thought I was nuts, and I needed to retain what little credibility I had left.

The cops had done their homework and found that pygmies did indeed fletch their arrows with leaves. The toxins they use in Africa are usually layered on the arrow points and made from insects, berries, and plants. They use them to hunt colobus monkeys, which are a good deal smaller than humans, so it takes several hits to incapacitate a human. In this case, the arrows were tipped with hemlock root, rendered salamander oils, and Drano.

Now, of course, I was more popular than ever with the authorities. I had not only Walker of the NYPD, and Renard of the New York State Department of Environmental Conservation, and Danny DA from Brattleboro, Vermont, but also the Wells Police and Maine State Police crowded around my bed, picking at my story. All while passing around two zip-seal evidence bags. One contained the remnants of the white crow. The other, a handful of tiny pygmy arrows. Each in turn gave the bird's remains and the arrows a squinty, skeptical examination.

I concentrated my story on Tex, MacTeague, and Flip. I mean, they were the ones who'd committed serious crimes, right? Murder, kidnapping, possibly arson. Isn't that enough?

Apparently not. The authorities kept trying to drag me into it, asking me where I got "the gun." I'd had a full day to muse over the particulars and was ready for them. I didn't have a gun, and I never saw Otto with one. All the guns, as far as I knew, belonged to Tex, MacTeague, and/or Flip.

Them: *But it was a Gapov, a Russian revolver, and your friend is Russian.*

Me: *I never saw Otto with a gun, not before or during the episode. He burst into the room and they shot him.*

Them: *From what we can tell, there were at least eight shots fired in there.*

Me: *I don't know what happened before I got there. As I said, there were a few shots fired while Flip and Tex struggled. And the two of them and MacTeague had obviously had a falling out of some kind. The pygmies were sneaking around somewhere ready to back up Flip and obviously finished off MacTeague.*

Them: *You went into the house without any weapon? Any weapon at all?*

Me: *That's right. No weapon. I'm a kung fu master.*

Them: *Wasn't that kind of foolish? And dressed as a clown?*

Me: *Angie was in there. I wasn't thinking about my personal safety. As for the clown getup, that was the result of a pen exploding red ink into my mouth after it got stuck in Walker's handcuffs.*

I mean, you'd think they'd be satisfied with what they had. When they searched the sideshow, they'd found the taxidermied remains of Gobo the gorilla Frankensteined to a grizzly bear pelt, the fur dyed to a uniform color and made into a Big Foot. Thus, the story of the conspiracy to sell Partridge a fake Sasquatch to collect the reward was substantiated.

But there were two—no, make that three—

things that bothered them, and in the interview, they kept returning to them.

1. What happened to Flip the Penguin Boy? How did he happen to be defenestrated, and why hadn't his body washed up? I told them I assumed that a rush of air from the fire broke the windows and sucked him out. I fell to the floor and was not sucked out. They didn't like this, and I think they thought I'd shoved him. They kept asking about "when you pushed him . . ." and I had to keep countering that "I never touched Flip, not once." As to why he hadn't washed up after falling one hundred feet into the ocean, I couldn't help but answer: "Well, he was part penguin. Maybe he migrated to the Shetland Islands?" If they were going to put me through the third degree while I was flat on my back in a hospital, I had to get my digs in too, didn't I?

2. Why did the carny gang want the crow? I replied that they never told me why. And that was true. I did mention that Flip said, "The kving-kie is mine," which I explained referred to an apparently extinct wild cow from Asia that Partridge had been after. But the crow was clearly not a kving-kie, so I didn't know what he meant. No doubt my pal Jimmy Kim could clear some of this up, if I ever saw him again. And I hoped I wouldn't.

3. Why was there a frozen penguin in my trunk? I explained that his name was Reggie and that this penguin wrangler owed me a penguin because his live penguins had attacked and killed my dead penguin, whose name was Sneezy on account of the fact

that I had seven penguins named after the seven dwarfs.

That shut them up for almost ten seconds.

Anyway, now the crow was destroyed and all opposing parties were dead. Bret, MacTeague, Tex, and Flip were all dead. Only the pygmies remained, and they'd lost their leader, Flip. So I was satisfied that this whole thing was over. However, the attending Steve McGarretts, Dannos, and the *Five-O* crew were not satisfied. They approached the issue of what the carny crew wanted at least thirty times. And I replied at least thirty times that I still had no idea what the unemployed traveling freak-show types wanted the crow for, or why it was valuable.

They finally left, convinced, I think, only that they needed to come up with some new needles of evidence to poke holes in the balloon that was my story.

After they'd left, Angie walked in with a guy named Frank Franks. No lie. He was a lawyer, one that actually cost money, and I gave Angie a sour look when I surmised that this shyster was going to fleece me. I'm suspicious of police, if for no other reason than they're always suspicious of me, but I'm not crazy about lawyers either. Remember Public Defender Phil? What a gem *he* was. Anyway, my prejudice was slightly assuaged by this guy Franks. First thing I liked about him was that he was trim and looked like a Marine. I've got a lot of respect for those who serve their country, and Marines have done more than their share. And unlike the cops, he seemed to *get it* right out of the box. He *got it* that

Angie and I were victims. Which is what you'd expect from your lawyer, sure. But he only needed it all explained once and didn't care one whit about Reggie or anything other than the salient details, like lack of motive or evidence against us. What's more, he said he'd have us on our way back to New York the next day. So he told me what I wanted to hear. If he delivered, so much the better.

Franks gave a casual salute and left. Angie and I were alone for the first time since the ambulance ride. She looked exhausted, circles under her eyes, and wasn't without her own bumps and scrapes. Ever have duct tape put over your mouth and then ripped off? You could still see the squared edges around her mouth. She was freckled with little blisters on her arms and face where burning ash had singed her flesh.

But thankfully, the nurses had managed to get the red ink off my face so I no longer looked like Krusty the Clown.

Angie tucked her hair behind one ear, and as she looked down at me, her brow furrowed.

I smiled. "I'm going to be fine, Angie. We'll be back home tomorrow night."

"I just feel like this is all my fault somehow."

"Your fault?" I snorted. "How do you figure?"

"Well, I was the one, when we picked up the skins from the state police, who said we should go back to Gunderson's, to Bermuda. If we'd only just gone home the way you wanted to . . ."

I took her hand. "Sugar lips, we're a team.

There's no me or you, just us. A year from now, we'll look back on this and—well, maybe we won't laugh. It's been an adventure, though, hasn't it?"

She was working her tear ducts with her fingertips, trying to stop them.

"All for what? That stupid crow. What did they want it for, anyway? We didn't even find that out."

"Who cares, at this point?" I wasn't about to start in on the kving-kie. No way. Next thing you know, she'd be out the door and on a flight to Korea. "Look, we escaped with our lives, my stuff, and even that nut Otto, all roughly intact. Lemme tell you, that guy Otto, for all his smoking in the house and wacky behavior, he came in real handy. Though I'm glad to know he's been separated from that gun. You know, his mother gave that to him. Or at least that's what he said."

I was trying to get her mind off the guilty jag. Wasn't working.

"And then the thing with the gallbladders a while back. I got you into that mess too."

Time for reverse psychology.

"Well, you're right, you did almost get me killed that time. Ow!"

She punched me in the shoulder. A real wallop too.

"It's not funny, Garth!"

She turned to the window, and silence overcame us, boxers in their corners waiting for the bell. During the intermission, I mused about the job offer. My guilt could certainly compete with hers. Maybe even cancel it out. I'd started composing my opening remarks and overall gambit when Otto burst into the room. Sometimes he had perfect timing.

"Garv, my friend!" He grabbed me by the face with his good hand. The other hand was wrapped in bandages. "How's lookink?"

I yowled—he was squeezing my burns. "You're killing me!"

"My Got!" He pointed at me. "Not lookink. Yangie, please to tell me my friend Garv not killed."

She didn't say anything, didn't turn, which Otto took as a bad sign. Falling to his knees, he literally howled, and broke into the most ferocious, soul-rending wailing I think I've ever witnessed. Imagine a coyote, a full moon, a brisk night, and a passing fire engine. Stirred from her reverie, Angie wheeled around and tried to calm him, to explain that I wasn't dying. But he was overboard. Off the deep end. Piloting a sub far below the Arctic ice. In a diving bell at the bottom of the Mariana Trench. Fathoms under Loch Ness with the monster.

It would have been comical had the ruckus not drawn a crowd of angry nurses, orderlies, and doctors who seemed to hold me accountable for this outburst, virtually dragging him out of the room by his heels, kicking and screaming. Angie, of course, went with them, still doing her best to quiet the tormented Russian wolf.

I heard his paroxysms trail off down the elevator and then outside in front of the hospital and for three blocks as Angie drove him somewhere to chill out.

Whew.

I hadn't slept much, as you might imagine. I'd no sooner get Sandman in my eyes than Belle Beverly's voice would surge up like a cauldron of magma in my subconscious. If that's not the stuff nightmares are made of, I don't know what is. I used to sorta like Belle's songs too, especially the "Mambo Rumba Two-Hand Jive."

At least the crow was away from me for good. Somehow, that thing was the cause, directly or indirectly, of everything that had happened.

That's when Renard walked into my hospital room.

Holding the evidence bag with the crow in it.

Renard didn't even ask if he could come in. Just made himself at home in the chair next to my bed, his blue plaid hat in his lap.

I sighed. "I thought you guys were through with me today."

A slight smile played on his lips, which told me he wasn't going to deign to reply.

"I have just a few more small questions. If you're up to it."

"And if I said I wasn't, would it stop you from asking them?"

"This Flip, the freak: Was he after you or the crow when he *happened* to fall out the window?"

I stared at the ceiling. "Didn't notice. All I was looking at was the knife."

"Were you holding the crow?"

"When?"

"When the two of you went toward the window."

I glanced over, and he was looking at the crow remnants, not me.

"I don't remember. A lot was happening, the room was on fire," I said flatly, as I had said before for the full audience. "Look, we just went over all this."

He sucked his cheeks, stroking the feather in his hat for a moment until his chocolate, half-lidded eyes lifted to mine.

"You really don't know what this is about, do you?"

"Look, Renard, *you* have the bird. *It's all yours.* Go test it, get the FBI to figure out what this is all about. Me? I'm through. So leave me alone already."

I detected the slightest glow in those damnable dark eyes. There was something else going on.

He looked away.

"We'll run some tests on this." He waved the bag nonchalantly before dropping it into his briefcase and locking it. "Where will you stay when they release you tomorrow?"

I felt like telling him off, bragging about how my mouthpiece Frank Franks was going to be sending me back home. But I was afraid I'd jinx it.

"A motel, somewhere."

He tucked the briefcase under his arm and went to the exit. Before the door closed behind him, I heard Renard say: "We'll find you."

Chapter 21

I half expected Jim Kim to show up at any turn. At the dry-ice distributor in Massachusetts (Reggie needed some new nesting material), at the Denny's we ate at in Connecticut, at the Westchester gas station, even at the tollbooths for the Triborough Bridge. That's right, Frank Franks got us out of there, bless his soul. Best $500 I ever spent. Well, next to the $500 I spent for a standing Kodiak bear. I've made over ten grand on that thing in rentals.

But no Kim. And why should I see him? The crow and I had parted ways, once and for all. Not that I didn't continue to have nightmares about Flip. Getting over that was just a matter of time, I hoped. Shelling out $500 to a barrister is one thing, but quite another to a shrink.

Once home, I quickly set Otto about the task of

cleaning all the pelts, the penguins, and generally getting the stock back in order. We wanted to get back to normal at chez Carson ASAP. No more episodes.

The job thing was still out there, and I knew I only had days to make a decision. But like an old cat with a new toy, I chose to ignore it no matter how much it was jiggled in front of my face. I'd been through too much over the last days to even contemplate more stress.

Angie and I had yet to resume our conversation from the hospital room. But it was still out there, the specter of self-recrimination dogging our every conversation.

On the second morning home, Angie went up to see Van Putin with boxes of her best jewelry. Meanwhile, I was cleaning receipts out of my wallet from our little murder tour of Vermont and Maine, trying to figure out if I could deduct any of it on my taxes, when I came upon Pete's folded piece of paper, the *MOOSE HEAD 4 SALE* ad. Believe it or not, so much had happened that I'd forgotten all about it. I wondered if that woman was awake yet. I dialed, with no little trepidation.

" 'lo?"

"Yes, I'm calling about the moose head. The fifty-dollar moose head?"

"Let's see . . ."

"The fifty-dollar moose head? Do you still have it?"

"Can you come get it now?"

"Yes, yes . . . you live on Dewberry Road. And I

know by the area code you live in Connecticut. But what town do you live in?"

"Connecticut? Oh . . . Greenwich."

Now we were getting somewhere. Greenwich is close to New York. Well, a lot closer than Brattleboro, that's for sure. "And the address?"

"What?"

"Your address?"

"Bring cash."

"Of course, five tens, two twenties and a ten, ten fives, fifty ones—however you want it. Give me your address on Dewberry Road and I'll come give you the money and take that nasty moose head away. What's your address?"

"Two twenty ten."

"Two twenty ten, got it. I'll come right up. See you soon."

I hung up.

Wait a sec . . . was she just parroting back to me what I said? When I said I'd pay her two twenties and a ten?

I tried calling her back. Busy. Ten minutes later, after some serious pacing? Still busy.

I called Dudley.

"Gawth, you ol' ragpicker!"

"Mind if I come over this afternoon and bring you a specimen for mounting? I think you'll be surprised."

"By all means. I was going to call you because—"

"Sorry to interrupt, Dudley, but I'm in a hurry. Can we talk this afternoon?"

"Why, certainly, I—"

"You online?"

"As a matter of fact—"

"Could you do an address search for me?"

"Gawth, when are you gonna get yourself on the Web? It's absolutely atrocious that you—"

"Please, save the lecture for this afternoon? The address is two twenty ten Dewberry Road, Greenwich, Connecticut."

I heard him loose a heavy sigh, followed by the clack of his keyboard.

"No such address. There's not even a Dewberry Road in Greenwich. Let me try a few variations. . . ."

I waited a few moments and heard him grunt.

"No such address."

"Rats!" I hit the table with my fist. "Okay, thanks. See you this afternoon."

I hung up.

I had an appointment with the body shop anyway, so I dropped the Lincoln off to get the trunk fixed. When I got back home, I tried the moose-head lady again and the number was still busy, so I set about taking Reggie out of the deep freeze and wrapping the penguin in newspaper. I paid particular attention to the sharp-edged beak and webbed feet, the former turbaned in about a half roll of toilet paper, the latter ensconced in bubble wrap. You'd be surprised how delicate the beak and toenails on a penguin can be once they're dead. In life they scramble all over the place, pecking and clawing without a thought. But Dudley would strengthen them up during the mounting using BeakRok and PoxieNail. In the meantime, I bedded ol' Reggie down in a big Styrofoam cooler full of peanuts, strapped him onto a hand truck, and headed out. Time to deliver the specimen to my friend Dudley.

He'd be beside himself. Puffins were in his repertoire, but I knew he was keen to try his hand at their larger cousin. He only collected specimens he mounted himself and did this as a favor now and again. He lives due south from our abode in an old carriage house near Canal Street. The downstairs is still barnlike, and stuffed with electronics. That's how he pays the bills, usually with some high-end, high-tech man-toys, the kind you can't even find in Schlemock and Hammer catalogs. Ever see a golf putter with a GPS guidance system built into it? A cell phone that's also a Taser? Pocket laser teeth whitener? Of course you haven't. You're not a billionaire, and even if you are, you need a referral. Some of this stuff isn't entirely legal.

Anyway, spring was much farther along in New York than up in Vermont, so I decided to walk, wheeling Reggie behind me. Trees were blooming, birds were chirping everywhere, and it was warm and sunny. There's a special sort of bonhomie among New Yorkers on these spring days. We'd toughed out another New York winter. Only we can truly appreciate days like this, the ones before the sweltering heat. I know, it's kinda sick, but New Yorkers are honestly proud of being long-suffering about certain things. Even elitist about it. Me included. So sometimes as we pass each other on gorgeous spring or fall days, we share a secret, snobby moment.

Dudley lives on a little angled street near some car-stereo shops, and I knocked on the door set into the barn doors of his carriage house. I was buzzed in almost immediately.

He wasn't downstairs, so I climbed the wooden steps up to his garret, the hand cart clunking its way up behind me. The bird didn't weigh much, but the ice did.

Dudley was at his rolltop desk, leaning back in a Windsor chair. This was his usual position for my entry, and I was convinced that he did, indeed, strike this as a pose. Why? I don't know. Maybe because when he's at his desk he's completely surrounded by his collection of birds, basking in their glory. The walls were lined with a high shelf displaying literally hundreds of birds. Many, like his electronics, were illegal, though I know he came by them more or less legitimately. His network of fellow bird taxidermists revere these creatures and trade specimens found dead. Dudley knows the maintenance staff at a dozen of New York's tallest skyscrapers. When songbirds migrate, they sometimes get confused by the shiny buildings and smack into them, falling onto a sidewalk or ledge.

"Gawth, you ol' ragpicker!" Dudley slapped his knees and smiled broadly. "My, my—you have been through the mill!"

Dudley is definitely the sort of man who is very

aware of his appearance, even if it's always the same. The uniform is khaki trousers, khaki shirt, red suspenders, and an open brown vest. He's thick, with oversize features, and brown. I know he sees himself as some kind of transplanted southern gentry, or the Mark Twain of Canal Street perhaps. But to me he looks like Deputy Dawg.

He held his hands up to my face, looking me over. I never fail to notice that his fingernails are always the picture of perfection. Possibly because he's a tactilaphobe and refuses to shake hands or touch anyone—or most things that other people have touched.

"Yeah, well, there have been a few bumps and scrapes. My face is still peeling a little from some burns."

"Hmm." He gripped his chin, his gaze drifting down to the package on my hand truck. "I look forward to hearing all about it. What have you got there?"

"See if you can guess." I grinned.

"I will not! You open that immediately, y'hear?"

So I gleefully opened the cooler, slipped the toilet paper off the beak, and folded the newspaper back from the face.

"You rascal! *Spheniscus magellanicus!*" He stood, and I thought for a second he might slap my back or even shake my hand. "But . . ." He stamped his foot.

"Problem?"

"My deep freeze is full." He looked genuinely pained. "A friend just brought me a baby ostrich."

"Who?"

A familiar voice startled me from the other side of the room.

"Waldo did."

He'd been sitting in a wing chair under an assortment of orioles, camouflaged against the leather and wainscoting in brown pants and brown Nehru jacket. He was stooped and lanky—his knees high in the air even when sitting. His head was completely bald—I don't even think he had eyebrows or eyelashes. His brow was furrowed, his nose beaklike. Not a Klingon at all. Mad scientist? Maybe. The Nehru jacket was a definite warning sign.

He unfolded and stood. Tall, all right, over six-six anyway, even stooped.

"Did Waldo startle you?" It sounded like a threat. He was holding a crumpled brown paper sack. You'd think a guy like that would have a *Twilight Zone* lunch box, complete with a Rod Serling thermos for his cocoa.

"Yeah, a little. I didn't see you sitting there." I stepped up and put out a hand. "Garth Carson."

He looked at my hand but didn't bother to shake it. "I know who you are."

A tactilaphobe convention in town?

I put my hand in my pocket. "What brings Waldo to town?"

He and Dudley exchanged glances but said

nothing. Well, this was a nice social event. Finally, Dudley evoked his southern charm.

"Gawth, you siddown for a minute. You want something to drink? A pop or somethin'?"

I thought about it and decided a beer—even at that early hour—was required to help navigate this situation. Dudley brought me one, some kind of rare microbrew. Tasted faintly of pumpkins. Why do some brewers have this compulsion to make beer taste like food?

"So stop stalling, Dudley. You guys clearly have something you want to discuss."

Dudley eased back into his chair with a creak, sighing and glancing once again at Waldo.

"Gawth, what happened up theyah in Maine?'

"You know, like I told you on the phone. These idiots, these carnies, went nuts double-crossing and then killing one another as they tried to sell the white crow. Angie and I got caught up in the middle."

"Kinda skimpy on detail, ain't it?"

"That's the short version, and to be honest, I'd rather not talk about it. Scared the bejesus outta me, if you must know."

"Mm hmm." Dudley shifted in his chair and avoided my eyes.

"Was he there?" Waldo boomed, clutching his lunch sack.

I was getting weary of this guy Waldo's eccentricities. I like strange people, as a rule. But I have a limit. I didn't even look at him. "Who?"

"You know who." Boris Karloff would have been proud, and I was about to say so.

"Flip, the Penguin Boy," Dudley said softly.

You could have shaken my blood with ice, added a dash of vermouth, and poured it in a chilled martini glass over an olive—and it would have been hot by comparison to what was coursing through my heart.

"I don't want to talk about it," I growled, slugging back some pumpkin beer. "Yes, you obviously know he was there. So what about it?"

Waldo was suddenly standing directly over me. He hissed, "Did he get it?"

I jumped to my feet, finger inches from his beak. "Back off, Waldo! That's it, Dudley, I'm outta here." I began packing up Reggie.

Waldo held out his lunch sack, slipped one bony hand in slowly. It didn't contain a ham sandwich after all. He held up what looked like a doggie's squeaky toy, a silly rubber penguin with the words *Flip the Penguin Boy* printed sloppily on its white belly.

I recoiled. "What the hell is that?"

His eyes bored into mine, and he gave the toy two squeezes. It squeaked, twice, like a mouse with whooping cough.

Squeak-hee, squeak-hee.

Believe it or not, this was scaring me. I didn't let on.

"Dudley, this guy is insane."

Waldo squeaked the toy again. "This is the only thing Flip fears."

"A doggie toy . . . This giant freak, this monster, this gorgon is afraid of that little rubber penguin?"

"Take it," Waldo commanded. "It may save your life."

Dudley interjected, thank God.

"Waldo was sent that from an elderly blockhead named Fuzzy in Gibtown, Florida. That's the town to which most freaks retire."

"A blockhead?" I winced. "Named Fuzzy?"

"He drives nails up his nose. Or used to."

"Oh, well, then . . . if it's from Fuzzy the blockhead in Freaksville, Florida, how could I possibly question the power of a kryptonite doggie toy from such a reliable source?"

Waldo was still right in front of me, the stupid rubber penguin held out like he was offering me a silver bullet to dispatch the Wolfman.

Dudley continued: "Apparently, these squeaky penguins were sold wherever Flip appeared, and he hated them. When he was a small child in the sideshow, gawkers use to hold out the toys and squeak them at him to try to make him move, to flap his flippers. He hated those squeaky toys and was traumatized by them. To this day, so they say, he's deathly afraid of squeaky toys. This one in particular."

"Oh, so now I'm Buffy the Vampire Slayer?" I was fuming at the absurdity. "And instead of a nice sharp stick, a mallet, and a silver cross, I get to slay my monster with a squeaky doggie toy. Terrific."

Dudley cleared his throat. "Waldo, please leave us alone for a spell."

I heard Waldo make giant strides to the door, open it, and stomp down the steps. He gave the penguin a few squeaks along the way, probably just to piss me off.

"I don't like that guy." I pointed at Dudley. "He can be weird if he wants, but he has to be civil or I'll clock him one, so help me. I've had about all I'm going to take. From anybody!"

That's when Dudley put a hand on my shoulder. Took a second to register the import of that. I stopped fastening the cooler with the bungee cords and looked up at him.

"Gawth, let me tell you a story. It's one you need to hear."

He retook his seat and I took mine, still astounded that he'd touched me.

"This ain't somethin' that's easy to tell. Outlandish as it is, it's what Waldo tells me he got through his connections. Flip the Penguin Boy isn't like the rest of us."

I rolled my eyes. "You don't say?"

"What I meant was, beyond his obvious congenital disorders, he has certain talents that set him apart."

"I know." I closed my eyes, trying not to visualize it.

"You saw him do it?"

"Yes. He sang just like Belle Beverly."

"Belle Beverly?"

"Yep."

"Remarkable." Dudley looked perplexed. "But that's not the talent I was referring to. Supposedly, Flip has psychokinetic powers."

I made a face. "Waldo has been filling you with a load of bunk."

"Could be." Dudley nodded. "But why would he come all the way here with the rubber penguin to do so?"

"How did he know about my run-in with Flip, anyway? And even if Flip is psychokinetic, what's he care?"

"Let us see if we can get to the bottom of that as well. Waldo hears things; he has connections throughout the carnival and sideshow community. Apparently, within that community, it has been widely held that Flip had real powers. Not hokum. As a community, they became wary of him. They honor and revere humbuggery—but fear the genuine. Flip became marginalized. But the sideshow pygmies stayed with him. They revered his mojo."

"Now, when you say powers, what do you mean? Bending spoons? Moving a marble across a floor by sheer will?"

Dudley looked thoughtful. "He was most noted for an uncanny ability to throw his voice, sometimes over distances that appeared to defy physics as we understand them."

I reflected on my sideshow visit, how the little

girl's voice came from the trailer. But then Flip was at the top of the hill before me, with a boulder. And, of course, he had Tex convinced he was on the other side of the door when he was actually behind the curtain.

Dudley continued: "What other powers he had I'm not entirely sure. Now, I know what you're thinking. These carnies are just flying off the handle. Superstitious people. But they are also dyed-in-the-wool skeptics. But all this is beside the point."

"Fine." I really didn't want to continue. "So, please get to the point."

"Did you ever stop to wonder how and why he was mixed up in this caper? This Big Foot gaff stunt?"

I shrugged. "I assumed even penguin boys are susceptible to avarice."

"Mm hmm. Could be. But what's got Waldo and some others worried is that he was there for an entirely different purpose."

I rolled my hand in the air. "Dudley, please, just tell me."

"He was there for the kving-kie."

"Yeah, I know." I shuddered. "He said that. But there was no wild cow around. I certainly didn't have one and no idea why he thought I would have it."

Dudley's eyes twinkled. "You know much about kving-kie?"

"Just that it's an extinct—or mythical—wild cow from Southeast Asia. That there are no preserved remains, no taxonomy."

"Mm hmm. Well, there's a little more to it. This diminutive wild cow had horns. Horns that supposedly empowered the possessor with strong psychokinetic powers. Ancient Asian armies and warriors used to take them into battle, as the story goes. They were so prized that the animal became scarce and then extinct. The horns slowly dwindled in the melee of war until all had been trampled into battlefields. There were none left. Supposedly."

I stood, frustrated. "Dudley, don't you see that this guy Waldo is a kook and this is a load of crap?"

"Did you have a horn?"

"No. All I had was the crow."

"Could it have been inside the crow?"

I shook my head. "No way, it was mostly destroyed by that point. Look, if Flip is truly telekinetic, or psychokinetic—"

"Same thing."

"Fine. Then what did he need with the horn?"

"It's widely believed that those with telekinetic powers are drawn to other people and objects with the same power. Even over great distances. The power can be multiplied. He sensed the kving-kie when Partridge brought it back from Korea, and he used those other carnies to get at it. To get into Partridge's house."

"He could just as well have read about it in the papers. It was widely published that Partridge was after the kving-kie."

"Point taken."

"And what would be the purpose of having telekinetic powers, anyway?" I flapped my arms. "So you don't have to get up and get a cup of coffee? Just have it pour itself and float over to you?"

Dudley looked at the floor. "The power is consuming; it promotes megalomania. You can only imagine how a severely deformed person might like the upper hand over 'normal' people. Instead of beneath, he's now above."

A sardonic smile flashed across my face. "Upper flipper, in his case."

Dudley just looked at the floor and sucked his cheek.

"Look, none of this matters." I was pacing now. "He's dead, okay? He fell out a window."

"Hmm."

I stopped. "What's that supposed to mean?"

"Hmm means *hmm.*"

"Not when you say it like that, it doesn't." I pointed at him. "He is dead, isn't he? I mean, he must be. He fell over a hundred feet into the Maine surf. Rocks, crashing waves. You know something, don't you?"

"They didn't find the body, did they?"

I sat back down with a groan. "No, they didn't find the body."

"Look, Gawth, what Waldo wants to know is that Flip did not get the kving-kie. I don't know anything about whether Flip is alive or dead. But if Waldo is concerned, that means Waldo thinks Flip is still alive. He might be in a position to know."

"I know, he's got his ear to the ground in Gibsville."

"Gibtown."

· "Whatever. But that could all be rumor. What's Waldo's stake in this, anyway?"

"He considers himself more or less at the top of the sideshow hierarchy. Believe it or not, he sees himself as the nexus between the show-people world and the 'normal' world. An interlocutor. The show people fear something bad will happen if Flip gets hold of the kving-kie. They are concerned enough that Waldo is investigating the matter on their behalf."

"I'm telling you, nobody could survive that fall. Even the Penguin Boy."

"Unless . . . unless he was able to somehow change the course of his fall . . ."

"Sure, the Flying Nun effect, with his flippers." I waved my arms in the air for comic relief but got none. My gut was in a knot. "I know what you're suggesting, Dudley, and it's utter nonsense."

"Who has the crow now?"

"New York State Department of Environmental Conservation. An agent named Renard is having it tested."

"Well, it's good, then, that you don't have it."

"Believe me, if I did, I'd throw it right into the river."

Dudley gave me a level look. "Did . . . did the crow impart any special . . . feelings? When you held it, I mean."

He saw me turn a shade whiter, and leaned back. "You want to tell me about it?"

"No, I don't. I was just scared out of my wits, that's all there was to it."

"Hmm."

"Don't start with that, Dudley!" I was shouting now.

"I'm sorry, it's merely an affectation, I assure you. Gawth, please sit." He gave me a curious look. "I daresay you're getting overly stimulated."

Now I felt he was patronizing me.

"That tears it." I grabbed the hand truck and wheeled it to the door. "Reggie and I are outta here."

He came to the door of the garret and watched me go without another word.

Outside, it was still a gorgeous, sunny day.

Inside, the storm clouds were gathering.

Chapter 22

What to do? Well, you know the mood I was in. PO'd, to put it mildly. I was tired of being pushed around, emotionally or otherwise. And I didn't have to take it from my friends or from oddballs like Waldo. I wanted my life back. Nice, predictable, day-to-day. I didn't want to hear or think about any psychokinetic freaks. I was back home, in New York City. Safe. Safe.

Like many a distressed male of the species, there was the notion that I should go to the corner bar and get seriously hammered. That's not something I do, mainly because I don't particularly like getting more than a three-drink buzz. Not that I didn't back when, college days and all that. The reasons are myriad, but among the demons beyond four drinks are a) drink five, b) drink six, c) confessional impulses, d) orneriness, e) hypersentimentality, f) hangovers. Last time I got seriously drunk was over ten years earlier, on my birthday, and in a pique of amorous devotion to Angie, I started to carve her name into my arm with the end of a comb. You can still faintly see the A on my right forearm.

Drinking was the wrong thing to do. Angie was upset, and I wasn't entirely sure it wasn't somehow my fault. I was soon to make a decision about the job that I would regret. No matter which direction I went on that one, I was terrified, both of my dreams and the possibility that Flip was out there somewhere. Jim Kim, he was out there too. My friend Dudley—even he was dragging me back into this. But perhaps even more disturbing was that there was something else out there, something that was pulling me back into the sinister cauldron of fire, flaming heads of taxidermy laughing. As I walked block by block toward home, looking for strength and determination around each corner, I only found self-pity lurking.

I slapped myself and gritted my teeth. What I needed to do was get hold of myself. Work—that's what I needed. Back to work, with lotsa coffee. Make some calls, rustle up some sales, some rentals. That would give me direction, the kind of purpose and escape that comes with the work-a-day whirl.

That's when a gray Crown Victoria screeched to a halt next to me. It was Walker. He got out of the car, face red and bloated like a giant tomato.

"Look, Walker, you had no right to handcuff me—"

He shoved me up against a shop window and it came seriously close to shattering.

"That's it, Carson. You are going down. You hear me? DOWN. Nobody does that to me."

"So you're going to arrest me? What charge?"

"Arrest?" He snorted, like a buffalo about to charge. "We're way beyond that now."

I thought his bloodshot eyes would burst, and for a moment I thought seriously about kicking him in the shin before he gave me a wallop. But that would have been the excuse he needed to arrest me and then probably have me "fall down the stairs, accidental-like" at the precinct. Psycho. Yet another one.

So I did nothing, just stared right back at him, and when he realized I wasn't going to move or do anything, he got back into his car and roared off.

An hour later I was under a full head of steam. At a place called Tiki Bob's Zombie Hut.

There'd been a small revival of tiki bars in New York—quaffing umbrella drinks from coconut shells under a thatched roof amid porcelain idols and blowfish lamps was on the upswing. Tiki Bob's on Eighth Avenue fit the basic kitschy Trader Vic's mold, replete with low blue and orange lighting, a loop tape playing waves, and lots of potted palms.

The late-lunch crowd was dispersing when I got there and ordered my first Suffering Bastard. Sure, I could have had a Mai Tai, Fog Cutter, Navy Grog, or Bob's signature Zombie, but an SB fit my mood and improved it almost immediately. To effect that change so quickly . . . well, it was plain that drinking was the thing to do. My mood needed a lot of improving.

I had myself a swell little pupu platter for lunch. For the uninitiated, these are served in large, compartmentalized wooden bowls with a small cauldron in the center that burns a pink, flammable jelly. In the compartments are savory appetizers such as chicken wings, teriyaki sticks, roast pork ribs, batter-dipped shrimp, and dumplings. Just the thing for someone downing a continuing succession of SBs.

The idea is that you warm up the treats over the cauldron. Maybe it's just me, but I prefer my food sans the piquant *je ne sais quoi* of Sterno. You never know with flammables—ingesting pink jelly-infused food and drinking Suffering Bastards could result in spontaneous gastric combustion. As if SBs weren't combustible enough. I kept my glass a safe distance from the pupu platter's cauldron.

There was only the barmaid Tommy and me and an old man with a magnifying glass and a racing form way down at the end. But I was fine being alone with strangers who knew nothing of Partridge, nothing of white crows, nothing of police, DAs, Bret Fletcher, Walker, Waldo, and all the rest. And Tommy is a pro behind the bar. A pal. Angie and I come in there often enough that she knows us. And she also knows when a guy needs a snootful, whatever the reason. And what's wrong with that, for Pete's sake? You know, you get all worked up about a burning mansion and these crazies . . . but that's over. Life is too short to spend worrying all the time—and Tommy agrees.

So when Jim Kim sat down next to me, I laughed. SB came up my nose, which was sure to stem any possible sinus infections for a while.

"Tommy, an SB for my friend," I said, wiping my nose with my sleeve.

Kim looked around warily. "So good to see you, Garth. Miss? I'd just like a light beer."

"Oh no you don't." I gripped his forearm. "I'm buying, and you'll have a Suffering Bastard. When was the last time you had an SB? They're . . . well, they're fantabulous is what they are."

Kim smiled politely. "Garth, we need to talk."

"Nooo. I knew you'd come and want to talk. Sooner or later. Sooner suits me fine. And I knew . . . I knew you'd want to talk about what *you* want to talk about. Can't we, for a change, talk about what I want to talk about?"

Kim looked around again, probably thinking he'd made a mistake in trying to talk to me while I was indulging at Tiki Bob's Zombie Hut. But he resigned himself and patiently leaned an elbow on the bar, his attention focused squarely on me.

"Okay, Garth, what do you want to talk about?"

"Not so fast! Not so fast!" Tommy set an SB in front of him and walked off. "First, we have to toast."

Kim sniffed suspiciously at his drink. "To what?"

"To Don Ho!"

"Don Ho?"

I leaned back.

"You know, 'Tiny Bubbles'? Reggie here wants to toast to Don Ho."

Reggie was propped up on the stool next to me, his head unwrapped, a lei around his neck and a cocktail umbrella in his beak. An SB was parked in front of him. Condensation beaded all over his feathers as he began to defrost. His feet were still wearing their bubble-wrap booties.

Kim actually betrayed a look of dismay, and I couldn't have been happier. Finally, I had him at some kind of disadvantage. Had someone—*anyone*—else at a disadvantage. And his unctuous fear-mongering was useless on me in my inebriated glow.

But he recovered quickly, too soon for my taste. Leaning in, he clinked his tiki mug with Reggie's and then mine.

"To Mr. Ho," he said, raising his glass.

"To 'Tiny Bubbles'!" I raised my glass and slurped.

"Now can we talk about what I want to talk about?"

"Oh no." I waved a finger. "When you buy the drink, then you get to talk."

He motioned to Tommy, but I held up my hand. "Doesn't work like that. Can't order . . . order another round until you finish yours. C'mon, loosen up, Jimmy."

Kim squinted with forbearance, but he did as instructed, while I talked.

"You know, Jimmy, it's a funny ol' world. Everybody runnin' around . . . and for what? Life's too short. You know what I mean?"

"I know exactly what you mean." He nodded. "And sometimes, lives get shorter unexpectedly."

"S'what I mean." I thumped the bar. "Get hit by a bus, and where are you? Right, Reggie?" I clinked glasses with the penguin. "Reggie here? Was in the beak of health. I mean *peak*. But beak works too, doesn't it? Then one day . . . one day Reggie—by accident, mind you—swallows a pen." I thumped the bar again. "Now look at him. Dead as an igloo. Never knew what hit him."

"A lesson for us all." Kim drained his glass and waved Tommy over.

Kim clinked a fresh glass with Reggie and then with me. "To Scott of the Antarctic!"

I raised my glass. "To Scott of the Attic! Hey, lookit this . . ."

I pulled out my wallet and peered into it with one eye. I removed a folded piece of paper and handed it to him. "Read that."

His eyes fluttered. *"WANT MY WHITE CROW BACK . . ."*

"Nah, not that one, *the other one.*"

Kim cleared his throat. *"MOOSE HEAD FOR SALE: MUST GO. YOU HAUL. NORTHEAST U.S."*

"You know what that is?"

He waited.

"That, m'friend, is a fifty-dollar moose head. I always wanted a fifty-dollar moose head, a moose head that somebody just wanted to get rid of. Y'understand? What I'm sayin' is that me, a dealer, waits his whole life for something like this to come along. . . ."

"It doesn't say it's fifty dollars." He handed the paper back.

"Ah, but I called. She said it's fifty dollars."

"So did you buy it?"

"That's the rub, Jimmy. I spoke with her twice, and she doesn't know where she lives. You think I'm kidding? Here . . ." I handed the paper back. "You call her. This woman doesn't know where she lives, so even though she wants to sell me a moose head for fifty dollars, she can't because I can't find her to take it off her hands. You see where I'm going with this?"

Tommy slid two more SBs in front of us and put a hand on my forearm. "Last one, Garth. Your pal Reggie is already cut off, and I gotta send you home while you can still stand."

I frowned, briefly, but was beyond being perturbed by anything.

"So you see where I'm going with this?"

Kim just looked at me in his mildly interested, insouciant way.

"Okay, lemme spell it out. I'm this close . . ." I held up my thumb and forefinger, like I was holding an invisible pebble. "Comes around only once inna lifetime, a fifty-dollar moose head. It's an opportunity, y'see? Like a job offer. Either you take it or you don't, but it won't be back again."

"So, I guess it's my turn?"

I shrugged. "Do your worst, Jimmy."

"Did you know Agent Renard is missing?"

I shrugged.

"He took the remnants of the crow and vanished."

I shrugged.

"You now know what this was all about, don't you, Garth?"

I shrugged.

"Not exactly fair, is it? When it was your turn to talk, we talked. Now that it's my turn, you won't talk."

"Look, Jimmy." I put my arm around his shoulder. "I have nothing left to say about any of that. It's out of my hands, see?"

"I know you *wish* that were so. But it doesn't *make* it so. You used the power of the kving-kie. That means you can locate it. You have a connection."

I sort of burped and laughed at the same time. "You guys are nuts, you know that? I never saw the magic cow, I never saw the magic cow's horn—"

"You used your mind to push Flip out the window."

"Ha."

"Ha?"

"S'what I said: *ha*. He was blown out. Boom, swish, plop! Snap, crackle, pop!"

"Now let me show *you* something." Kim pulled a piece of folded paper from his pocket and handed it to me. A sense of déjà vu rippled through the lipid pool of SBs in my brain as I unfolded the paper and saw a photocopy of an old Korean manuscript. In the center of the Korean writing was a picture of what looked like a stick, pointed at one end, slightly corkscrewed. Even in that state I recognized it. This was the same thing Smiler had shown me two years before. Even in that state, I realized this probably meant Kim worked for Smiler.

I handed it back to him.

"That's a gallbladder."

"It's a horn." He handed it back to me, and I squinted at the illustration.

"Okay, it's a horn." I shrugged for about the hundredth time.

"A kving-kie horn."

"A cow horn? It's all bumpy an' irregular, like a friggin' stick."

"Exactly." Kim took the page back again, patting me on the shoulder. "Look, Garth, I have to run. You think about what we talked about, okay? I'll be in touch." He stood and turned to go.

Then Kim paused and leaned in to the penguin.

"Nice to meet you, Reggie. I like your shoes."

He left.

I couldn't have been there much longer. But I'm not entirely sure.

arth!"

Was I back on Partridge's stoop?

"Garth!"

Yep, that was Angie's voice, all right, and my head hurt, and my mouth was dry as a mummy's, and I was being tugged.

She shook me and my eyes creaked open. I was home, in bed. I knew because I could see the buffalo head on the right, the sailfish tail to the left, and the bearded gnu chin directly overhead. Angie was all the way at the end of the bed, and she was pulling on my feet, doing her darnedest to pull me out of bed. Her progress in this effort had my calves and knees off, but the rest of me was still nailed to the sheets.

"Sit up. We need to talk."

The glare of the sun from the small, grimy bedroom window stung my eyes. That's right, I'd been at Tiki Bob's. And now? I was in dutch.

Confront a man with a knife-wielding freak singing Belle Beverly in a room full of flaming taxidermy, and still his worst fear is to hear his mate utter the words: *We have to talk.* Times two if you're hung over. Times three if you don't remember coming home.

I sat up, my feet dropping to the floor at the end of the bed. My eye caught the time: 12:01 P.M. I was still wearing my shirt, but my pants were slumped in the corner.

She looked me over, hands on her hips. The body language of disappointment.

But in these chilling confrontations—which are few and far between—I've found contrition a poor overcoat. I had nothing to be ashamed of. I'm allowed to feel sorry for myself every blue moon. It was unavoidable. Kismet, thy name is SB.

So I shrugged on the overcoat of unrepentant and glib perspicacity.

I expected her to say something like: *What the hell is wrong with you? You come home drunk with a half-dressed penguin? Is that any way to act?*

I'd bet a million dollars that no man has ever been lambasted for coming home with a half-dressed penguin. But I'm a special case.

And I'd say something like: *There's nothing wrong with me that some aspirin, some coffee, and a half gallon of water won't cure. As to the penguin and his state of undress, he's an adult. And this is no act. I was depressed and I got drunk, an age-old phenomenon that I reserve the right to practice, from time to time, when under extraordinary strain.*

But Angie didn't say what I thought she would.

"What's this about you being offered a job?"

My eyes went from slits to saucers.

My mouth moved, and when it failed to make any intelligible sound, my hand came up and started waving the air in a way to suggest the glib perspicacity I was unable to deliver.

There was a cup of coffee on the dresser, and she handed it to me, then put her hands back on her hips. I drank and tried to collect my thoughts.

Hers were already collected.

"Look, Garth, I know we've been through a lot this week, but for God's sake, did you ever think I might like to get a little hammered myself now and again?"

I blinked, still sipping, wondering where this was going. I'd have curled up inside that cup if I could.

"I mean, you might have called me from Tiki Bob's, and I'd have come down. Instead, I'm sitting here staring at the TV wishing I was somewhere having a drink. Several, in fact. Instead, you're drinking with a frozen penguin. Why didn't you call me? I'd have called you if I was alone drinking."

I shrugged, still hiding in the mug of coffee. Man, was she hard to predict sometimes.

"And if it isn't enough that you're getting looped with a dead penguin instead of me, I answer the phone yesterday afternoon and it's some guy from

Fish and Wildlife wanting an answer from you about the job offer. What job offer? Wouldn't I discuss that with you? Am I your partner or what?"

I lowered the mug and put it on the floor. While I'd been trying to work angles on what she was saying and what I should say, my heart suddenly shoved my brain aside and spoke up.

"You're the best thing that ever happened to me, Angie, and I love you more than anything, even my own life."

I paused. Men are virtually incapable of baring their feelings while looking someone in the eye, so I cast mine to the floor.

"And that's the problem. I sometimes think I'm *not* the best thing that ever happened to you. Not that you don't love me, and not that you don't think, maybe, that I'm the best thing that ever happened to you. But I know I'm not all I should be. For you. I love you so much that I'd rather see you happier, more successful, with someone else than with"—I waved my hand at the buffalo to my right—"a taxidermy bum. I feel I've held you back from being the art jeweler you always wanted to be. Had I been more successful, a lawyer or doctor or something, you could have had the time and resources to say no to piecework and invest time and money in your own stuff."

I finally looked up at her. Now I remembered why men don't look at women while baring their feelings. The waterworks were in progress, tears streaming down her cheeks. When I see that, my heart bottoms out and I want to cry. I suspect many women find crying can be a welcome release. For most men it's an excruciating, gut-wrenching indulgence. Once I start, it takes days for me to recover.

I looked away, lockjaw of emotion strangling my words.

"I need to take that job. For you. So I can hold on to you. Because I'm terrified that one day you'll wake up and see what I see. That you deserve better."

"Ding bust!" She grabbed me by my shirtfront, and when I looked up, my temples and tear ducts throbbing, I thought she was going to belt me one. She doesn't say *ding bust* unless she's really mad.

"Don't you *dare* take that job, Garth Carson. This is the man I love, taxidermy and all, not some state functionary. Not some doctor or lawyer. You didn't just choose me, *I chose you*, just the way you are, and anything more or less isn't what I signed on for. I'm the only one responsible for my career, the only one responsible for whether I'm successful or not. You got all that?"

I tried to say something, but didn't. She continued.

"My career is my doing." She wiped tears from her eyes. "And as it so happens, Peter Van Putin called. I got the job doing his piecework. Without you being a doctor or lawyer."

I put my hand on hers and pulled her to me.

That was one strong, long hug. It was the kind of hug where two people love each other so much that, if it's strong and long enough, the embrace might actually meld them into one being, one heart, one love. Be a cynic if you like, but there are such things as soul mates.

Well, it was going to take days for me to recover. So be it.

An hour later, we were eating cheeseburgers. Not just any cheeseburgers. These were from a place called Houston Smith, over on Eighth Avenue, and their burgers make Mickey D's look like they came from a rendering plant. And like many self-indulgent New Yorkers on a Saturday morning, we ordered in. New Yorkers may act elitist sometimes, but never so much as when they glory in the variety of take-out menus at their disposal. Knowing that ninety percent of the U.S. is relegated to emollient, cheese-heavy take-out pizza fills us with quiet glee. It's the little things that make life worth living.

And finding myself in bed after noon with Angie, eating Houston Smith cheeseburgers and fries with chipotle mayo, is one of those little things.

As we ate, I filled her in on all the latest developments, and when I finished, she had a finger to the curl of her lips, her gaze distant. This was the posture she assumed while doing crosswords or watching quiz shows. Her brain was calculating.

"The horn of a kving-kie . . ." she muttered. "Hokey smoke!"

I looked up from my burger, mostly in wonder at the vast range of her dopey expletives. Her eyes were wide, and I thought she might be choking. But I heard her swallow. Hard.

"Garth! You did have the kving-kie in your hand when the windows exploded!"

"I was holding the crow . . ."

She tossed her burger down and we locked eyes.

"The stick."

"The stick?"

"The branch, the stick the crow was standing on. That was the horn."

I blinked, brow furrowed.

"Remember? When we went to Remington, to the auction house, the log said it was a white crow on a rock in a bell jar. Partridge buys the crow, replaces the rock with a stick."

I set my burger down and heard myself swallow. Hard.

"Why would he do that?"

"To hide it. He knew it was valuable, and he hid it somewhere nobody would think to look for it. You know the picture Jim Kim showed you, of the horn, and you said it looked like a stick, right?"

"Sort of. But when I first saw that picture, years ago, I thought it was an illustration of a gallbladder or something. So when Kim showed it to me . . . of course. How could I have been so stupid? The crow was holding the horn, which just looked like a stick."

"Garth? Is it possible you really did make those windows explode?"

I suddenly felt very warm. "I don't know. I mean, there was so much going on, what with the fire and that horrendous freak coming at me."

"Is there something that happened that was, you know, strange? I mean, stranger than Belle Beverly."

I found myself standing. "Well, as I said, there was a lot going on. But . . . there was a moment where I thought I was dead, because I could look down and see me and Flip, him doing that little dance in front of me with the knife."

She gasped. "An out-of-body experience."

"I dunno about that."

"And that's when the windows exploded?"

I nodded. "And I saw Flip go out the window while I watched myself just stand there, smoke and ashes flying all around me."

"What about what Dudley said?" She had her finger back to her lips. "And about what Jim Kim said. Do you feel any connection with the horn?"

My appetite was suddenly shot. "Not unless that connection feels like fear."

"Do you get any feeling about where the horn is now?"

"And if I did?"

She looked up at me, and then away, adjusting her robe.

"I'm sorry. You're right. We've had enough trouble for a while."

"A long while, I hope." I sat on the bed, my back to her. Her hand gripped my shoulder.

"Let's forget about it. The horn is someone else's problem now."

"Renard's problem."

Chapter 24

The night I got in from my bender at Tiki Bob's, there was a message on my machine from Rodney. For some strange reason I'd completely forgotten about this. Once Angie and I finally got out of bed, I noticed that there was an unerased message on my machine, and gave a listen.

He was in town, which meant only one thing: He wanted to collect on the Chinese meal and beer I'd promised. So I gave him a ring.

"Tonight?" I half-moaned. The SBs were still resonating throughout my body, and I didn't really feel like drinking beer. With or without a penguin.

"Has t'be. I just ran some sea chests down an' go back tomorrow. You have other plans, do you?"

"No, I just—"

"Not gonna welsh on me, are you, Garth?" He chuckled, knowing he had me.

"I'm a man of my word, Rodney," I sighed, but tried to sound enthusiastic.

And so it was I met him down in Chinatown at the Golden Frog, two six-packs under my arm. This was a ritual between me and Rodney. Whenever he ran his circuit of Manhattan antiques stores, he never failed to give me a ring for a Chinatown repast. Especially when I owed him a free dinner. Especially when the beer was included.

Like most New Yorkers, I have a couple shabby little Chinese greasy spoons I like to think have the world's best Szechuan. One of those drab, BYO places Asians actually go to. That's not to say they don't have their charms. They typically have various Chinese prints on the beige walls, some paper lanterns hanging from the fluorescent lighting on the ceiling, and a giant algae-filled aquarium full of carp in the front window. These are eating carp, so when you order *live carp* from the menu, it's one of these poor devils you get to choose from. Chopsticks are an automatic—you have to ask for a fork and then hope they can find it.

Chinese food in Chinatown is a completely different cuisine from the usual grist of restaurants in other parts of town: moo goo gai pan, General Tsao's chicken, kow pung beef, pork fried rice, etc. The non-Chinatown joints have essentially sold out to American tastes. I mean, what is it with broccoli in almost everything? And yet in Chinatown, I'm not sure they even know what broccoli is.

Anyway, on this night I chose the Golden Frog. It's not my favorite, but it boasts a menu with some of the most original, hideous-sounding treats you can imagine. *Cold jelly with spicy sauce. Duck blood and intestine in sour cabbage. Spicy duck tongue with green sauce. Sautéed stinky to-fu*—no lie. *Double-cooked lamb stomach in ma-la sauce. Shrimps and pork groin. Spicy duck feet with mustard.* Mind you, I don't order any of those things. I don't go to the Grand Canyon either—but it's reassuring to know it's there if I ever want to go. My tastes are a tad more pedestrian, like shredded beef with dry bean curd, rabbit tenders in red chili sauce, diced duck with basil and green pepper, Chinese string bean with minced pork.

This hole-in-the-wall is on Division Street, just off Kimlau Square, and that's where I found Rodney just around dusk. We were soon settled into a booth with some hot and sour soup spicy enough to etch glass. The beer was slow going for me; not so for Rodney. Funny, as much beer as he drinks—which he does almost constantly—I don't think I've ever seen him drunk. Then again, I've probably never seen him with a 0.0% blood-alcohol level, so I have no basis for comparison.

He naturally wanted to be updated on all the latest with the white crow. I gave him the quick version, concluding with the notion that the stick the crow had been mounted on was actually a horn. I did not touch on any of the psychokinetic stuff, at least not from my personal experience. What was the point? Besides, the very thought of it turned my stomach.

"Bloody 'ell, Garth. You do get yourself into int'restin' situations, don't you?"

"Interesting? Not interesting when Angie's neck is on the line."

"I mean, first you had that thing a couple years back. That shoot-out over bear gallbladders. Now this."

My mind flashed to Smiler handing me the photocopy, and then to the same one Jim Kim had shown me. I forced it from my mind.

"Which reminds me of the one about the hunter and the bear. This hunter goes into the woods, finds this bear, see? The bear puts up his paws, the hunter takes aim and pulls the trigger. But the gun misfires, so the bear swats the gun to the ground and says . . ." The rest of the three encounters between the hunter and the bear were licentious in the extreme, enough so to make a grizzly blush. Good thing the other patrons probably didn't speak much English. It ended with the bear saying, "You don't come out here to hunt, do you?"

Rodney loosed his cannonade of laughter, but stopped abruptly. "Maybe, Garth, you don't do this for the taxidermy. You have a knack for scrapes."

"I know. Believe me, if I could possibly avoid this sort of thing . . . but you just don't see it coming. C'mon—this could happen to you. You buy a sea chest, and there's something hidden in it, and people come looking for it, and—"

He was wagging his head, polishing off his third beer.

"Somehow I don't think so, Garth. Luck runs different ways for different blokes. Mine doesn't run that way. Yours obviously does."

"Ah, that's right, you and luck. I'd almost forgotten about your luck theories."

"You think it's all probability, then? That it's all random?"

"No." I sipped my beer. "We make choices. From the choices we make, there are consequences and happenstance associated with it. I come to an intersection. I make a right turn, and I get into an accident with an old lady in a Studebaker. I make left turn, and there's no old lady in a Studebaker so there's no accident."

"Aha, yes, but what if the old lady made a different turn that resulted in her being beyond the left turn?"

"Then if I made the right, no problem."

"But don't you see? What about when you both happen to make the decision to end up at the same place and have that accident?"

"Now, that's random."

"Is it?"

This was beginning to make me uncomfortable. We were straying toward more spooky stuff, the stuff of which wild bovid horns are made.

"Look, you're depressing me. If you're right, I'm

in deep shinola, because it means things will keep happening to me. Right?"

He nodded.

"If I believed that, I'd end up in a mental institution." I shook my head. "So if you don't mind, I'd very much like to hear everything that's going on in your life, where luck doesn't run the way it does in mine."

He let the luck topic go.

For the next hour, he regaled me with the intricacies of the antique sleigh and wagon market. Somehow he managed to quaff seven beers to my three, all the while pontificating seamlessly on troikas, felloes, whiffletrees, and spokeshaves. Slurping through the soup, we shoveled dumplings, rabbit tenders, sizzling war bar, and a happy family. In the end, we found ourselves like a couple of happy, teetering gourds.

"Bloody 'ell, Garth, what I wouldn't do for vittles like that in the North Country." Rodney grinned, engulfing a fortune cookie. "I'd say this Golden Froggy is better than Wong's."

"I'd say. Um, Rodney, you didn't take out the fortune."

"Never brought me any luck readin' 'em, now, did they? So now I got a theory that if you don't read the fortunes, maybe they'll come true."

I knit my brow. "How would you know if it came true? I mean, if you don't read it . . ."

"That's the point, dear boy. When somethin' good 'appens, you chalk it up to the fortune cookie."

"You really enjoy deluding yourself, don't you, Rodney?" I snapped open my cookie, hoping it would say something innocuous like *Avoid gas-station bathrooms.*

"So whatsit say?" Rodney held out his hand, but I didn't offer the fortune. "You opened it, now you have to tell me what it says. That's the rules. If you eat it whole, you don't have to tell."

"It's stupid." I tossed it in front of him.

"Aha!" He squinted at the slip of paper, and read, *"Never trouble trouble until trouble troubles you."*

I slid out of the booth and staggered up to the cashier. In the time it took me to pay, Rodney opened and downed the last beer. His nine to my three. And he seemed no worse for wear.

Standing at the register, I was inserting a piece of bubblegum in my mouth when I happened to look out the front window at a limousine parked across the street.

I blinked hard and began choking on my gum.

Under the glow of a streetlamp, I clearly saw Agent Renard and an Asian man in a double-breasted suit emerge from a small office building. They ducked into a limousine, and a waitress started smacking me on the back.

"Awright, lad?" Rodney took over patting my back, and I pushed his arm away, gurgling and pointing. The limo zoomed off down the street and the pink gum shot from my mouth into the open register.

"It's Renard!" I barked, darting out into the street.

"Hey!" I heard Rodney holler. "Garth, what the 'ell are you doin', y'bloody fool!"

Here I was, running through the streets of Chinatown after the limo, my meal rolling around my gut like a water balloon.

Rodney had a very good question: What the bloody hell *was* I doing? Here I'd just gotten through saying that I didn't want any more trouble, ever. *But they had the horn, right there in that limo.* How did I know that? I just did. And for some reason, that was enough.

A glint of hope that I might catch up kept me in track-star mode. A red light at Bowery let me gain a few strides before the long black car turned right. I could hear Rodney calling after me as I avoided a near collision with a delivery bike, weaved around a knot of German tourists, and ducked right on Catherine Street. I thought I might just be able to cut the limo off before it could reach the Manhattan Bridge.

My thoughts flew by like cards in a shuffling deck. Who was Renard with? Where was he going? How would I catch him? Should I stop and make a phone call? To whom? Would the police help me? Would they believe me? Of course, the one card I don't remember pulling from the deck was the question of how I planned to stop the limo when I caught up with it.

Traffic was snarled at Canal Street, and the limo

was inching its way between a stalled cab and some construction barricades when I threw myself on its hood. All I could see of the limo's occupants was the driver, a guy decked out in black chauffeur duds, a big black mustache, and black wraparound sunglasses. He put the car in park and got slowly out of the limo the second before a loud buzz filled my head.

The chauffeur grabbed me by the collar and said, "Garth, what do you think you're doing? You're going to blow the whole thing. Garth? Garth?"

Headlights and neon blinked out. My eyes shut. I guess I fainted.

Never trouble trouble until trouble troubles you. I haven't opened a fortune cookie since.

Chapter 25

I awoke slowly, and I had to work at making my eyes open.

"This is actually rather opportune, don't you think?" It sounded like Agent Renard.

"I don't get you," a grumpy voice replied. "How can we know he won't bolt?"

"Mr. Park, I think he'll make the perfect go-between. If he runs, either we'll shoot him or they'll shoot him. He's expendable."

Mr. Park harrumphed. I could make out two blurs seated across from me, and I felt the scrunching of soft leather upholstery on my cheek. I was in the limo, and it was in motion. Had I been out moments or hours? The sense of lost time made me feel a little panicky, and I forced myself upright. My neck felt like a Slinky, and it took both hands to hold my head still.

"Honestly, Mr. Carson," Renard tsked. "Why do you insist on getting yourself killed? Why couldn't you have stayed home with your collection?"

I slumped to steady my head against the seat back, squinting my eyes into focus. Yup, I was in the limo, two goose-neck lamps illuminating my captors. Across from me: Renard in his trench coat and blue plaid porkpie with the red feather. His sleepy eyes considered me like I was a pesky alarm clock. And the pinstriped Asian? Pinky ring, gold cuff links, sideburns, a pompadour, and tinted, oversize black-framed glasses. You got it: Smiler, a.k.a. Mr. Park.

To my right and left were two Asian thugs in turtlenecks and dark blazers. They were big and fat, looked like identical twins, and I could feel their body heat radiating. So much for Sweater and Vest.

Tinted windows kept me from getting any clue as to where we were, though I could feel the limo rumbling over cobblestones. That meant we were probably still in the city, doubtless in one of the older parts of town. Great, like down by the river. I was mildly encouraged by the absence of any cement bags in the limo, though that talk of shooting somebody had me on alert.

"Now, you're going to be a good messenger, aren't you, Mr. Carson? We have a little job for you, and if you do it well, perhaps you'll survive."

I cleared my head. "Where's the horn?"

"Here." Renard held out a painted red box decorated in Chinese designs, the kind you get when you buy a jade curio in any of a gazillion dime stores throughout Chinatown. "But what do you want with it? Honestly, your predilection for getting in trouble astounds me."

"I . . . I don't want. I don't want anybody to have it," I heard myself say. I suddenly felt like an idiot. Here I was, deep in it again. For what?

Smiler did his best to pretend I wasn't there.

Renard graced me with a slim, patronizing grin.

"Let me guess. You felt the kving-kie was here, didn't you?"

"No."

"Please, Carson. You held the horn, you blew out those windows, you killed Flip. Hideous freak. At least *that* connection is broken."

"No, it wasn't me. That's not possible."

"Oh, but it is possible. Why on earth do you think everybody wants to get their hands on a tiny cow horn?"

He lifted the box, and I stared at it, eyes watering. He continued.

"The truth is, Mr. Carson, once you held and used the kving-kie—"

"Yeah, I know, I supposedly have a connection."

He nodded. "Why else did you throw yourself on the hood of the car? Hmm? And this is precisely why there are so few kving-kie left. Ancient Asians used them in battle, yes, but the power was corrupting, and they fought tirelessly among themselves just to possess the horn. And yet, one by one, the horns found their way to the ocean. All it takes to destroy the ridiculous horn and its power is to throw it in salt water. Rather fragile, all said and done."

"Were you there that night, at the mansion? Did you drag me out of that fire?"

"I'm sure I don't know what you mean. Had I known that deal was happening, I would have had the whole department come down on it. In the end, the result would have been the same. A broken bird clutching a stick in a plastic evidence bag, in my hands."

"And you and Smiler here"—I gestured at his companion, who frowned at his nickname—"how long have you been working together?"

"Not long. This was purely a crime of opportunity on my part. Who but a DEC agent such as myself knows how valuable a commodity this horn is, what the market will bear, and the right black-marketeers for this sort of thing?"

"Enough!" Park barked. "Tell him nothing more, Renard."

I didn't like his tone. Smiler already had me for dead.

Sitting there in the limo between the two Asian hoods, I rode on with just the sound of the rumbling cobblestones under me. I stared at the red Chinese box on Renard's lap, and in so doing somehow cleared my head of the cobwebs. Which got me to wonder why I'd passed out. Hell, just like Bret Fletcher passed out at Gunderson's.

That's right. I had my hand on the bell jar when Bret

*passed out. Did I make that happen? And did Renard
make me pass out in the same way?*

It was then that the limo came to a stop. The
driver came around to the back of the car and
opened the door for Smiler and Renard. Then the
two turtlenecks and I got out, more or less as one
unit. They now had matching silver automatics in
their hands. No mix-matching here. These two
were color-coordinated all the way.

It was night and we were by the river, just as I'd
feared. The Statue of Liberty was visible dead
ahead. I could see ferries crisscrossing the bay and
Manhattan twinkling off to the right. Warehouses
blocked my view, but I could hear a highway somewhere behind me. I was in Brooklyn, in a disused
port that's usually desolate at night.

But right before me, in front of a long wooden pier,
were the festive lights, whir, and fun hum of a traveling carnival. I'd seen them appear on Manhattan's
West Side before, near the Intrepid museum.
Brightly twirling rides, rattling spook houses, midway
games, funnel-cake stands, and the screams of spinning thrill-seekers. Then just as suddenly they pack
up and vanish, the litter of paper cotton-candy cones
and ride tickets the only evidence of their passing. But
tonight, crowds were streaming in and out of the carnival, and my companions kept their guns underneath
their jackets.

The chauffeur with the handlebar mustache was
standing nearby. I suddenly remembered that he
had said something to me just before I fainted. But

the spring in my brain's Victrola was wound down, and his voice played back like a bassoon in a tar pit. What was it he said? I scrutinized his sunglassed visage but got nothing for it.

The turtlenecks clasped hands on my shoulders and marched me in the wake of Renard and Smiler, who growled in a Far Eastern tongue to a third turtleneck, waiting at the entrance to the carnival.

We were quickly engulfed in the controlled mayhem, the surrounding gaiety oblivious to the squadron of thugs marching through their midst. The smell of popcorn and candy apples turned my stomach, the garish wail of piped-in calliope music from the carousel an irritating counterpoint to the laughter and shrieks. Of all these people, wasn't there someone, anyone to intervene? They were too busy having fun, toting gaudy plush toys, doing the ring toss, working the crane games, waiting in line for the Sky Diver. Heavily tattooed ride operators were too harassed processing customers, game operators too consumed with suckering the witless. Where in the heck were we going? For a jump in the Moon Bounce?

As I scanned my surroundings, I gratefully noted the lack of any sideshow attractions, Flip the Penguin Boy in particular.

At the far end of the carnival, backed up against the pier, was a spook house. It had a fake stone facade, like a castle, with the words CASTLE CREEP in Halloween orange blazoned across the top. The lights around the sign were dark. Loudspeakers that probably reverberated with eerie noises were silent. The ride's cars: idle. No carny was in attendance, and there was a yellow rope across the entrance, a sign hanging from it that read CLOSED FOR MAINTE-NANCE. THANK YOU!

The lead turtleneck lifted the rope and held it for the rest of us to pass under.

I never liked spook houses, and this one even less. They were always so lame. You get in a rickety car and half the time they get stuck, whereupon some smelly grease monkey with *Cooter* stitched on his coveralls has to come in and push your car back on the tracks. A light pops on, there's a raggedy statue of a werewolf. A strobe light flickers on a wall painted with goofy ghosts. Usually, one of the "boos" is a loud noise that's more annoying than anything else. Or maybe a burst of air that hits you right in the eyes. They tend to be musty and ill-maintained, and those sparks jumping from the track are the real scary part. At any moment you expect to get electrocuted, for real. And when finally you emerge, banging through the doors at the end, you say, "Is that it?" It is roughly equivalent to or-dering a specialty sandwich at a fast-food joint. What you unwrap is haphazard, undersize, and nothing like the picture up on the menu.

Would that I were a kid again and would come out merely disappointed. This time I feared I might come out dead.

The wiry chauffeur was walking close behind me. *That's right—he called me by name when I was on the limo hood.* I glanced back at him as I ducked under the rope, forming a mental picture of him. That's when it hit me: Pete Durban!

My brain bulged with the possible combinations of events that might unfold with Undercover Agent Peter Durban at my back. Perhaps this should have been reassuring. It wasn't. Not after what happened two years ago. Was he armed with cone snails?

We pushed through the doors, walking between the car tracks. I recognized that musty smell, that odor of ozone given off by sparks from the cars. There was a light at the far end, two men holding flashlights flanking one in the middle with a suitcase. As my eyes adjusted to the darkness, I could make out the oval of the track and the silhouette of four statues or "boos" at each corner. I couldn't make out what they were, but I really wasn't concerned about that. I was concerned about those three men.

I was thrust forward. Renard pressed the Chinese box into my left hand.

"I warn you, Mr. Carson, don't toy with us," Smiler hissed. "You don't know what you're dealing with, believe me." I glanced at Renard, who was sweating almost as much as I was.

"So it's a swap?" I looked back at Smiler. "The horn, for money?"

His answer wasn't one. "When he puts down the suitcase, hand him the box. Come back here with the suitcase. Renard will accompany you, to validate the transfer. And to keep an eye on you."

The box shook slightly in my trembling hand. I'd really put my foot in it this time.

"You forgot about the part where you let me go when I get back." What is it with the wisecracks just when I can least afford them?

Smiler unwrapped a piece of Fruit Stripe gum and started to chomp on it. "See you when you get back."

"Can I have a piece?"

Smiler frowned.

"A piece of gum." My mouth was filled with the sand of dread, and I was dying for some bubblegum. "I'm all out."

Smiler actually smiled, slowly unwrapping a plank of gum and placing it on my tongue. It was like he was giving me last rites. Sacrament of the Eucharist in the form of Fruit Stripe gum.

The turtlenecks gave me a shove, and I found myself walking toward the three men at the far side of the spook house, Renard just footsteps behind me. I assumed he must have a gun. Heck, everybody but me seemed to have one.

Buoy horns sounded in the distance, and I could hear the river lapping against the pier just behind the spook house.

I struggled with an internal dialogue, the clomp of my feet on the wood floor like a metronome counting down the seconds. Dead man walking.

Just do what they say, Garth, and this'll all be over, for good. Yeah, over for good is right. They can't let you

live once you've witnessed this crime. How else to keep
you from talking?

Clomp, clomp, clomp . . . I passed a witch on my
right, stock still in the dark holding a broom.

Pete was there. He must have a plan, right? The
place must be crawling with agents with night
scopes and plenty of firepower, ready to pounce.
Oh, yeah, great, firepower. With me in the middle.
Again.

Clomp, clomp, clomp . . . I passed what looked
like a group of crouching goblins.

My hand holding the box was still trembling and
more than a little sweaty. With my left thumb, I
flipped the catch open on the box.

Clomp, clomp, clomp . . . I passed a large boo on
my left, which was covered with a sheet. A ghost, I
guessed.

Clearly, I was certifiable, ready for a rubber rum-
pus room at the booby hatch. I was pinning my
hopes on a magic horn? They were imagining this.
I was imaging this.

How I wished I were, and that I was still with
Rodney at the Golden Frog. Had I chosen the
Golden Frog because I sensed it was close to the
horn?

I flashed on the image of those flaming gazelle
heads, the windows exploding, me just standing
there.

I pried the box lid open and shoved my thumb
inside. As I touched the cold, bumpy horn, I shivered.

Orderlies? Get the straitjacket.

We reached the approaching party much sooner than I would have liked. I needed more time to think.

By the flashlight, I could see that the flanking men were both Asian, in military uniforms, with red stars on their hats.

I blinked.

Hard.

You've got to be kidding me. The Chinese military? How in hell did they get here? Well, they probably believe in the curative powers of gallbladders too. Orderlies, round up some more straitjackets.

The one counterpart looked like a common soldier, and his eyes betrayed that he was as scared as I was. The other was clearly an officer of some kind and looked calm and collected. The one in the middle wore an outdated black suit, a thin black tie, and a face like an angry toad, replete with bumps and warts. It was a woman, I think. Her black hair was shoulder length with strict bangs, but she was bulky and bosoms weren't immediately evident, not in that light, not in that Blues Brothers' suit.

Could she be a freak too? *TOAD WOMAN... Eats Flies Right Before Your Eyes... Genuine, Direct from the Orient!*

I remembered what Pete had said when we had lunch: *All I can tell you is that there's some guys from Korea coming to town with alligator briefcases so full of money it looks like a Brinks truck crashed into the Everglades.* Not Chinese soldiers. They were Korean.

We stopped three paces apart, and the toad set the suitcase before me. Renard stepped up to it and knelt. He set the suitcase on its side. Two snaps and it was open, displaying a full load of U.S. currency. He looked up at me and nodded in the direction of Toad Woman, who had her hand out for the box. Renard motioned for me to hand it over.

I hesitated. Yes, I had some crazy idea about using the power of the horn, the power I didn't really believe in. But I didn't get the chance.

The scared Korean soldier started to hum.

Toad Woman gave him a stern look and shone the flashlight on the soldier's face, whose eyes were glassy, focused somewhere off in the middle distance.

Renard and I exchanged glances just before the soldier broke into song. Song in the voice of a little girl.

> *"Watch me, swingers, and let's all strive*
> *To do the Mambo Rumba Two-Hand Jive*
> *Get down low, and back up high*
> *Shimmy those hips, give it a try."*

Toad Woman looked like she'd just swallowed a bad bug. I'm sure the soldier had probably never uttered a word of English in his life, and here he was doing Belle Beverly, right out of the blue.

Drawing the suitcase of money closer to him,

Renard reached out and smacked me in the leg. "Give them the horn, you idiot!"

But I wasn't about to do anything. In my mind, I was surrounded by flaming heads of taxidermy, a flippered freak coming at me with a knife. There's paralyzed with fear and then there's comatose with fear. I knew Flip was nearby.

The soldier continued:

> *"Feel the music in your feet*
> *The gang on the beach has the beat*
> *Let your hands show your honey*
> *You're no square, on the money."*

Toad Woman swallowed her bitter beetle and grabbed the soldier by the collar. She slapped him hard, three times. A burst of Korean admonishments followed, but the soldier was still in a trance. I could only imagine that her husband—perhaps Toad Man—was kept on a pretty short leash. Or in his case, in a small terrarium.

Renard stood and grabbed the box from my hand, thrusting it toward Toad Woman.

She shoved the singing soldier aside with a sneer, snatching the box and turning a flashlight beam on the horn.

From inside his tunic, the officer pulled a slender feather and a pocket-size ultraviolet lamp, the kind you can use to check currency. Toad Woman took the feather and stroked the horn. Then she examined it under the ultraviolet lamp. The black horn glowed white.

She grunted with satisfaction.

But then the officer began to sing. And the soldier chimed in. They sang together.

> *"C'mon, Cats, work those mittens*
> *These ginchy girls are all but kittens*
> *Doin' the Mambo Rumba Two-Hand Jive*
> *Way out, Daddy-o, it's a dance alive."*

Toad Woman looked not just unhappy but scared by the impromptu karaoke duet. The little blue lamp fell from her chubby hand and hit the floor. The feather wafted slowly to her feet. Eyes ping-ponging from one singing soldier to the next, she snapped the box shut and clasped it to her chest. She started to back up. There was an emergency exit behind her, and she put a hand on the door handle.

From behind me, I heard what sounded like someone spitting, and then something whizzed, a speeding bee right past my ear.

Toad Woman paused. It looked like a toothpick was sticking out of her forehead, and she reached up to pull it out. Blood trickled down her broad nose.

Those goblin statues—pygmies! The realization and shock made me inhale my gum, and I started to choke.

I could hear Renard scrambling back toward Smiler and the gang, but a series of other spitting sounds and some shouts came from behind me. I had trouble making out what was going on back there—I was gagging on my gum and bent over in an effort to dislodge it. First the gum at the restaurant, now this.

Good thing, because when I finally managed to eject the Fruit Stripe gum from my epiglottis and glanced up, Toad Woman had two more toothpicks, this time in her chest. If I'd been standing, those toxiferous toothpicks would have been in my back. The toad fell to her knees—the poison from the darts was working its magic.

Time for Garth to vamoose. The exit was right in front of me, the soldiers were in a trance, Toad Woman was out of the game, and the pygmies were probably coming after me next.

You know, of all the things in this modern world to worry about, like slipping in the tub, falling from a ladder, being attacked by a rabid squirrel, I never thought I'd have to worry about pygmies. Bring on the squirrels, any day.

Glancing back into the dark, the only thing I could make out was the statue with the white sheet closing in on me. The ghost had big, blocky, corrective shoes.

Flip.

I lunged forward, snatched the Chinese box from Toad Woman's grasp, and shouldered open the exit.

I fell down some wooden stairs but came up on my feet and ran down the dark pier.

The air was briny, mixed with the smell of creosote from the wood pilings. The stars twinkled dully behind New York's gauzy glow, and navigation lights from boats tracked across the twinkle of Governor's Island and Manhattan's downtown. I always used to like the combination of these sensations. Now the bayside ambience was a trap, water ahead and on both sides, Flip and his pygmies behind me.

"Garth!"

I made out a figure before me, but the voice wasn't immediately familiar. Jim Kim? Should I race back toward the carnival, try to get past Flip and company? Was Smiler still back there with his goons?

Skidding to a stop a few strides from the stranger, I recognized his silhouette—tall, bald, gaunt, commanding: Waldo.

"Give Waldo the horn!"

In my panic, I was gasping for breath and beyond having any discussions. The freak show just kept getting freakier.

Shirley Temple exclaimed from somewhere behind me, "Well, if it isn't Waldo! The King of Gaff!"

I turned. Framed by the kaleidoscope of rainbow lights from the carnival, Flip emerged from the gloom, his blue eyes glowing almost as white as the horn had, his flippers flexing menacingly at his sides like a pair of antsy boa constrictors. Behind him, a knot of small potbellied figures crouched, their blowguns at the ready.

"You shall not have it, Flip," Waldo commanded.

"Who's going to stop me?" Flip giggled.

There was a pause, and from Waldo's direction I heard:

Squeak-heez, squeak-heez.

Flip's clunky shoes stopped dead in their tracks.

Squeak-heez, squeak-heez.

Waldo Van Helsing—no kill saw and crossbow, just a penguin squeaky toy to destroy the monster and his goblins. My confidence level was running somewhere between zero and zero point zero. Flip might be afraid of the squeaky toy, but I doubted the pygmies were. These people were all nuts, I had to get out of there, and I wasn't sure Waldo would let me pass without handing over the horn. Fine. You know, that's what I should have done. But what did he want it for, really? Perhaps I actually did have enough of a connection with the horn to know it was bad and that nobody should have it. Let's face it, even if it was all hokum, look how much trouble it had created already.

"You son of a bitch," Flip's little-girl voice stammered. "That asshole Fuzzy gave that to you, didn't he?"

Squeak-heez, squeak-heez.

I wasn't sticking around for this encounter. I had only one direction to go, and that was toward the end of the pier. Football style, I tucked the box in my armpit and made like Walter Payton. Waldo threw his arms in the air as if to scare me back, but I zigged, I zagged, I rolled, and made it past him. Who knew all those Sundays watching football might actually have a practical application?

I admit I was feeling somewhat exhilarated as I raced down the wooden gridiron, even more so when I saw the silhouette of a boat at the end of the pier. It looked like a tugboat because only what appeared to be a control tower was visible above the pier—must be low tide. There were some small murky lights on, but otherwise it was dark. Even if nobody was aboard, at least I might be able to hide there. Launch a rubber raft. Grab a life ring and dive overboard. Radio for help. Run up the Jolly Roger and sail for Danger Island, just me and Chongo, whatever. But it held possibilities.

A tugboat? By the city's orange glow, I could see the deck as I approached. It was very long, narrow, and the sides sloped precipitously to the water. In the center was a wide, narrow coning tower. Hey, I may not be Howard Hughes, but I've been subjected to a number of *Ice Station Zebra* screenings myself. I know a submarine when I see it.

That's when I dropped the Chinese box.

Was it the shock of being confronted with a North Korean submarine docked at a Brooklyn pier that made me drop it? Don't ask me how, but it fell from my hand onto the dark pier. I heard it snap open, and I heard the horn tumble out. I slammed on the brakes, spun, and dropped to my knees in the vicinity of where I thought the horn might be.

I felt boots on the pier, not running, but at a quick pace. The vibrations were getting stronger. My hands raced around the rough wood and crannies of the pier, splinters pricking me and the smell of creosote stinging my sinuses.

My hand brushed the box, I picked it up: empty, as I knew it would be. But I was close. I heard myself groan with frustration.

If I had a psychic connection with the thing, why couldn't I find it?

That's when the first boot kicked me, hard in the ribs. I didn't know you could have the wind knocked out of you from the side, but trust me, you can. Both of my hands came up to my sternum as I rolled on my back. I could see the silhouette of two soldiers standing above me, against the orange haze of the New York night. They muttered something derisive in Korean and raised their submachine guns, but today must have been Boot Day aboard the *Sea View* because they kicked me again. I tried to roll away from them, my lungs still seized, searing pain in my sides from the beating my ribs were taking. Why hadn't I just jumped off the side of the pier into that filthy water and made a swim for it?

I felt a lump under my face. My hand scrambled, grabbed hold of the lump.

My brain had just been feeling sorry for its miscalculations and the pain it was enduring, when I felt a familiar impulse. An overwhelming, consuming, volcanic loathing. Hatred and rage.

In my hand was the kving-kie horn, and the image of flames and glass exploding from Partridge's windows gripped me.

I heard a shout, and the kicking stopped. I got to my hands and knees. *This time you go for the water, Garth, before they start kicking you again.* But when I glanced back to where the soldiers had been, they were gone. Their boots were still on the pier, but they were gone.

What the . . .

I looked around feverishly. *Yes, but where is Flip?* I could hear more shouting aboard the submarine, and a spotlight came on from its upper deck. Fortunately, it was focused farther down the pier. I looked back. No Waldo, no Flip, no pygmies. The path was clear, and I could see a torn fence next to the Castle Creep where I could get back into the lights and laughter of the carnival.

A loud ratcheting sounded, like a giant machine gun about to open fire. I don't have any military training, unless you count the Weeblos, but I've watched enough war flicks and *Rat Patrol* to know what one sounds like. Could I somehow make it off the pier without them shooting me? It was only a matter of time before the spotlight's sweeping beam came to rest on yours truly.

But somewhere back at the fair would be the cavalry. Had the pygmies got all of Smiler's troop? Including the chauffeur, Pete Durban?

I eyed the water instead. No doubt a gauntlet of dirty Pampers, Optimo butts, greasy Q-tips, and used Band-Aids floated next to the pier. I was trying to get over my revulsion toward diving into that flotsam when Flip the Penguin Boy, Koreans with boots, and a giant machine gun tipped the balance in favor of immersion in briny ejecta. But my Pampers baptism wasn't going to happen as long as that spotlight was on. It spilled enough light that I was plainly visible now to anybody on the submarine.

Two sets of boots were still sitting where the soldiers had been kicking me mid-pier. What was up with those boots, anyway? Had I made the soldiers disappear with the help of the horn? Or had Flip grabbed them? The main thing was that Flip was nowhere to be seen.

The kving-kie was still tight in my fist. I winced, and I held it out at the spotlight.

Please, if this thing works, let it be now!

I heard a pop, like the sound of a firecracker, and the light went slowly out, only a purple blotch where the bulb cooled. Excited voices shouted disappointment and anger from the submarine.

Had I done that? Did it do that? Or had they just shut off the light? Forget making a swim for it. Hightail it back to that hole and the fence.

But it was a long way back to terra firma, and I could hardly see in the sudden darkness.

How had I gotten into this jam? How could I keep this from happening again? If there was an again.

I realized that the answer was in my grasp. The damnable kving-kie, of course. Nobody wanted me—they wanted the horn. That's what got me into this mess. The question of what to do? Pellucid.

After dragging myself to the pier's edge and seeing that there actually were Pampers down there, I tried to stand and immediately doubled over. My gut was in a bad way, worse than I knew. So I scuttled crablike, cursing a blue streak, not a *ding bust* in the bunch.

Dyep deya vya boga duga seraza mat! Habit sometimes prevails, even under duress. I managed to get to my feet and began loping away from the pier's edge toward the lights of the carnival. No more Walter Payton. More like Walter Brennan with a thumbtack in his shoe.

My eyes were blinded by the bright lights of the carnival, and I hoped that my silhouette wasn't visible to the machine gunner.

It seemed impossibly far, loping like that, pain knifing my sides. Broken ribs for sure.

Squeak-heez.

Something was under my foot, and I knew what it was. I stooped and picked up the toy, shoving it in my pocket. Hell, it couldn't hurt to have it on hand. It had caused Flip to stop in his tracks, though what ultimately transpired between him and Waldo was anyone's guess. Mine was that the pygmies got Waldo and that he'd run back to the carnival before collapsing. But if so, why wasn't Flip out here after me? He must have known about the submarine. Even he wouldn't try to go up against all that.

From behind me I heard shouts and a few stray gunshots. I glanced back. Flashlights were bobbing along the deck of the sub and the end of the pier. The tromp of boots on the pier was like a stampede headed my way. They were giving chase.

It was like a nightmare where I couldn't run, and the harder I tried, the farther away that hole in the fence seemed. Here I was in the good ol' USA being chased down by Korean troops. It just didn't seem possible. This couldn't be happening.

Twenty feet from the fence, a figure appeared in the opening. The figure was surrounded by several men holding guns.

"Garth!"

It was Pete Durban. He trotted forward, grabbing my arm to help support me.

"Pete, the Koreans, they're right behind me!"

He chuckled. "It's going to be okay, Garth."

"But . . ." I twisted my head back toward the squad of men approaching the carnival.

My eyes were blurry with the tears of pain and panic. All I could see were men in uniform. Except one. He had a tennis sweater tied over the shoulders, and when he stood before me, I could smell cloves. Sure enough, it was Jim Kim, and he was surrounded by soldiers. Even with my vision blurred, I could see that the soldiers were in commando gear, with ropes and night vision goggles. I could hear them talking into radios saying things like "target secure" and "captive hostiles" and "perimeter." They were Americans.

Like butter in a microwave, I melted with relief, but Pete kept me from collapsing into a pool at his feet. I was surrounded by good guys for a change and wanted to burst out in tears. I was safe from Flip.

"Medic!" Kim yelled over his shoulder. Then to me: "Hey, buddy. You okay?"

I tried to speak but broke into a coughing fit instead.

"Garth, do you still have it?" Kim patted me on the shoulder. "The kving-kie? Do you still have it?"

I ignored the question. "Did you get Flip?"

"We will. Got the nasty munchkins." Pete held up one of their toothpicks. "One of the little buggers hit me with this."

"How come . . ."

"Hey, I get bit by snakes and poisonous critters all the time. I have a high tolerance for toxins. So, amigo, tell us—where is it?"

We stepped into the light of the carnival, Kim following. His troops stayed out on the pier, searching it with flashlights.

"Did Flip have it?" Kim grabbed my elbow. "Did Renard have it? Is it out on the pier somewhere? Who had the kving-kie last?"

"I did."

"Great!" Kim's smile faded. "Did?"

"Did," I repeated. "All I've got now is this."

Squeak-hee, squeak-hee.

They stared quizzically at the rubber penguin.

"So who has it now?" Kim persisted. "The horn—what happened to it?"

"I dropped it out there, then they started kicking me. Maybe it fell in the river, I dunno."

Kim cocked an ear closer to me, like he hadn't heard right. "You—"

"I don't have it, I dropped it out there."

Kim looked at me like I'd just told him his mother was actually a secret agent. Hmm. Maybe she was.

"Divers!" He dashed back out through the hole in the fence and started shouting orders to the troops. "Get the SEALs over here!"

Pete tightened his grip, helping me along. And I felt him vibrating. Deep in his chest, he was laughing.

"Garth . . ." he began mirthfully. Then he leaned in and whispered in my ear: "Good job."

Chapter 26

As the Navy medics looked me over, wrapping my torso and ribs in Ace bandages, the carnival was almost cleared of revelers and employees. NYPD was all over the place and had created a gauntlet at the exit. I saw them crowd the pygmies in a paddy wagon, their heads down and shoulders drooping like kids caught sneaking into the drive-in. The cops were still looking for Flip, but I couldn't have been safer with so many of them around. Anyway, I was sure he must have escaped. Perhaps he swam off as he did in Maine. The horn was gone, I didn't have it, and Flip—wherever he was—must have known that. No reason to come after me anymore.

A makeshift first-aid center had been set up in the ring-toss concession, and Waldo was laid out on a stretcher waiting for an ambulance. He was still alive, probably because he was such a big man that the poison from those little arrows wasn't sufficient to do him in. He was unconscious, arms folded across his chest like Bela Lugosi taking a catnap. I hoped they'd cart him off before he came to and started up with his Svengali act. A series of ambulances had already come and gone to take away the more-serious victims, like Renard, Smiler, Toad Woman, and the turtlenecks. I had no idea what their conditions were and, frankly, didn't care.

What I cared about was Angie. Using Pete's cell phone, I briefed her on what had happened and let her know I was okay. But to be on the safe side, I asked her to go stay with friends. If Flip had escaped the carnival grounds and still had it in for me, he might go to my place of residence. Who knew what he might do? He might go after Angie. I wasn't taking any chances.

"No way! I'm coming right down there this instant!"

"Sugar, they won't let you in. This place is sealed tighter than a diving bell. They're still looking for Flip. The police will give me a lift to the hospital in a little while, just to have me checked over. I'll call you when I get there, and you can come meet me. How's that?"

She groaned stubbornly. "Are you sure you're okay?"

I smiled. Hearing her voice, and its familiar cadence, was like a Christmas tree lighting up in my heart.

"Positive. Just hang out and I'll call and then you can see me at the hospital. Just a couple hours, that's all. I'm surrounded by police, federal agents, and Navy SEALs. I couldn't be safer."

"Garth, you have to be more careful. In the future, I mean."

Don't trouble trouble unless trouble troubles you.

"Believe me, no more chasing taxidermy. Or limousines."

"I feel somehow responsible."

"Not at all. Now, I'll call you in a little bit, okay?"

There was a pause, and then she sighed.

"You better be all right." I could hear her choke back tears. "Or I'll kick your butt."

"Been done." I laughed and hung up.

Fully bandaged, I was excused, so I stepped out into the midway. All the lights were still on. The Ferris wheel's multicolored fluorescent tubes festively illuminated its spokes, running lights along the sides of the Octopus still flickered maniacally, the sign for the Round-Up still flashed, bumper cars still hummed, the neon on the Salt N' Pepper shakers still glowed red like hot licorice. It seemed strange having the place all lit up but almost empty, like something from a dream. Of course, police and soldiers crisscrossed the midway, so I wasn't exactly alone, and as I made my way toward the exit, hoping for that ride to the hospital, I strolled past all those wonderful rides I enjoyed so much as a kid. I was exhausted but so relieved that I was actually in a mellow mood.

The Sky Diver! I marveled at the huge wheel, with its cars with steering wheels. Man, I used to spin my car on that ride so fast that when I came close to the ride operator he'd shout at me to cut it out. And to think there was only a big-ass cotter pin holding the doors shut on those things. Same with the Zipper, which was there too. That ride has cars facing out that revolve around a bean shape that also twirls. Sometimes, at the top, your car does a triple flip. I didn't know that I would enjoy these rides anymore. Well, not tonight, surely. I didn't need any excitement in my life for a while.

Then there was the Matterhorn, with its alpine facade and glitter snow peaks. I never liked those rides much. First of all, they're a lame excuse for a roller coaster. The set of cars just goes around in an oval, and the big thrill is supposed to be the little hills and dips. Well, there was a small cave you went through in the back to give you that rush of thinking you're going to be decapitated. And for some reason that I have yet to fathom, these rides always blared disco music, often a version without lyrics. It was supposed to be a ride for older teens or Disco Stu or something. Though the cars were stationary and it was twenty-five years later, the damn thing before me was still blaring disco.

The disco craze never did much for me as a kid. In fact, I hated it. Pounding electronic music, fluff. It was still tawdry stuff, but I now thought it kitschy. I even danced to it on occasion, more as a gag than anything else.

But seriously: Like Frank Sinatra's "New York, New York," how many times must I be subjected to "Can't Stop Me Now"? I'm ashamed to say I even remember it was by Boogie City Express, a wailing Cecily Trieste singing lead.

You got it. "Can't Stop Me Now" was blaring from this contraption, without the words.

I looked at the entrance to the carnival. The cops had their hands full discharging customers and checking IDs. I wasn't going to get a ride to the hospital any time soon.

The music was disturbing my mellow mood, so I stepped up and looked at the ride's controls to see if I could nix the sound system.

"Garth!" Pete called.

I looked around.

"Pete?"

"Muchacho, come up here, you gotta see this."

He was calling from the ride's tunnel, which ran through the fake mountain.

"In there?" I couldn't see him, so I squeezed along the side of the cars. They were halfway into the tunnel, and I had to skirt along with one hand on the wall.

"C'mon, hurry!"

I stepped into one of the cars and began clambering from one to the next, into the dark tunnel.

"Pete? My side hurts too much to be doing this."

A loud alarm bell sounded. The cars jolted forward, and I somersaulted onto my back into the next car. Someone had started the ride, and the coaster lunged farther into the tunnel. It was dark, and the coaster's wheels were drumming along my spine, which was pressed into the seat. I could feel my ribs click, and my chest was afire with pain.

"Pete!" I shouted.

I kicked my legs and pushed against the side of the car to right myself, shrieking with agony from my broken ribs.

Gripping my side, I pushed myself upright and saw the flashing lights at the end of the tunnel ahead.

And then I didn't.

A pair of hairy cactuses clamped over my eyes from behind.

"Guess who?" A little girl's voice giggled over the growing roar of the coaster.

I didn't have to guess. What I had to do was get my heart to start pumping again.

The coaster rumbled around a curve as I gripped the stubbly flippers, trying to pry them from my head and eyes.

Flip was giggling hysterically in the car behind me. Then he broke into his best Cecily Trieste:

> *"At first I said no, I cannot hide*
> *He's the man, the one I need by my side*
> *Let him get away*
> *I'll die right here, today*
> *Then when I saw him in her arms*
> *I got mad, I swore I'd do him harm*
> *Can't stop me now!*
> *Can't stop me now!"*

I think you'll understand if my hatred of disco and Boogie City Express was forever reaffirmed at that moment.

His grip on my head made it seem like those flippers were bolted in place; Flip was incredibly strong. But as we hit the next curve, he was thrown to one side. His grip loosened, I yanked myself forward and was free.

We approached the tunnel again, and I vaulted into the car ahead of me, yowling from the spikes of agony driven into my sides.

Flip was at least one car away now but was still singing above the coaster's clamor:

> *"I turned and ran, fast as I can*
> *But turned to fight for my lovin' man*
> *Walked up to him, pulled him away*
> *Instead of hitting him I soon began to sway*
> *Magic worked within my body*
> *And showed him I'm not shoddy*
> *The music raged, we danced all night*
> *In his arms I found the morning light*
> *Can't stop me now!*
> *Can't stop me now!"*

Gasping for breath, I looked back as we entered the tunnel again. I could only see his hideous form framed by the receding light at the entrance to the tunnel. His flippers were waving a carving knife in the air like a diva on stage. All he needed was a feather boa and he'd have been a shoe-in for *La Cage aux Mort.*

We came back out of the tunnel.

And there was Walker, standing in front of the ride, his gun drawn. Smiling.

I was like George Jetson on his treadmill: "Jane! Stop this crazy thing!" I wanted to crawl farther away from Flip, but I couldn't entertain the idea of tumbling onto my ribs again. I might just pass out from the pain and then would be completely at Flip's mercy.

But I was already at his mercy. I braced my back against the front of the car, watching Flip wriggle into the car behind me, the blade of his knife pulsing with the flash of the strobe lights as we passed yet again into the dark tunnel. I ducked, fearing I might hit my head.

Surely the police would shut this thing down any second.

But as we came back out of the tunnel, I caught the jittery image of cops pounding on the controls while others dumbly watched the ride with guns at their sides. We were going too fast for them to try and shoot Flip.

But that didn't stop Walker. I saw a flash from his gun at the same instant a spark exploded on the car's handrail with a loud ping. The handrail next to me, not Flip.

Other cops were running every which way, maybe to try to find the master switch to shut down the power.

It would be too late. Flip's tiny glowing blue eyes and smiling kewpie-doll lips rose in the seat behind me, a flipper holding the knife, Cecily Trieste at full throttle:

> *"Did you think I'd let you go?*
> *That I'd let her have your soul?*
> *Can't stop me now!*
> *Can't stop me now!"*

I was thrust to one side by a turn and felt something in my pocket press against my thigh. Careening around the next turn, back toward the tunnel, I managed to reach into my pocket.

Flip stood and made his move.

And I made mine.

Squeak-hee! Squeak-hee!

He howled, recoiling.

I caught a glimpse of a scripted sign that said: *Please remain seated at all times for your safety.*

Then the tunnel entrance zoomed overhead, and the roof chopped Flip just under the chin.

It was like he'd been shot from a cannon, catapulting backward and out of view, blood spattering my face. The knife hit the roof butt-first and ricocheted.

I didn't have time to react, except to put my hand up and duck my head. I felt the blade's icy slice on my hand. The darkness of the tunnel prevented me from seeing how bad the cut was, but I felt the knife fall into my lap—blade flat, thank God.

The coaster jolted, and as I came out of the tunnel, the lights and disco music were no more. I was slowing down. They'd found the master switch.

My hand had a nice slice in it and was bleeding all over the place. The knife lay in my lap, the blade stuck right through the belly of the squeaky penguin toy.

Sorry about your toy, Fuzzy.

A squad of cops and SEALs grabbed the slowing cars as they rumbled toward the controls, bringing it to a stop before it entered the tunnel again. They were all shouting, asking me questions that I could neither understand nor answer. I felt their hands on me, someone wrapping my hand with a handkerchief. Blood was all over my shirt. I was lifted out of the car and handed man-to-man like a bale of hay. And I was just about as animated as one.

My head rolled, the flash of the pretty carnival lights blurred with the fake mountain scenery of the Matterhorn.

Just before being carried down to a stretcher, my eyes focused on the last car. On the seat there was something odd, and it took me a moment to realize what it was. It looked like a big broken egg full of ground chuck. Tiny blue eyes stared back at me. Unblinking. I felt like he could still see me.

I awake in a sweat late at night sometimes, and think Flip still can.

redictably, I wound up back in the hospital, at a trauma center somewhere in a traditionally very bad neighborhood in Brooklyn. This may not sound like the optimal place to be, but the reverse is actually the case. Because of the rough neighborhood, these guys see the most gunshot and beating victims of almost anywhere in the country. That was reassuring, except for the fact that I was a beating victim myself.

The phalanx of police of every shape and form surrounding my room was not as reassuring. Acronyms abounded: USFW, FBI, NYSDEC, NYCPD, even CIA.

No, I didn't have a lawyer. I had something better: Angie. She was glued to my side, fending them off, the way you hold off a pack of wolves with fire. Well, the doctor assigned to my case, Dr. Singh, was right in there. Singh was an Indian woman, with a long black braid. I'm used to seeing doctors being composed and often distracted, if not detached. This woman was consumed with trying to figure out what had happened to my internal organs and wouldn't stand for the acronyms pestering me and getting in her way as she rushed me through a battery of tests. But mostly she kept coming in with other surgeons, poking my black-and-blue side and belly, watching me yelp with pain, and muttering terms like *peritoneal lining* and *rebound tenderness* that didn't mean anything to me. But they also did a CT scan and what they called a *lavage*, in which giant needles were inserted into my belly so they could wash out my gut looking for telltale blood, bile, and what have you. I took some comfort in her headstrong manner and thoroughness but also knew that meant there might be some cause for alarm. It meant she had reason to worry my injuries might turn fatal.

Words like *peritonitis* were mumbled here and there, as was *colostomy*, but after two days they calmed down and decided exploratory surgery wasn't necessary. While there was blood in my urine, it seemed my kidney was only bruised. My liver and spleen each took the equivalent of a black eye, and they marveled that my pancreas came through without so much as a broken fingernail. There was a minor tear of the bowel, and they began focusing on that and talking about a colostomy. It would have been temporary, but I didn't relish the thought of having my droppings collected in a bag on my belt. In any case, the nick to my colon was eventually assessed as inconsequential. In time, I was expected to have a complete recovery without any surgery at all.

Dr. Singh told me that stomping victims, as one of them called it, are often some of the most severely injured.

"Were you not a young man," she said, "you might not be so lucky."

Lucky? Sure, all things considered.

Young man? Hey, beats the hell out of *mister*.

Relieved? In spades. But I still felt like hell.

Angie, as I said, was a champ, keeping her considerable fortitude focused on making sure I got the best treatment possible. She managed to not cry in front of me while all this was going on. And to not ask any questions about what happened. Until the second night in the hospital. She told me I'd have to talk to the acronyms the next morning.

"I'm ready," I whispered.

"I brought you some bubblegum." She held out a pack. "Thought it might make you feel better."

I thought about Smiler putting that Fruit Stripe gum on my tongue, about gagging on it in the spook house.

"I think my gum days are over."

My bed was cranked up a little, and there was a tray with some really bland, really bad food on it in front of me. Untouched.

"Well, how about some ice cream?" Angie held up a tub of banana ice cream, my favorite.

I smiled faintly. "Now you're talking."

She drew her chair next to the bed, pried open the ice cream, and spooned some into my mouth.

"Garth, they think you know where it is." She slipped another spoonful of ice cream into my mouth. "Pete told me they checked everywhere."

I'd surmised that Pete had filled her in on the essentials. Of course, I had questions of my own.

"Renard is dead?" It still sometimes hurt to talk, so mostly I whispered.

"Under arrest. Only Park and one of his bodyguards were killed. The other two are cooperating, and they think they can get to Park's chop shop through them."

"And the Koreans?"

"All that was reported in the papers was that there was a drug bust or some such thing at a Brooklyn carnival that night. That explains away the commotion. They're keeping a lid on the Koreans. I guess there's some behind-the-scenes stuff going on, diplomacy. Pete suggested that we 'seriously consider' keeping this to ourselves in the interests of national security. I think the idea is that if we keep our traps shut they won't press any charges against you."

"Charges?"

"You know that if they wanted to, they could make things difficult." She shrugged, spooning some more ice cream into my mouth. "They could think of something."

"Yeah, I'm sure Walker could think of something. Like an execution. He tried to shoot me on that ride."

"I don't think you have to worry about Walker," Angie snorted. "He got hit by the ricochet."

I rolled my eyes. "How fitting that he should get hit by his own bullet."

"Not a bullet," she said, spooning more ice cream into my mouth.

"Hmm?"

"Flip. His body landed on Walker after bouncing off the wall of the ride."

I began to chuckle. It hurt my sides but made my intellect dance.

"It's not funny." She withheld the next spoonful. "His neck is broken. Looks like he'll be on disability for some time."

"Sorry, but you've got to admit," I whispered, "it's kinda absurd, and I have a hard time feeling sorry . . . How about some more ice cream?"

"Garth, what did happen?" She shoveled in another spoonful. "I know, you ran into Renard and Park down in Chinatown, and they kidnapped you, and then they tried to make you a go-between to sell the kving-kie horn stick thing to the Koreans. But how did Flip suddenly show up? And how did you get out of this . . ."

"Alive?" I whispered.

She nodded, looking at the floor.

"I don't know how to answer that." I sighed.

She looked at me, eyes wide, but said nothing.

"I could tell you that I got lucky. I can't say for sure that what happened out there, whether any of it was directly related to the horn. When I wanted to make it to the water and wanted the spotlight to go out—that's probably just when the commandos charged the sub and shut it down. Did I make the two Koreans who were kicking me disappear?"

I didn't have a rejoinder for that one.

"But?" she prompted.

"But . . ." I sighed again. "Perhaps the squeaky toy was more powerful than the horn."

"To think he was afraid of that cute little toy," she whispered back.

I closed my eyes. "There's no doubt in my mind that Flip had powers. He made the Korean soldiers sing."

"Sing?"

I opened my eyes. "Belle Beverly."

Her jaw dropped. I continued.

"And it wasn't just throwing his voice. Their mouths moved, and his voice came out."

"Which song?"

"Does that really matter?" I rolled my eyes. "I don't even like thinking about it. The point is he definitely had telekinetic powers. And he felt that the kving-kie had power, and that's why he was there. Maybe even how he was there. And maybe . . ."

She let that sit for a second, looking at me intently. I had to continue.

"Maybe that's why I chased the limo. Maybe, just

maybe, I felt some connection to the kving-kie. I mean, what the hell was I thinking?"

"Rodney says you lit out after that limo like a track star."

"I saw Renard and Smiler—I mean Park—and, well, I knew he must have it. But that didn't mean I had to chase them down." I closed my eyes, my brow furrowed.

I felt Angie's hand on my forehead, massaging the wrinkles of consternation away. "Anyway, it's not important. What is important . . . As your partner and protector here, I need to know what happened to the kving-kie. You had it last, didn't you?"

I opened my eyes and looked deep into hers.

"Yes. I was lying there on the pier, trying to figure a way out, and it was still in my hand. That gnarled, stupid horn was still in my grasp."

"What did you do with it?"

"I was thinking about the whole mess I was in, about how all this happened, about what people believe . . . believe about the power of a cow horn. And it became suddenly clear to me that the truly destructive power was probably not in the horn but in what people believed about it, regardless of whether it had any power. Like the way people kill, and steal, for diamonds and money, things that in and of themselves are essentially worthless."

I could see she was getting impatient. But I wasn't going to rush it. She wanted to know what happened, and this was probably the most important part. At least to me.

"And then I realized—in an instant—that the only thing, for me, that really holds any power over anything, over me, is my love for you."

She made a gentle gasp, but held her tongue.

"It was then, while holding the kving-kie—which I'd held on to for dear life, for reasons I can't explain—that I was able to let it go."

"Go?"

"Pampers."

"Pampers?"

"I dropped it in the river."

She put her hand over her mouth. "But they looked there. . . ."

"Believe me, it's gone." I shook my head gently. "For good."

"It could wash up on a beach in Staten Island, or on Coney Island. How do you know it's gone for good?"

I closed my eyes again. I reflected on what Renard said about salt water destroying the horn. But that wouldn't have reassured me. What did reassure me was that the vision of flaming gazelles, of Flip, of exploding windows did not come. And thinking of it no longer frightened me.

I smiled weakly.

"I just know."

Epilogue

Keep your Gobi and Sahara deserts. Death Valley? Laughable. Take it from me, there is no hotter place on any continent on Planet Earth than Massachusetts. Specifically, Brimfield Antiques and Collectibles Show in July. Well, it certainly seems that way. Dusty and crowded as any Tunisian bazaar, the miles of aisles with hundreds of vendors' tents are a course through which nomad shoppers tramp. Some, like so many Foreign Legionnaires driven mad by the relentless heat, foolishly gulp down soda pop and wallow in french fries, only to be stricken down by bloating. Others lose their way, Aussies staggering deliriously across the Gibson's sandy scrub, searching vainly for that tent with the cheapest *Cowboy in Africa* lunch box.

I dress for safari, all khakis and a canvas fedora,

and keep bottled water close at hand. But by the time the sun gets over the yardarm and starts blinding the already heat-stricken crowd, even an old hand like me is worn down to the very nub of my wits. Like a hunter on the savanna, relentless scanning of the tents' merchandise is required, looking for my taxidermy prey. Seven hours of this have my eyes unable to hold still in their sockets. I've walked probably six miles through row and row of tents, haggling and marking my map with the location of my latest kill. By day's end, the Lincoln and I have crawled the congested byways back to collect my trophies. With the car's radiator about to boil over, I end my sojourn at Rodney's oasis, his Brimfield tent, for the best beer of the year. Like Chinese food, the Brimfield beer was a ritual of Rodney's and mine.

This year, Angie joined me. I tried to dissuade her, or at least get her to train for this demanding ordeal, but she wanted to go. Since our fiasco with the kving-kie two months before, she'd been spending more time with me as a matter of habit, even though Van Putin had her busier than ever with the art of jewelry work. And I'd been spending more time with her. Mortal danger has a way of defining what's important in life.

I'm proud to say she was holding up well and made my hunt much easier. We'd bought walkie-talkies so that she could scout one area while I scouted another. You come to get a feel for the shopping terrain year to year at these fairs. Some areas are hot for taxidermy, others not. I more or less had her troll the historically less productive shoals, where every once in a long while you hook into a whopper.

When Angie targeted something of interest, she'd call in her coordinates by row and aisle. Instead of my safari garb, Angie had opted for all-white cotton shorts and blouse, enormous round sunglasses, and a straw hat with a red bandanna on it. The bandanna was so I could spot her in the crowd.

It was about two weeks since Dr. Singh said my liver and I could resume the regular consumption of alcohol. Except for the occasional (if regrettable) SB binge, I don't consider myself a big drinker, but apparently it was enough that I lost ten pounds in those six weeks. Either that or I eat more when I drink. Probably a little of both. Anyway, I was in fighting trim for the summer's antiques fairs.

My trailer was loaded with some new pieces and a few I had brought to trade but hadn't managed to move. Among the large new pieces was a hammerhead shark (a whopper Angie found), a zebra shoulder mount, a kangaroo pelt, a full-body mountain lion, a standing black bear, and a peacock. Among the stuff I had left to trade: Reggie.

I know, he was supposed to replace Sneezy, and Otto was very upset I was taking the new penguin away to trade. Dudley did a superb job, as always. But John Mason, one of the big taxidermy dealers at Brimfield, was hot for my penguin and had promised me a trove of stuff in trade. Let's remember that I'm a businessman. One with some considerable hospital bills to pay. Unfortunately, Johnny came down with shingles and sent his cousin in his place. Without telling him anything about the penguin deal. So once again I was chauffeuring a dead penguin.

Angie and I draped a tarpaulin over our horde to protect them from the sun but lifted the penguin from the backseat. He was too delicate for this heat, had been out in it too long as it was. I could hear Dudley admonishing me for abusing his work of art. Reggie needed shade to conserve the natural oil in his feathers.

Rodney was sitting on an old sea chest in the musty canvas shade of his tent, a wet bandanna tied to his wide forehead and a pile of beer cans at his feet. I hadn't seen him since Chinatown, though we'd spoken briefly on the phone.

"Angie!" he bellowed. "Can't believe Garth's been leavin' this ravishing woman alone in New York all these years. How do you like Brimfield?"

"I've always wanted to go on safari with Garth." She leaned down and gave him a peck on the cheek. "But next time we bring bearers."

"Pick me a cold one," I rasped, and stopped mopping sweat from my face just in time to catch an incoming Schlitz.

"Bloody 'ell, Garth. Was wonderin' whether you'd make it. Thought maybe you'd seen just about enough of me for a while."

"Don't kid yourself. I'm here strictly for your beer, you know that."

Rodney got up and cleared off an old wooden rocker for Angie. "So the liver seems no worse for wear, 'eh?"

"Haven't sprung any leaks."

It was about a hundred degrees cooler under the canvas. I sat on a sea chest next to Rodney and placed Reggie on a milk crate next to me.

Angie settled into the rocker. "Where's my beer?"

Rodney plunged his hand into the cooler and handed her a cold one.

"You two been keepin' the bad luck at bay, have ya?" Rodney opened another beer for himself, then shook his head. "Sorry, I promised myself I wouldn't start in with that. Well, damn luck and all. I'm grateful that my friend Garth has pulled through."

The three of us clunked beer cans in a toast.

"I'll drink to that," I sighed. "Everything is back to normal. The cops are off my back. No more carnies with gaffs, no more kving-kie." I leaned against a Hoosier cabinet and cooled my neck with my beer.

"See you and Angie found some merchandise," he said, gesturing to my trailer.

"Yep, what you see there plus a water buffalo–hoof lamp and an old, old vulture mount."

Rodney snorted. "A vulture? People'll buy a moth-eaten vulture?"

"Yup. Thing is a goner too. I'll pluck it and sell the feathers to Native Americans for use in folk art. Don't laugh. This southwestern art thing is big. I can get a pretty penny for the feathers, while some Santa Fe buyer glues them to a soup bone and sells them to spiritually enlightened gringos. Feel free to stock up on old tennis rackets, but I'm putting more chips on birds of prey. Of course, I'll have to be careful to document what I buy and sell, keep it all on the up-and-up."

"And that." He gestured to Reggie. "Is it the new one? Sneezy's replacement?"

I didn't get a chance to answer.

"Have you heard the one about the penguin driving his convertible to Las Vegas?"

"Uh . . ."

"Well, there he is, driving across the desert. Sunglasses, one flipper on the steering wheel and the other on the door, when all of a sudden like—BOOM—steam pouring out from under his hood. As luck would have it, he's just closing on a little town, a filling station on one side and ice cream stand on the other. . . ." This one would make a polar bear blush. He ended it with the penguin saying, "I did not! That's ice cream!"

Rodney grabbed his belly, put his head back, and howled with laughter. To my surprise, Angie was once again in a fit of laughter over one of Rodney's racy jokes, so much so that she had to steady herself on his shoulder.

"Well, looks like I missed a good one!" a voice

from behind me said. "Hello, Garth. This must be Angie."

Rodney and Angie's runaway hilarity skidded to a stop.

I smelled cloves. A familiar chill weeviled up my neck. Jimmy Kim ducked into Rodney's tent.

"This fellow must be Rodney." Kim, seemingly fresh from the golf course in a sport shirt and pleated tan slacks, came forward and forced a handshake on the yeasty Brit, whose eyes shifted to mine. "I can see what they say is true. You tell one heck of a good joke."

"This the happy Korean bloke?" Rodney asked guardedly.

"That's me," Jimmy laughed. "I was in the neighborhood and thought I'd stop in, join your chat." He pulled a forearm across his brow and took a swig from a bottle of mineral water. "Hot one, eh?"

Kim was the only loose end from the kving-kie imbroglio. I never did find out exactly for whom he worked, though in as much as he was with the cavalry that rescued me, I subscribed to Dudley's dark prediction that Jimmy was from one of our own government's shadowy inner workings. I hadn't seen him since that night on the pier. And hoped I'd never see him again.

"Still following Garth?" Angie gave him the evil eye. "We ought to call the police."

"Angie, please. I'm not following Garth. He's just a man of habit, which makes him easy to find.

As I said, I thought I'd stop in and see how you two are doing."

"So let's 'ave it, Jim," Rodney snorted. "Who are you? What's your part in all this, then?"

"My part in this was to keep Garth from getting in the way. Anyway. What I came to talk to Garth about is to make sure he takes the proper perspective on that ugly business two months ago. With the white crow, all that. Rodney, Angie: You mind if I talk to Garth in private?"

"They stay." I shook my head. "Say your piece, Jimmy."

His smile wavered, but his eyes brightened. "Very well. I suppose you think all that nonsense out on the pier was about the kving-kie, about the North Koreans wanting to buy it."

We just looked at him. He continued.

"Well, it was and it wasn't. The idea was to fool the North Koreans into buying a bogus magic horn. No easy feat, let me tell you. In the process, we had to convince U.S. Fish and Wildlife and particularly Agent Renard."

"And Partridge?" Angie asked.

"A swell guy too." Jimmy shook his head. "No, he was in on the game. Anyway, the idea was to get this on the market. We knew there was a rotten apple in the barrel, we just didn't know it was Renard. We wanted him and his North Korean connections. Especially Park. Well, things went off track when Flip and his crew stole the crow standing on the horn. No sooner did we lure them in than Fletcher's mother took the thing to Gunderson's and Garth bought the crow. If I'd interceded, the whole ball of yarn would have unraveled. I wanted the carnies to sell it to Renard, keep the whole thing natural and out of my hands. Had Renard or Park sensed my hand in this, they would have scattered."

"But you were the one who put the ad in the paper," Angie said. "The *want my white crow back* ad."

"Well, when I saw Flip's profile, I knew he was just using the carnies to get the horn for himself. He had no intention of selling it to Renard or the North Koreans."

"So you were the one who was going to meet them and buy it at Partridge's mansion? Then what?"

"Well, the plan was to take out Flip and scare Tex Filbert and MacTeague back toward Renard. Flip trying to kill them before I got there didn't figure into the plan."

"Take out?" Rodney squinted. "You mean kill, don't you?"

Jimmy ignored him. "Flip was a pretty cagey customer. By the time I got there, all hell had broken loose, they had Angie . . . Well, I managed to slip in and save Garth."

Angie gasped. "You dragged Garth from the burning room?"

Kim brandished a smile that was only half bashful. "I couldn't let my friend Garth die."

"I guess I should thank you, though I can't help but feel you had another motive." I stood up. "Like you needed me to draw Flip back so you could take him out. You knew he'd come back for me to get at the horn."

He sucked his cheeks. "If you want to take the cynical view, I can't stop you."

"Well, I'm cynical too." Angie stood next to me. "So in essence, you're saying it was a fake kving-kie that Flip the Penguin Boy was after, that the Koreans handed over suitcases of cash for?"

"Exactly." Jimmy gave us a big smile. "Just to flush them out. What I came to let Garth—and now you and Rodney—in on is that it was all a hoax, orchestrated to fool the North Koreans. The magic horn was a fake, and Partridge's trip to Korea to find it was backstory."

"But why?" Rodney stood and joined our ranks. "And who do you work for?"

"Why? Who? Those are things I'm not at liberty to divulge. But honestly, can't you guess?"

"CIA, NSA, like that, eh?" Rodney volunteered.

"Nothing so pedestrian." Kim winked. "Anyway, all you need to know is that this was all part of the continuing brinksmanship between the United States and North Korea. It's really that simple."

"But is it?" I put a hand on his shoulder. "I have to wonder, Jimmy, why they would send you to tell us this."

"We don't want people going away from this convinced there are magical horns." He grinned, and I thought I detected the slightest unease in his smile. "The idea could spread. And, well, to appeal to you not to compromise national security."

Rodney, Angie, and I exchanged glances.

"Couldn't it be, guys"—I grinned—"that Kim here represents our government's efforts to procure a *magic* horn? That they thought it might be able to be used as a secret weapon, just like the North Koreans thought they could use it for a secret weapon? I mean, who were all those different police that showed up down at the pier? Not all were U.S. Fish and Wildlife and NYCPD. There were commandos. And you seemed awfully concerned out there on the pier about the whereabouts of the kving-kie. A fake kving-kie. You know what I think?"

Nobody said anything, so I continued.

"I think Jimmy is here because he's convinced that I may still know where the horn is."

Kim laughed softly, shaking his head. "Really, Garth, that is so far-fetched. We saw you throw it in the river."

"I told the police and all the other government types who would listen that I dropped the horn on the pier, in the dark, and never saw it again. I never, not once, said I threw it in the river. But that's what you want to believe, isn't it? To confirm that nobody else has it?"

"You guys are comedians, I'm serious." Kim chortled. "Besides, who would ever believe—"

"And that's exactly what you're counting on, isn't it?" I volleyed. "In the ocean of conspiracy theories out there, who would believe this one more than any other? But you were sent down here to chum the waters with doubt."

"Or to confirm that nobody has it," Angie added.

"All right, you two kidders, you've had your fun." Jimmy took a few steps back, laughing with all the mirth of someone confronted by the absurdities of the tax code. "Nice chatting."

"Jimmy." I grabbed his elbow just as he tried to slip out of the tent. With a hard, intent look into his eyes, I said, "I don't have it. Maybe it did fall in the river. I don't know where it is. And I don't *feel* it out there anywhere, if that's what you're thinking."

"I know, Garth," he said with a brittle grin.

"Am I going to be seeing you again? More little chats?"

"I shouldn't think so." He pulled his elbow from my grip, and almost winked. "But I left you a parting gift, something to remember me by."

Jimmy Kim stepped out into the heat and was gone as quickly as a mirage.

"A parting gift?" Rodney belched. "Where?"

"The car?" Angie suggested.

The three of us stepped out into the heat and turned the corner of the tent.

On the hood of the Lincoln was an immense moose head. It was laying plaque flat so that it was staring into the scorching summer sky.

Antlers: sixty-plus inches, masterful, imposing, threatening.

Pelt, Ears, Dewlap, Eyes, Nose, Lips: Superb.

Pose: Moose-head quintessence.

The three of us stood gaping at it, until Angie reached out and looked at the tag hanging from the antler. Rodney and I leaned in. It read:

~~$50.00~~ SOLD.

Confronted by this massive beast on the hood of my car, a contemplative silence followed.

"Well, paint my bottom and call me Horace!" Rodney finally bellowed, raising his beer can for another toast. "Here's to a fifty-dollar moose head."

Angie held up her can. "Here's to throwing that darn horn in the river!"

My beer can met theirs.

I winked at Angie.

"Here's to love."

About the Author

Brian M. Wiprud

Home: New York City

Age: Wears red tennis shoes

Physical Description: Diabolical

Profession: Mystery Author, Outdoor Writer, and
Photographer

Publisher: Bantam Dell

Agency: Trident Media Group

Latest Accomplishments:

    *2002 Lefty Award for Most Humorous Novel

    *2003 Barry Award Nominee for Best Paperback
      Original

    *2004 Independent Mystery Booksellers
      Association Bestseller

Favorite Books: *I, Squid,* Chuck Flink
    Tubing Badgers for Fun and Profit, Bubbles Tenzer

Favorite Movies: *Bowanga! Bowanga!*
    Eegah!

Favorite Albums: *Arrrg!* Johnny Neanderthal and
the Cave Dwellers

Hobby: Cutting-Edge Top-Secret Devices

Favorite Lines: "What a gorgeous day. What effulgent sunshine. It was a day of this sort the McGillicuddy brothers murdered their mother with an axe." W.C. Fields.

Favorite Scotch: Bourbon

Don't miss

BRIAN M. WIPRUD'S

next comic mystery

Coming in Summer 2006
from Dell Books

Read on for an exclusive sneak peek—
and look for your copy at your
favorite bookseller.

Nicholas stepped under the awning and into the full bare-bulb glow of a fish stand. Light rippled up his overcoat, reflected from water-filled buckets.

Behind him, Asians flooded the sidewalk, a turbid river of shoppers wielding pink plastic bags laden with pea pods, bok choy, mung beans and squid. The night air was filled with rain, blinking signs, exhaust and the sour vowels of vendors bickering with customers. Cars and semis crept by on Canal Street, a traffic jam headed for the Manhattan Bridge in one direction, for the Holland Tunnel in the other.

Nicholas zeroed in on the fish shop proprietor, a blind old man with a wispy beard, skullcap and pernicious smile who waved his cane through the air with the determination and panache of a maestro before his choral group. Even blind, the shop-keeper knew the locale and price of each variety of fish. The wares wriggled and squirmed in old lard buckets tiered five deep. He was clearly capable of pricing and protecting the wares with his baton, while his harried niece was relegated to making actual exchanges. A pair of crones would double-team the geezer, singing their demands and gesturing with fists at a lard tin full of writhing hornpout. Smacking the edge of a fish tin with his cane, he'd bark a price at the chorus, only to be flanked by the staccato of two other women yowl-ing and pointing to the sea robbins or spiny urchins. The piscatorial patriarch would swing his baton, thwack the bucket to which they pointed, and bark a price. Upstarts would not be tolerated in this glee club.

Two hours earlier, Nicholas had been on the phone with a man who called himself Dr. Bagby, a guy with a hot painting and a penchant for a noisy part of town. The background clamor was famil-iar—the honking, the cane smacking metal buck-ets, the yammering. Two hours and seven cabs later, Nicholas's search brought him to the Canal Street fish stand. He'd finally pegged the market din not because he spent any appreciable time shopping Chinatown but because of Figlio's, a lo-cal lounge around the corner. Courthouse-types watered there, and he'd sometimes had occasion to buttonhole young ADAs for information. He'd stood many times in front of the fish stand to hail a cab.

February bowled a wet ball of wind under the fish stand's awning, and Nicholas turned away from the tin bucket ensemble, water beading on his glasses and close-cropped hair. He waded back through the pedestrian current to a phone booth on the corner where he sought refuge from the tide of pink bags and two-dollar umbrellas.

Dr. Bagby hadn't called from a cell phone. Background noises were always strangely garbled in digital signals. No, this had been clear—a land line, but on the street.

There was a vendor close to the phone booth. The shop was comprised of a huge golfers' umbrella, a Coleman lantern and a peach crate, all assembled in the threshold of a defunct savings and loan. Huddled beneath the umbrella, an Asian dwarf woman buzzed away with a hobby tool fashioning netsuke from chunk plastic. The finished product hung by threads from the spokes of her umbrella. It was as if a tornado had lifted a yurt from a Mongolian bazaar and dropped it in downtown Manhattan.

"How much?" Nicholas stepped forward and poked at the carving of a peanut, which twirled in the light of the lantern. "How much for this one?"

Magnifying goggles made the dwarf woman's eyes the size of fried eggs. Her tool buzzed to a stop.

"That special. Twenty buck." The eyes vanished and the tool buzzed, puffs of dust pluming from where she crouched.

"Here." Nicholas held out a twenty, which fluttered

slightly to the rhythm of grocery bags whacking him in the shins. The tool stopped buzzing, and egg eyes reappeared. The woman sniffed, looked at the twenty, wiped her hand on the top of her woolen cap and snatched the bill.

"Tank you. En-joy." Wind battered her umbrella and Nicholas turned up the collar of his tweed overcoat. He admired the twenty-dollar peanut between thumb and forefinger.

"I'd like to buy something else. I want to buy what you know about a man who made a call from that phone booth. That phone booth there. Did you see a man? He coughed. He's sick."

She scratched her head in thought, wiping her nose with the back of her glove.

"Man? Sick man?"

"Yes. Sick." Nicholas demonstrated, coughing and holding an imaginary receiver to his head and pointing at the booth.

Her face sprouted a smile as wide as she was tall.

"I see. Sick man. I see all time. I see come, go, all time. Sick man. Twenty buck." She put out a hand, but Nicholas held the bill out of reach where the damp winter gusts looked they might just blow it away, to be lost forever in the expanses of the Gobi. Or at least Canal Street.

"Where does he live?"

The building was a pre-war four-story. Spanish American War, that is, and every year seemed to weigh heavily upon its frame. Nicholas stood in the foyer dripping water, wiping the rain from his glasses, razzing the damp from his bristly hair and re-flipping the small curl that formed at his widow's peak. He'd long since abandoned umbrellas, preferring to tough it out with just an overcoat. He'd spent considerable time in the tropics, where one gets used to being wet, and where being caught in the rain provides welcome relief from the heat.

Ancient shellac had beaded on the chipped woodwork of the vestibule like yellow sweat. A low-watt bulb illuminated an amber tulip sconce and little else. Mailboxes were all unlabeled, flanked both by ancient buzzer buttons and hailing tubes. Nicholas wanted to arrive unannounced, so he tried the door's rusty knob. The oak door creaked, but it wouldn't budge. He put his face up to the murky glass and peered beyond the shredded lace curtain.

The door opened suddenly.

"Yahj!!" gasped a Chinese gent in a porkpie hat. A carpetbag fell from his grasp as he staggered back in alarm, hand raised defensively. Looked like he'd almost given the poor guy a heart attack.

"It's O.K... It's O.K..." Nicholas took the opportunity to step past the door. He picked up the carpetbag and held it out to Porkpie.

Porkpie quickly recovered from his cardiac infarction and snatched the bag back. His malady was replaced with indignation, and he wagged a threatening finger, scolding Nicholas in Cantonese. Nicholas shooed him out into the foyer with reassuring gestures.

German Expressionists seem to have designed the staircase; the whole shebang looked as though it might spiral in on itself like a collapsing cup. Nicholas ascended carefully, each step voicing a creaky complaint. One dim sconce at each landing barely lit the way. Scents of sesame oil and soy grew stronger the higher he went. At the top landing, next to a sconce, was a door without a Confucian icon thumb-tacked over the number. He put an ear to the door. A gentle steam-heat slurping came from within. He turned the knob and the latch clicked.

Peering into the apartment, Nicholas had a view along a crooked, dark hallway that terminated in an illuminated kitchen. It was there that a man sat slumped at a table with a towel over his head. Wisps of steam snaked from under the towel. The man was dressed in a worn terry bathrobe and grimy slippers. Bagby sleeping? Next to him, leaning against the stove, was a large, square, flat wooden crate, one that might hold, say, a painting. Somewhere a radiator valve hissed like a snake ready to strike.

Nicholas slid quietly in and pushed the door closed. It was roasting hot in the apartment, and he loosened his trench coat. It didn't help that he was wearing a tweed suit. He pulled the neatly folded handkerchief from his top pocket and mopped the back of his neck as he made a quick survey of his surroundings. The place was stacked with old newspapers and magazines like some kind of recycling center. Clearly Bagby was one of those freaks who couldn't throw away reading material of any kind. Furniture must be in there some-where, along with legions of roaches. Chinatown was rife with roaches. Nicholas expected the place to smell musty, of decay. But instead it smelled of menthol.

His eyes latched back onto Bagby. A few steps in that direction and the floor squeaked a loud warning—but the man at the kitchen table didn't stir. Nicholas approached more swiftly, and real-ized that the man was more than asleep. A hypo-dermic needle stuck out of one side of the man's neck, a large bruise graced the other. Clubbed and stuck.

Nicholas circled to the side and lifted the towel. The corpse fit the dwarf's description of the man from the payphone. Heavyset. Dark curly hair. Eyebrows pierced by small silver rings. He may have once been swarthy, but his complexion now was waxy. Eyes open, dilated, dead. His cheek smooshed against a croup kettle, like wet clay. Droplets, condensed steam, clinging to the stubble of his beard.

Bending over to raise one of Bagby's pant legs, Nicholas noted that the ankle over the white sock was just turning purplish. Blood beginning to pool in his legs. With the back of his hand, Nicholas felt the hairy leg. Warm. Bagby had been kaput for a half hour or less.

He stood. The top of the table was strewn with nasal sprays, cold formulas and lozenges, some of which had been knocked to the checkered tile floor by the victim's sprawled arms. One bottle had the old-fashioned label "Doctor Bagby's Croup Elixir;" the source of the dead man's alias. A used Kleenex was clenched in his extended hand.

Time to watch the prints. With his handkerchief, Nicholas tilted the nearby crate towards him for a look-see. Just an empty frame where the Moolman had been. He lifted out the familiar gilt frame and saw the ragged ends of the blue canvass where it had been hurriedly cut from the frame. Sloppy, but quick. The frame had held the 24" x 36" painting *Trampoline Nude 1972*, which had been lifted from a private collection in Westchester six weeks earlier by a man posing as an exterminator. Nicholas let the frame drop back into the crate with a thud.

"Just super." He snorted.

Had Chinatown been first on his dance card, Nicholas would probably have had the canvass in hand. Sorry son-of-a-bitch. Bagby would still be suffering from his head cold. Only someone else got to him first.

A door slammed at street level. Heavy footsteps sounded on the stair. As did the squelch of a police radio.

Nicholas didn't have to think about what his next move was. He operated on instinct and turned to the kitchen window. Flipping the catch on the security gate with a forearm, he opened the grimy window with his palms and crawled out onto the fire escape. Flower pots and a mop tripped him up in the gloom, and he had to grab the railing to keep from cartwheeling down the metal steps. Would have been a long hospital stay, and that he couldn't afford. Cautiously, Nicholas sidled down each flight towards the backyard, keeping his weight mostly on the railing. Rusty old fire escapes—he knew from experience that the steps sometimes snapped unexpectedly.

No sooner had Nicholas jumped from the fire escape to the backyard than he glanced up to see a cop appear in Bagby's kitchen window, talking into a radio. He turned his attention back to his escape. The backyard wasn't some grassy nirvana with sprinklers, lawn gnomes and azaleas. It was more like a small prison yard, a patch of broken concrete surrounded by a wall topped with razor wire. Broken beer bottles and cigarette butts blanketed the ground. Nicholas skirted the wall, trying to stay out of view, his footsteps crunching lightly on the faintly glittering glass. As he stole quietly around the corner into a blind alley that stabbed between two buildings, he could see a basement walk-down near the end. He tried the door, but it was locked. A few shoves of his shoulder and the moldering jamb gave way like stale bread. A wave of sewage reek flushed from the dark.

Streetlight spilled into the rank basement through a coal grate at the far end of the long, black space, a grim beacon. What sounded like a dozen rats scuttled for the corners. By the sound of them, he gauged they were welterweights compared to the wharf-bruisers down near the Brooklyn Bridge where Nicholas lived. And certainly neither as fleet of paw as the upper west side rail yard variety, nor as insouciant as the Tompkins Square model. Even as the bear was friend to Grizzly Adams, the rat was a pal of Nicholas Palihnick. He took a shine to their independent nature, their tenacity, their gritty lifestyle. But he knew enough to respect the domain of the cellar rat. Generally slow, mid-size, and shy, they also have a tendency to be defensive, if not openly hostile on their home turf. Nicholas recalled the story of a man trapped in a Chicago basement who was reduced to a paraplegic before he was rescued. Nibbled around the edges like a saltine.

But Nicholas's years in gritty third-world slums had taught him not to fear places that were merely dark, squalid or rat-infested. Worldly battle scars that broke some men had armored him for a new lease on life. Disillusionment and subsequent hard lessons about human nature had warped idealists into cynics, and Nicholas into a practical solipsist. Whatever New York could dish out, Nicholas had decided to bottle and turn into a buck. So a stroll through Ratville was little more to him than a Park Avenue jaunt. It might be hard on his tweed suit, but he had a lot of them.

Making a bee-line for the coal grate's light at the far end of the blackness, he managed to cross the room without stepping on any rats, though one brushed by his leg, perhaps a coy test of his resolve. Drawing near, he could see bright lines that could only come from the underside of sidewalk cellar doors to the right of the coal chute, and steps leading up to them. His ears rang with the clicking of palm-sized roaches scattering as he climbed the steps.

A padlock sealed the cellar doors.

Eyes still adjusting to the gloom, Nicholas spied the shadow of another stairway hunkering mid-basement, and the dark forms of rats trundling from his path as he headed for it. He heard a roach flying toward his head and batted it away. He remembered the halcyon days, back when roaches in New York didn't fly, before the euphemism "waterbug" came to replace "big fat disgusting roach." Having tangled with giant Columbian spiders that feasted on birds, roaches were nothing to him now.

A dull amber light spread from under a door at the top of the stairs. Surveying his location, Nicholas reasoned the door probably opened to the building's ground floor, under the Fritz Lang staircase. He paused and listened: just creaking, several floors above.

The door was secured with an eyehook latch on the outside. A credit card flipped it. Nicholas pushed the door open an inch and peeked through. Then he grinned.

He exited the cellar with a whistle on his lips, a song in his heart, and a roach on his lapel. He jettisoned the latter, maintained the former.

Emerging from the vestibule onto the stoop in front of Bagby's building, Nicholas found himself confronted by a cop leaning on her patrol car. One upstairs, the partner downstairs. Crap. Ditching any sign of alarm, he innocently pretended to search the heavens for clearing skies, meanwhile whistling tunelessly.

The cop watched him walk down the steps, smile, say "h'lo," and turn toward the flow of pink bags at Canal Street.

"Sir . . ."

Nicholas kept whistling, walking. Just a gent out for a stroll.

"Sir. Hey, you. Mister, stop." He heard the sound of her holster unsnapping.

Damn snap. An unmistakable cue that he had to turn. Gun leaves the holster, a cop stops listening and starts cuffing. No talking your way out then.

Nicholas turned. Eyebrows raised, he displayed a helpful smile for the nice police lady.

She approached, her hips' sway made huge and duck-like by the citation binder, flashlight, handcuffs, and radio stuffed in her trousers.

"Yes, officer?" It seemed to echo in his head. He flashed his most charming smile.

"Where you comin' from?" She sniffed, chewing hard on her gum, looking him up and down. Her eyes settled on his face, and she didn't return the smile. But she put a hand up to check her hair just the same.

"Me?" He let slip a sly grin, as though she were approaching him in a bar.

"Yeah." She considered him sidelong, eyes guarded. "You."

He sighed. Sometimes Nicholas's charms betrayed him.

It was the beginning of a long night that would turn into a longer day.